Kelly Ruth Winter

MARILYNNE ROBINSON is the author of the novels
Home, Gilead (winner of the Pulitzer Prize), and
Housekeeping, and four books of nonfiction, *When I
Was a Child I Read Books, Mother Country, The
Death of Adam,* and *Absence of Mind.* She teaches at
the University of Iowa Writers' Workshop.

ALSO BY MARILYNNE ROBINSON

FICTION

Home

Gilead

Housekeeping

NONFICTION

When I Was a Child I Read Books: Essays

*Absence of Mind: The Dispelling of Inwardness
from the Modern Myth of the Self*

The Death of Adam: Essays on Modern Thought

Mother Country: Britain, the Welfare State and Nuclear Pollution

Additional Praise for *Lila*

"Radiant . . . [*Lila* is] a mediation on morality and psychology, compelling in its frankness about its truly shocking subject: the damage to the human personality done by poverty, neglect, and abandonment."   —*The New York Times Book Review*

"*Lila,* Marilynne Robinson's remarkable new novel, stands alone as a book to read and even read again. It's both a multilayered love story and a perceptive look at how early deprivation causes lasting damage. . . . Robinson is a novelist of the first order."
                                                        —*The Seattle Times*

"Emotionally and intellectually challenged, it's an exploration of faith in God, love, and whatever else it takes to survive."
                                            —*Entertainment Weekly* (Grade: A)

"Gorgeous writing, an absolutely beautiful book . . . This should come as no surprise to anyone familiar with Robinson, a novelist who can make the most quotidian moments epic because of her ability to peel back the surfaces of ordinary lives. . . . [A] profound and deeply rendered novel."   —*Los Angeles Times*

"An unflinching book."   —*The New Yorker*

"[A] brilliant and deeply affecting new novel."   —*The Atlantic*

"Marilynne Robinson has written a deeply romantic love story embodied in the language and ideas of Calvinist doctrine. She really is not like any other writer. . . . Robinson has created a small, rich, and fearless body of work in which religion exists unashamedly, as does doubt, unashamedly."
                                            —*The New York Review of Books*

"Lila's journey—its darker passages illuminated by Robinson's ability to write about love and the natural world with grit and graceful reverence—will mesmerize both longtime Robinson devotees and those coming to her work for the first time."

—*Elle*

"Robinson's genius is for making indistinguishable the highest ends of faith and fiction. . . . The beauty of Robinson's prose suggests an author continually threading with spun platinum the world's finest needle."

—*Bookforum*

"Don't hesitate to read *Lila*. . . . It's a novel that stands on its own and is surely one of the best of the year."

—*St. Louis Post-Dispatch*

"Glorious . . . *Lila* is—at once—powerful, profound, and positively radiant. . . . Life, death, joy, fear, doubt, love, violence, kindness—all of this, and more, dwells in *Lila,* a book, I will venture, already for the ages, its protagonist engraved upon our souls."

—*The Buffalo News*

"*Lila* is a dark, powerful, uplifting, unforgettable novel. And Robinson's Gilead trilogy—*Gilead, Home,* and *Lila*—is a great achievement in American fiction."

—*The Dallas Morning News*

"[*Lila* is] a masterpiece of prose in the service of the moral seriousness that distinguishes Robinson's work. . . . A superb creation."

—*Publishers Weekly* (starred review)

"Robinson has created a tour de force, an unforgettably dynamic odyssey, a passionate and learned moral and spiritual inquiry, a paean to the earth, and a witty and transcendent love story—all within a refulgent and resounding novel so beautifully precise and cadenced it wholly transfixes and transforms us."

—*Booklist* (starred review)

"A lovely and touching story that grapples with the universal question of how God can allow his children to suffer. Recommended for fans of Robinson as well as those who enjoyed Elizabeth Strout's *Olive Kitteridge,* another exploration of pain and loneliness set against the backdrop of a small town."

—*Library Journal* (starred review)

LILA

Marilynne Robinson

Picador

———

Farrar, Straus and Giroux

New York

LILA. Copyright © 2014 by Marilynne Robinson. All rights reserved. Printed in the United States of America. For information, address Picador, 175 Fifth Avenue, New York, N.Y. 10010.

www.picadorusa.com
www.twitter.com/picadorusa • www.facebook.com/picadorusa
picadorbookroom.tumblr.com

Picador® is a U.S. registered trademark and is used by Farrar, Straus and Giroux under license from Pan Books Limited.

For book club information, please visit www.facebook.com/picadorbookclub or e-mail marketing@picadorusa.com.

Designed by Jonathan D. Lippincott

The Library of Congress has cataloged the Farrar, Straus and Giroux edition as follows:

Robinson, Marilynne.
    Lila / Marilynne Robinson. — First edition.
        p. cm.
    ISBN 978-0-374-18761-3 (hardcover)
    ISBN 978-0-374-70908-2 (e-book)
    I. Title.
PS3568.O3125L57 2014
813'.54—dc23

2013038776

Picador Paperback ISBN 978-1-250-07484-3

Picador books may be purchased for educational, business, or promotional use. For information on bulk purchases, please contact the Macmillan Corporate and Premium Sales Department at 1-800-221-7945, extension 5442, or write to specialmarkets@macmillan.com.

First published by Farrar, Straus and Giroux

First Picador Edition: October 2015

10 9 8 7 6 5 4 3 2 1

To IOWA

LILA

The child was just there on the stoop in the dark, hugging herself against the cold, all cried out and nearly sleeping. She couldn't holler anymore and they didn't hear her anyway, or they might and that would make things worse. Somebody had shouted, Shut that thing up or I'll do it! and then a woman grabbed her out from under the table by her arm and pushed her out onto the stoop and shut the door and the cats went under the house. They wouldn't let her near them anymore because she picked them up by their tails sometimes. Her arms were all over scratches, and the scratches stung. She had crawled under the house to find the cats, but even when she did catch one in her hands it struggled harder the harder she held on to it and it bit her, so she let it go. Why you keep pounding at the screen door? Nobody gonna want you around if you act like that. And then the door closed again, and after a while night came. The people inside fought themselves quiet, and it was night for a long time. She was afraid to be under the house, and afraid to be up on the stoop, but if she stayed by the door it might open. There was a moon staring straight at her, and there were sounds in the woods, but she was nearly sleeping when Doll came up the path and found her there like that, miserable as could be, and took her up in her arms and wrapped her into her shawl, and said, "Well, we got no place to go. Where we gonna go?"

If there was anyone in the world the child hated worst, it was Doll. She'd go scrubbing at her face with a wet rag, or she'd be after her hair with a busted comb, trying to get the snarls out. Doll slept at the house most nights, and maybe she paid for it by sweeping up a little. She was the only one who did any sweeping, and she'd be cussing while she did it, Don't do one damn bit of good, and someone would say, Then leave it be, dammit. There'd be people sleeping right on the floor, in some old mess of quilts and gunnysacks. You wouldn't know from one day to the next.

When the child stayed under the table they would forget her most of the time. The table was shoved into a corner and they wouldn't go to the trouble of reaching under to pull her out of there if she kept quiet enough. When Doll came in at night she would kneel down and spread that shawl over her, but then she left again so early in the morning that the child would feel the shawl slip off and she'd feel colder for the lost warmth of it, and stir, and cuss a little. But there would be hardtack, an apple, something, and a cup of water left there for her when she woke up. Once, there was a kind of toy. It was just a horse chestnut with a bit of cloth over it, tied with a string, and two knots at the sides and two at the bottom, like hands and feet. The child whispered to it and slept with it under her shirt.

Lila would never tell anyone about that time. She knew it would sound very sad, and it wasn't, really. Doll had taken her up in her arms and wrapped her shawl around her. "You just hush now," she said. "Don't go waking folks up." She settled the child on her hip and carried her into the dark house, stepping as carefully and quietly as she could, and found the bundle she kept in her corner, and then they went out into the chilly dark again, down the steps. The house was rank with sleep and the night was windy, full of tree sounds. The moon was gone and there was rain, so fine then it was only a tingle on the skin. The child was four or five, long-legged, and Doll couldn't keep her covered up, but she chafed at her calves with her big, rough hand and brushed the damp from her cheek and her hair. She whispered, "Don't know what I think I'm doing. Never figured on it. Well, maybe I did. I don't know. I guess I probly did. This sure ain't the night for it." She hitched up her apron to cover the child's legs and carried her out past the clearing. The door might have opened, and a woman might have called after them, Where you going with that child? and then, after a minute, closed the door again, as if she had done all decency required. "Well," Doll whispered, "we'll just have to see."

The road wasn't really much more than a path, but Doll had walked it so often in the dark that she stepped over the roots and around the potholes and never paused or stumbled. She could walk quickly when there was no light at all. And she was strong enough that even an awkward burden like a leggy child could rest in her arms almost asleep. Lila knew it couldn't have been the way she remembered it, as if she were carried along in the wind, and there were arms around her to let her know she was safe, and there was a whisper at her ear to let her know that she shouldn't be lonely. The whisper said, "I got to find a place to put you down. I got to find a dry place." And then they sat on the ground, on pine needles, Doll with her back against a tree and the child curled into her lap, against her breast, hearing the beat of her heart, feeling it. Rain fell heavily. Big drops spattered them sometimes. Doll said, "I should have knowed it was coming on rain. And now you got the fever." But the child just lay against her, hoping to stay where she was, hoping the rain wouldn't end. Doll may have been the loneliest woman in the world, and she was the loneliest child, and there they were, the two of them together, keeping each other warm in the rain.

When the rain ended, Doll got to her feet, awkwardly with the child in her arms, and tucked the shawl around her as well as she could. She said, "I know a place." The child's head would drop back, and Doll would heft her up again, trying to keep her covered. "We're almost there."

It was another cabin with a stoop, and a dooryard beaten bare. An old black dog got up on his forelegs, then his hind legs, and barked, and an old woman opened the door. She said, "No work for you here, Doll. Nothing to spare."

Doll sat down on the stoop. "Just thought I'd rest a little."

"What you got there? Where'd you get that child?"

"Never mind."

"Well, you better put her back."

"Maybe. Don't think I will, though."

"Better feed her something, at least."

Doll said nothing.

The old woman went into the house and brought out a scrap of corn bread. She said, "I was about to do the milking. You might as well go inside, get her in out of the cold."

Doll stood with her by the stove, where there was just the little warmth of the banked embers. She whispered, "You hush. I got something for you here. You got to eat it." But the child couldn't rouse herself, couldn't keep her head from lolling back. So Doll knelt with her on the floor to free her hands, and pinched off little pills of corn bread and put them in the child's mouth, one after another. "You got to swallow."

The old woman came back with a pail of milk. "Warm from the cow," she said. "Best thing for a child." That strong, grassy smell, raw milk in a tin cup. Doll gave it to her in sips, holding her head in the crook of her arm.

"Well, she got something in her, if she keeps it down. Now I'll put some wood on the fire and we can clean her up some."

When the room was warmer and the water in the kettle was

warm, the old woman held her standing in a white basin on the floor by the stove and Doll washed her down with a rag and a bit of soap, scrubbing a little where the cats had scratched her, and on the chigger bites and mosquito bites where she had scratched herself, and where there were slivers in her knees, and where she had a habit of biting her hand. The water in the basin got so dirty they threw it out the door and started over. Her whole body shivered with the cold and the sting. "Nits," the old woman said. "We got to cut her hair." She fetched a razor and began shearing off the tangles as close to the child's scalp as she dared—"I got a blade here. She better hold still." Then they soaped and scrubbed her head, and water and suds ran into her eyes, and she struggled and yelled with all the strength she had and told them both they could rot in hell. The old woman said, "You'll want to talk to her about that."

Doll touched the soap and tears off the child's face with the hem of her apron. "Never had the heart to scold her. Them's about the only words I ever heard her say." They made her a couple of dresses out of flour sacks with holes cut in them for her head and arms. They were stiff at first and smelled of being saved in a chest or a cupboard, and they had little flowers all over them, like Doll's apron.

It seemed like one long night, but it must have been a week, two weeks, rocking on Doll's lap while the old woman fussed around them.

"You don't have enough trouble, I guess. Carrying off a child that's just going to die on you anyway."

"Ain't going to let her die."

"Oh? When's the last time you got to decide about something?"

"If I left her be where she was, she'da died for sure."

"Well, maybe her folks won't see it that way. They know you took her? What you going to say when they come looking for her? She's buried in the woods somewhere? Out by the potato patch? I don't have troubles enough of my own?"

Doll said, "Nobody going to come looking."

"You probly right about that. That's the spindliest damn child I ever saw."

But the whole time she talked she'd be stirring a pot of grits and blackstrap molasses. Doll would give the child a spoonful or two, then rock her a little while, then give her another spoonful. She rocked her and fed her all night long, and dozed off with her cheek against the child's hot forehead.

The old woman got up now and then to put more wood in the stove. "She keeping it down?"

"Mostly."

"She taking any water?"

"Some."

When the old woman went away again Doll would whisper to her, "Now, don't you go dying on me. Put me to all this bother for nothing. Don't you go dying." And then, so the child could barely hear, "You going to die if you have to. I know. But I got you out of the rain, didn't I? We're warm here, ain't we?"

After a while the old woman again. "Put her in my bed if you want. I guess I won't be sleeping tonight, either."

"I got to make sure she can breathe all right."

"Let me set with her then."

"She's clinging on to me."

"Well." The old woman brought the quilt from her bed and spread it over them.

The child could hear Doll's heart beating and she could feel the rise and fall of her breath. It was too warm and she felt herself struggling against the quilt and against Doll's arms and clinging to her at the same time with her arms around her neck.

They stayed with that old woman for weeks, maybe a month. Now it was hot and moist in the mornings when Doll took her outside, holding her hand because her legs weren't strong yet. She walked her around the dooryard, cool under her bare feet, smooth as clay. The dog lay in the sun with his muzzle on his paws, taking no notice. She touched the hot, coarse fur of his back and her hand was sour with the smell of it. There were chickens strutting the yard, scratching and pecking. Doll had helped to start the garden, and how had she done that, when the child thought there had always been someone holding her? But the carrots were up. Doll pulled one, no bigger than a straw. "It's soft as a feather," she said, and she touched the child's cheek with the little spray of greens. She wiped the dirt off the root with her fingers. "Here. You can eat it."

There was an ache in the child's throat because she wanted to say, I guess I left my rag baby back there at the house. I guess I did. She knew exactly where, under the table in the farthest corner, propped against the table leg like it was sitting there. She could just run in the door and snatch it and run off again. No one would have to see her. But then maybe Doll wouldn't be here when she came back, and she didn't know where that house was anyway. She thought of the woods. It was just an old rag baby, dirty from her hand, because mostly she kept it with her. But they put her out on the stoop before she could get it and the cats wouldn't even let her touch them and then Doll came and she didn't know they would be leaving, she didn't understand that at all. So she just left it where it was. She never meant to.

Doll took the child's hand away from her mouth. "You mustn't be biting on yourself like that. I told you a hundred times." They put mustard on her hand once, vinegar, and she licked them off because of the sting. They tied a rag around her hand, and when she sucked on it the blood came up and showed pink. "You might help me with the weeding. Give you something to do with that hand." Then they were just quiet there in the sunlight and the smell of earth, kneeling side by side, pulling up all the little sprouts that weren't carrots, tiny plump leaves and white roots.

The old woman came out to watch them. "She don't have no color at all. You don't want her getting burned. She'll be scratching again." She put out her hand for the child to take. "I been thinking about 'Lila.' I had a sister Lila. Give her a pretty name, maybe she could turn out pretty."

"Maybe," Doll said. "Don't matter."

But the old woman's son came home with a wife, and there really wasn't enough work around the place for Doll to be able to stay there anymore. The old woman bundled up as many things as Doll could carry and still carry the child, who wasn't strong enough yet to walk very far, and her son showed them the way to the main road, such as it was. Then after a few days they found Doane and Marcelle. Doll might have been looking for them. They all said Doane had a good name, he was a fair-minded man, and if you hired him you could trust him to give you a day's work. Of course it wasn't just Doane. There was Arthur with his two boys, and Em and her daughter Mellie, and there was Marcelle. She was Doane's wife. They were a married couple.

There was a long time when Lila didn't know that words had letters, or that there were other names for seasons than planting and haying. Walk south ahead of the weather, walk north in time for the crops. They lived in the United States of America.

She brought that home from school. Doll said, "Well, I spose they had to call it something."

Once, Lila asked the Reverend how to spell Doane. What had he thought she meant? *Done? Down?* Maybe *don't*, since she didn't always sound her *t*'s? He was never sure what she knew and didn't know, and it pained him for her sake when he guessed wrong.

He paused and then he laughed. "Mind putting it in a sentence?"

"There was a man called himself Doane. I knew him a long time ago."

"Yes. I see," he said. "I knew a Sloane once. S-L-O-A-N-E." Old as he was, the Reverend still blushed sometimes. "So it might be the same. With a *D*."

"When I was a child. I was thinking about old times the other day." She wouldn't have told him even that much except that she saw the blush deepen when she said once she knew a man.

He nodded. "I see." The Reverend never asked her to talk about old times. He didn't seem to let himself wonder where she had been, how she had lived all the years before she wandered into the church dripping rain. Doane always said churches just want your money, so they all stayed away from churches, walked right past them as if they were smarter than the other people. As if they had any money for the churches to want. But the rain was bad and that day was a Sunday, so there was no other doorway for her to step into. The candles surprised her. It might all have seemed so beautiful because she'd been missing a few meals. That can make things brighter somehow. Brighter and farther away. As if when you put your hand out you would touch glass. She watched him and forgot she was in the room with him and he would see her watching. He baptized two babies that morning. He was a big, silvery old man, and he took each one of those little babies in his arms as gently as could be. One of them was wearing a white dress that spilled down over his arm, and when it cried a little from the water he put on its brow, he said, "Well, I bet you cried the first time you were born, too. It means you're alive." And she had a thought that she had been born a second time, the night Doll took her up from the stoop and put her shawl around her and carried her off through the rain. She ain't your mama, I can tell.

It seemed like that girl knew everything. Mellie. She could bend over backward till her hands were flat on the ground. She could do cartwheels. She said, "I know that woman ain't your mama. She telling you things your mama would have told you already. Don't go sucking on your hand? Like you was a baby? You probly an orphan." She said, "I used to know an orphan once. Her legs was all rickety. Same as yours. She couldn't talk neither. That's probly why she was an orphan. She sort of turned out wrong."

Mellie was curious about them, if the others were not. She would drift back to walk with them, and she would put her face close up to the child's face, to stare at her. "She got that sore on her foot. That's one thing. Put some dandelion milk on it. I got some here. I bet I could carry her. I could." She'd be eating the bloom of a dandelion, the yellow part, or chewing red clover. She was pretty well brown with freckles, and her hair was almost white from the sun, even her eyebrows and eyelashes. "I hate these old coveralls. The boys about wore 'em out and now I'm wearing 'em. They're mostly just patches. Doane says they're better for working. I got a dress. My ma's going to let the hem down." And then she'd be off, walking on her hands.

Doll said, "She likes to pester. Don't you mind."

Lila didn't talk then. Doll said, "She can. She just don't want to." It was partly that Doll gave her anything she needed. She still woke her up in the night sometimes to give her a morsel of cold mush. And Lila never even knew there was such a thing as cussing, till that old woman told her. It just meant leave me alone, most of the time. Once, she told that old woman she wisht she was in hell with her back broke, and the old woman yanked her up and gave her a swat and said, You got to stop that cussing. She'd gone off somewhere and come back with a little bottle of medicine for the sore on the child's foot that didn't heal, and it did smart when she put it on, but it hurt her feelings that the child would be hateful about it. Lila didn't know where to hide, so she just went into a corner and curled up as small as she could, with her eyes shut tight. The old woman said, "Oh, mercy! Doll, come in here! She's back in the corner again. Was there ever such a child!"

Doll came in and knelt down by her, smelling of sweat and sunshine, and lifted her into her lap. She whispered, "What you doing now, biting on that hand like a little baby!" The old woman brought the shawl, and Doll put it around her. And the old woman said, "She's your child, Doll. I can't do a thing with her."

They never spoke about any of it, not one word in all those years. Not about the house Doll stole her away from, not about the old woman who took them in. They did keep that shawl, though, till it was worn soft as cobwebs. But she felt the thrill of the secret whenever she took Doll's hand and Doll gave her hand a little squeeze, whenever she lay down exhausted in the curve of Doll's body, with Doll's arm to pillow her head and the shawl to spread over her. Years after she had become an ordinary child, if there were going to be people to deal with, Doll would whisper in her ear, "No cussing!" and they would laugh together, enjoying their secret. They didn't even mention the nights they spent bedded down beyond the light of Doane's fire, or the days walking behind Doane's people, at a distance, as if they only happened to be going along on the same road.

They could keep to themselves because they had a bag of cornmeal and a little pot to cook it in. Every night Doll made a fire. As she walked she'd be looking for things they could eat. She caught a rabbit in her apron and killed it with a stone, and cooked it that night with a mess of pigweed. She found a nest of bird's eggs. She found chicory and roasted the roots, which were medicine, she said, a cure for the bellyache. Then finally one morning she took up the child and walked after Doane's people into a field of young corn and started pulling weeds in the rows where their hoes couldn't reach, and they didn't say a thing to her about it. The child stayed beside her, holding on to her skirt. When Marcelle brought a pail of well water for the others, she brought it to them, too. Doll thanked her, and held the cup to the child's lips, and then she wiped her hand on her dress and dipped her fingers into the cup to wet them and rinse dust from the child's face. Cold drops ran down her chin and throat and into the damp of her dress, and she laughed. Doll said, surprised, "Well, listen to you now!"

Marcelle was standing there, watching them, waiting to get the cup back. "I guess she been poorly for a while?"

Doll nodded. "She been poorly."

"She could ride in the wagon. You got a lot to carry."

"I keep her by me."

"Then set your bedroll in the wagon."

Doll never did put herself forward, but the next morning, when she had everything bundled up, Doane came and took it and set it on the wagon bed. He said, "We got some spuds in the ashes, ma'am. If you care to join us."

And after that she and Doll were Doane's people, too, most of the time, for as long as the times were decent. That would have been about eight years, counting backward from the Crash, not counting the year Doll made her go to school. Their own bad times started when the mule died, two years or so before everyone else started getting poorer and the wind turned dirty. It seemed like the whole world changed just at that time, the mule gone first, which made the wagon useless. They couldn't even sell it, and they had to leave most of their things behind. The creature died on a lonely piece of road where they would not have been in the first place if it had shown any sign at all of what was about to happen to it. It just sank down on its knees and went over on its side while Arthur was trying to put it in the traces.

Lila heard about the Crash years after it happened, and she had no idea what it was even after she knew what to call it. But it did seem like they gave it the right name. It was like one of those storms you might even sleep through, and then when you wake up in the morning everything's ruined, or gone. Most of the farmers that used to know Doane and Marcelle sold up and left, or just left, and the ones who stayed didn't want any help, or couldn't pay for it. But there were those few years when it seemed that they knew who they were and where they should be and what they should be doing. There were those few years when the child began to be strong and to grow, when Doll was still herself, when Mellie still pestered and played her pranks like some half-grown devil trying to mind its manners. Evenings Doane might be away from the camp a while, somewhere trading one thing for another for some small mutual advantage or settling terms with somebody for the work they would do. When he came back again he'd look for Marcelle, never saying a word, but when he saw her he would go and stand near her, and then whatever else might have been on his mind you could tell he was pretty well at peace.

They all thought it was a fine thing to live the way they did, out in the open like that, when the weather was tolerable. It seemed true enough as long as the good times lasted. If they were tired and dirty it was from work, and that kind of dirt didn't even feel like dirt. Work meant plenty to eat and a few pennies for candy or ribbons or a dime for a minstrel show when they passed through a town. They never camped by a stream without bathing, and washing their clothes if the weather was good and they could stay long enough to let things dry. That was before the times when they began to be caught in the dust, and it would make them cough and cough, and the wind would blow it right through the clothes on their backs. But in those days they were proud people. If they could, they patched and mended and hemmed whatever needed it. They looked after what they had. Anybody could see that.

Lila did like to work in the Reverend's garden. He hardly ever set foot in it. It used to be that somebody from the church would come in now and then to keep the weeds down. When she came there at first to tend the roses and clean things up, she had made a little garden in a corner and planted a few potatoes, just for herself. A few beans. She didn't see any reason to let a sunny spot like that go to waste, and the soil was good. It had been a while. She loved the smell of dirt, and the feel of it. She had to make herself wash it off her hands.

Now that she was the Reverend's wife she had made the garden much bigger. She could get all the seeds she wanted. She still liked to eat a carrot right out of the ground, but she knew that wasn't what people did, so she was careful about it. She thought sometime she might just let the boy try it, to see how it tasted. (Two or three times she had even had the thought of stealing him, carrying him away to the woods or off down the road so she could have him to herself and let him know about that other life. But she imagined the old man, the Reverend, calling after them, "Where are you going with that child?" The sadness in his voice would be terrible. *He* would be surprised to hear it. You wouldn't even know your body had a sound like that in it. And it would be familiar to her. She didn't imagine it, she remembered that sadness from somewhere, and it was as if she would understand something if she could hear it again. That was what she almost wanted.)

No, it was just a dream she had had a few times, two or three times, a kind of daydream. And it was the dream that stayed in her mind, not any real thought of taking the child away from his father. If he knew what she was thinking he would probably say, Soon enough you'll have him all to yourself. Sometimes she wished he could know her thoughts, because she believed he might forgive them. Because the Good Lord would forgive them, practically for sure, she thought. If the old men knew anything about the Good Lord. If there was a Good Lord. Doll had never mentioned Him.

Lila's thoughts were strange sometimes. They always had been. She had hoped getting baptized might help with it, but it didn't. Someday she might ask him about that. Well, Doll always said, Just do what you're told and be quiet about it, that's all anybody ever going to want from you. Lila had learned there was really more to it than that. But she was very quiet. He didn't ask much of her, though. Anything, really. In those first weeks she could tell he was just glad to find her there at the house when he came home, or in the kitchen when he came down from his study. Even a little relieved. Maybe he knew her better than she thought he did. But then he might not have been so glad to find her there. She wished sometimes he would tell her what to do, but he was always so careful of her. So she watched the other wives and did what they did, as well as she could figure it out.

There was so much to get wrong. She came to that first meeting at the church, after he had asked her to come, and when she walked into the room, all ladies there except for him, he stood up. She thought he must be angry to see her, that he was going to tell her to leave, that she should have understood it was a joke when he invited her. So she turned around and walked out. But two of the ladies followed her right into the street to tell her how happy they were that she had come and how they hoped she could stay. Kindness like that might have made her angry enough to keep walking if she hadn't had that idea in her mind about getting baptized. And when they came back in, he stood up again, because the kind of gentleman he was will do that when ladies come into a room. They almost can't help it. How was she supposed to know? They have to be the ones to open a door, but then they have to wait there for you to go through it. To this very day, if the Reverend happened to meet her out on the street he took off his hat to her, even in the rain. He always helped her with her chair, which amounted to pulling it out from the table a little, then pushing it in again after she sat down. Who in the world could need help with a chair?

People have their ways, though, she thought. And he was beautiful for an old man. She did enjoy the sight of him. He looked as if he'd had his share of loneliness, and that was all right. It was one thing she understood about him. She liked his voice. She liked the way he stood next to her as if there was a pleasure for him in it.

Once, he took her hand to help her up the steps at Boughton's house, and Boughton winked and said, "'There are three things which are too wonderful for me, yea, four which I know not,'" and they both laughed a little. She thought to herself, No cussing. But the Reverend could see it bothered her when they talked that way, making jokes they knew she would not understand. So when they were home again he took the Bible off the

18

shelf and showed her the verse: *The way of an eagle in the air; the way of a serpent upon a rock; the way of a ship in the midst of the sea; and the way of a man with a maiden.* That was the joke. A man with a maiden. They were laughing because he was an old preacher and she was a field hand, or would be if she could just find her way back to that time. And she was old, too. For a woman being old just means not being young, and all the youth had been worked out of her before it had really even set in. So Lila had been old a long time, but not in a way that helped. Well, she knew it was a joke. People were still surprised at him, that he had married her.

She could see it surprised him, too, sometimes. He told her once when there was a storm a bird had flown into the house. He'd never seen one like it. The wind must have carried it in from some far-off place. He opened all the doors and windows, but it was so desperate to escape that for a while it couldn't find a way out. "It left a blessing in the house," he said. "The wildness of it. Bringing the wind inside." That was just when she began to suspect she was carrying a child, so it frightened her a little to realize that he knew she might leave, that he might even expect her to leave. She only remembered afterward that the first time she crept into bed beside him it had been the dark of the moon. It was the black-haired girl who told her about that, the one who called herself Susanna. She had three or four children, all staying with her sister or her mother, she said, so maybe she didn't know as much as she thought she did. Still, here Lila was with something more to worry about. The old man could have been telling her she should leave, she didn't belong in his house. Maybe that's how a gentleman would say it. If he wanted to, he could say, This was your idea, you're the one who said I should marry you. Maybe a gentleman couldn't say it. Sometime he might be angry, though, and forget about his manners, and that would be hard to live with. Doll always said, Just be quiet.

Whatever it is, just wait for it to be over. Everything ends sometime. Lila thought, When you know it will end anyway, you can want to be done with it. But if you're carrying a child, you'd best have a roof over your head. Any fool knows that.

One evening they went to old Boughton's house and the two men talked about people she didn't know and things she didn't understand. What else was there, after all? But she didn't mind listening. And soon enough they forgot she was listening. They had read about missionaries back from China, about how they had converted hundreds, and that was a drop in the bucket compared to all the people who had never heard a word of the Gospel and probably never would hear one. Boughton said it seemed to him like a terrible loss of souls, if that's what it was. He was not one to question divine justice, though sometimes he did have to wonder. Anyone would. Which was really not the same as questioning. And the Reverend said, When you think of all the people who lived from Adam to Abraham. Boughton shook his head at the mystery of it. "*We're* a drop in the bucket!" he said. "It's an easy thing to forget!"

The next day was a Sunday, and she had waked up early and slipped out of the house and walked away past the edge of town and followed the river to a place where the water ran over rocks and dropped down to a pool with a sandy bottom. She could watch the shadows of catfish there once the sun came up. She sat on the bank, damp and chilly, smelling the river and barely hearing the sound of it, hidden in the dark, not because she thought anyone would be there, but because she always liked the feeling that no one could see her even when she knew she was alone. The old man would wake up to an empty house, and he would dress and shave as he always did, and make his coffee and toast and gather up his papers and go off to church by himself to preach his sermon as he always did, and sing the hymns and pray the prayers and speak afterward with ladies who wouldn't ask how she was or where she was, because they knew his marriage was a sorrow to him, one more sorrow.

She meant to do better by him. He was always kind to her. But she felt strange in the church. And the night before, lying beside him in the dark, she had asked him a question about China. He tried to explain and she tried to understand. He said, "I believe in the grace of God. For me, that is where all these questions end. Why it's pointless to ask them." But he seemed to be telling her that Boughton might be right, that souls could be lost forever because of things they did not know, or understand, or believe. He didn't like to say it, he had to try different words for it. So she knew he thought it might be true. Doll probably didn't know she had an immortal soul. It was nothing she ever mentioned, if she ever thought about it. She probably wouldn't even have known the words for it. All those people out there walking the roads all those years, hardly a one of them remembering the Sabbath. Who would know what day of the week it was? Who wouldn't take work when there was work to be done? What use was there in calling a day by a certain name, or thinking of it as anything but weather? They knew what time of the year it was when the timothy bloomed, when the birds were fledging. They knew it was morning when the sun came up. What more was there to know? If Doll was going to be lost forever, Lila wanted to be right there with her, holding to the skirt of her dress.

She had put on her own dress, not one of the nice ones from the Boughtons' attic or the new ones from the Sears, Roebuck catalogue, and her own shoes. No need to worry she might dirty them. When she stepped out the door she felt that good chill, the dark of the morning she used to wake up to every day. The trees stirred in the darkness, and birds made those startled sounds they do when the stars are gone and there is still no sunrise. The river smelled like any river, fishy and mossy and shadowy, and the smell seemed stronger in the dark, with the chink and plosh of all the small life. She eased herself down to the edge of the water and put her hands in it. She took it up in her cupped hands, poured it over her brow, rubbed it into her face and into her hair. Then she did the same thing again, wetting the front of her dress. And again. Her hands were so cold she felt them against her face as if they weren't hers at all. The river was like the old life, just itself. Nothing more to it. She thought, It has washed the baptism off me. So that's done with. That must be what I wanted. Now, if I ever found Doll out there lost and wandering, at least she would recognize me. If there could be no joy for her in whatever was not life, at least she might remember for one second what joy had felt like. Lila thought about that for a while, seeing Doll walking ahead on some old dusty road, nothing on every side of her, and calling out her name so she would turn, and then running into her arms. No, Lila would be sitting on those steps, after it was dark, long after, and then Doll would be there, all out of breath, saying, "Child, child, I thought I was *never* going to find you!" When the sun had been up a little while she decided she could go back to the Reverend's house. Maybe no one would see her. They would all be in church.

She put on the blue dress she had found in the mail order catalogue he gave her. It was the first time she had taken the dress out of the box it came in. And she put on the white sandals, and she brushed her hair. In St. Louis one of the girls had said to her, Just pretend you're pretty so they can pretend you're pretty. The old man would come home, or stay in his study at the church. Someone might invite him to dinner, which they ate in the middle of the day on Sunday. And he might say yes rather than come back to his own house, which would still be empty, or where he would find her and have to think of a way to speak to her. When she did something wrong, something that made him unhappy, he was embarrassed by it, and he would smile and say, "Perhaps you could help me understand . . . you are so quiet . . ." But she would not know how to explain, and if she told him how strange and alone she felt, and wanted to feel, he would wonder why she stayed with him at all. Now that there might be a child she'd best try to act like she belonged there, at least for a while. Her hands still smelled like river water, and her hair. She still felt a little more like who she was. That was a help.

She could read. Doll had seen to that. She might sit on the porch with a magazine and wait for him there. Then he could ask her what she was reading, or she could tell him that there was a word she didn't understand, as there certainly would be. So she was sitting with a copy of *The Nation* in her lap, when, hours after church would have ended, she saw the Reverend walking up the road, Boughton beside him, the two of them talking together as they always did, and listening to each other, as if, so far into their lives, some new thing might still be said, something not to be missed. Boughton saw her first and said a word to the Reverend, who glanced up, and then they stopped in the road to say goodbye and the old man came on alone. His body still had the habits of largeness and strength, as if he had learned to be a little slow when he moved, out of consideration for whatever might be around him, whatever he might bump or displace. Still, he was slower than usual, taking his time, approaching his own door with a reluctance she saw and regretted, since this time might be the time that he would not forgive her, or at least the time that he would have decided he did not want her to stay.

He took off his hat as he came up the steps. Then he stood there a moment, turning the brim of it in his hands, just taking her in. "*The Nation*," he said, as if that was as strange as anything else that had happened to him lately.

So she said, "I got to do more reading. It's something I been meaning to do for a while now."

After a moment he said, "Yes, well, that's always worthwhile, I guess." His voice was mild, almost amused. He shifted his weight, the way he did when something surprised him a little.

So she said, "Seems like I'm carrying a child." She had not meant to tell him then, but she couldn't very well wait until he decided to be angry to tell him, or until he told her he just wanted his life to himself again, as she expected him to do any day. If that happened, her pride would make her leave, without a mention of it, and there was no telling what would become of her and the child, if there was a child.

He said, "Really." He sat down on the porch swing beside her, at a little distance from her. He said, "Is that a fact." Then he said, "This is not at all how I thought this day would end."

She had not looked at his face yet. She was watching the wind move the trees. It was a soft evening wind, and the trees were darkening, filling with shadows. It would be time to stop working, not soon but sometime. A wind like that used to mean the day isn't endless, sometime there'll be supper and talk and sleep. So many things they knew together and never spoke about at all.

He said, "So, then, you've decided to stay."

"I never did plan on leaving." For a town it wasn't such a bad place. The trees were big enough that it was almost like living in the woods. There was no reason not to make another garden. She could plant some flowers.

After a minute he said, "When you go off like that, you might leave a note. I don't always know what to think. You left your wedding ring."

"I just forget to put it on sometimes."

"Yes. I guess I knew that."

"I'm always wearing that locket you give me."

It seemed strange to her to wear a ring. It was a gold ring. She might harm it in some way. It might slip off her finger and be lost.

"Lila," he said, "I'm glad to know you aren't planning to leave. But if you ever change your mind, I want you to leave by daylight. I want you to have a train ticket in your hand that will take you right where you want to go, and I want you to take your ring and anything else I have given you. You might want to sell it. That would be all right. It's yours, not mine. It doesn't belong here—I mean it wouldn't—" He cleared his throat. "You're my wife," he said. "I want to take care of you, even if that means someday seeing you to the train." He leaned forward and looked into her face, almost sternly, so she would know he meant what he said.

She thought, We would be safe here. He would be good to a child. But if he was going to put her on the train, where would the child be then? Would he expect her to leave it behind when she left? Or did he think there wasn't going to be any child? Well, sometimes you expect you're going to have a baby, then nothing comes of it. You can't set your heart on it.

"I can't yet know for sure," she said. "Whether there's going to be a baby."

"I understand that."

"You might think it's a story I made up to smooth things over. If it don't turn out to be true." She didn't want to have to worry about what he might think if a day came when he stopped trusting her. *When* that day came. She was sure it would.

He said, very gently, "I would never suspect you of such a thing," as if a lie like that would be too low for her even to think about.

She thought, If it *was* a lie, and if it had come to mind, I just might have told it. It surely did smooth things over. She said, "I ain't what you seem to think I am. I done some things in my life.

25

Like I told you." The time would come when he would understand that, too. Better that he shouldn't be too surprised. She knew he wouldn't ask for more particulars, not now.

He was quiet, and then he said, "You are the only person in this world I want to have sitting here beside me. That isn't what I think, it's what I know. I guess it doesn't explain anything. Have you had supper?"

"Some bread and jam."

He patted her knee. "I wouldn't call that supper. We have to take care of you." The kitchen was empty, so he went to the neighbors and came back with a bottle of milk and a can of baked beans. He laughed. "We'll do better tomorrow." She knew about that other wife and that other baby. If she had given herself some time to think, she'd have realized they would be on his mind.

She was there in Gilead in the first place because once when she was walking along the road, probably hoping to get to Sioux City, tired of walking, tired of carrying her suitcase and her bedroll, she had noticed a little house sitting a way off by a cluster of cottonwood trees, a sort of cabin someone had built and abandoned along with the fields around it. So she thought she'd take a look. Then she knew for sure it was abandoned because people had camped there and left clutter behind, and broken up the stoop for firewood, and no one had ever fixed any of it or cleared it away. The people who left the mess might come back and tell her it was their place—just look at the beer cans and the snoose tins, who you think put them there? She had seen that happen before. You seen them spent cartridges out by the trees? You think it was squirrels dropped them? Nothing to do then but move on.

But she had been there for weeks and so far no one had

come. She knew how to get by so long as nobody bothered her. Plenty of fish in the river. There were dandelion greens. Mushrooms. You can chew pine sap if you want to. You can eat the roots of things. Cattails. Wild carrot. Nettles are very good if you know how to pick them and cook them. Doll said you just had to know what wouldn't kill you. Most folks don't eat squirrel, but you can. Turtles. Snakes, if need be. Lila couldn't really live that way for very long, only until the weather turned cold. But she wanted to stay in one place for a while. The loneliness was bad, but it was better than anything else she could think of. It was probably loneliness that made her walk the mile or so into town every few days just to look at the houses and stores and the flower gardens. She never meant to talk to anybody. She had a dress she wore and a dress she saved, and she was wearing the good one, the clean one, the one she kept a little nice so that she could go walking where people might see her, when she got caught in the rain that Sunday and stepped into the church, just to save her dress. And there was that old man, speaking above the sound of the rain against the windows. He looked at her, and looked away again. "Blessed be the name of the Lord."

They didn't really ask for money. They passed a plate, but nobody made you put anything in it. She began counting up the days, so she would know when it was Sunday again. She lost count once. People living the way she was could go crazy. She began to wonder if that had already happened to her. She thought, If I'm crazy, I may as well do what I feel like doing. No point being crazy if you have to worry all the time about what people are thinking anyway. There were ten or twenty good reasons why she would not go to church. Doll never did. The place was full of strangers. She had only the one dress to wear. They all knew the songs, they knew what they were supposed to do and say and what it meant. They all knew each other. The preacher said things that bothered her, she couldn't make sense of them. Resurrection. But she guessed she liked the candles and the singing. She guessed she didn't have a better place to be.

She was probably crazy, and she was probably leaving, so she decided she would talk to that preacher. There were a hundred reasons why she would never go to his house, in that same old dress, and ask him a question. She was never one to put herself forward. But there was no way to keep the mice out of that shack. The fields around it were going all to tansy. In St. Louis they gave them tansy tea, and she hated the smell of it. So she had decided to leave. Then why not ask him? He would just say, That crazy woman came to my door with something on her mind, and then I never saw her again after that. Soon enough he'd forget it ever happened. He wouldn't know what to tell her. But who else was she ever going to ask?

When he saw her at the door he looked surprised and not surprised, as if he had no reason to expect her and there she was anyway. He was in his shirtsleeves and house slippers, looking older than he did in the pulpit, and she thought she had come too early in the morning. But what did it matter.

He said, "Hello. Good morning," and waited, as if he expected her to explain herself. Then he said, "Please come in." When she stepped inside the house, he began to apologize for how bare it was. "I'm not much for keeping things up. I suppose you can see that. Still—" and he gestured at the sofa, which was covered with papers and books. "Let me make a little space for you here. I don't have much company. You can probably see that, too." She didn't know then that it would have embarrassed him to have her there, a woman alone with him, a stranger. But he didn't want her to leave, she did know that. "Can I get you a glass of water? I could make coffee, if you have a few minutes."

She had a day, a week, a month. She said, "I got nowhere to be."

He smiled at her, or to himself, as if he saw that the mystery of her presence might just be something a few dollars could help with. He said, "Then I'll make coffee."

She stood up. "I don't even know why I come here." She recognized that smile. She had hated people for it.

"Well— We could talk a little. Sometimes that helps. I mean, helps make things clearer—"

She said, "I don't much like to talk."

He laughed. "Well, that's fine, too. A lot of people around here feel that way. But they do enjoy a cup of coffee."

She said, "I don't know why I come here. That's a fact."

He shrugged. "Since you *are* here, maybe you could tell me a little about yourself?"

She shook her head. "I don't talk about that. I just been wondering lately why things happen the way they do."

"Oh!" he said. "Then I'm glad you have some time to spare. I've been wondering about that more or less my whole life." He brought her into the kitchen and seated her at the table, and after he had made coffee they sat there together for a while, saying practically nothing. Yes, the weather had been fine. He traced a scratch on the table with his finger. And then he began to tell her about the brother and sisters who died before he was born, and how his mother said once that the stairs were scuffed by the children's shoes because she could never keep them from running in the house. And when she found a scrawl in a book, she said, "One of the children must have done it." There was a kind of fondness and sadness in her voice that he heard only when she mentioned them. So when he found a scratch or a mark on something, he still thought, One of the children. His brother Edward, the oldest, was spared the diphtheria that took the rest of them. So Edward knew the children, and he had stories about them. One, closest to him, was named John, a family name. Once, he heard his brother call him Non-John, thinking he was too young to understand. Because Edward missed the brother he had lost, he always did miss him. He was—very loyal to him. Their mother and father and grandfather seldom mentioned those children. They could hardly bear to think of them. "There's been a good deal of sorrow in this old place," he said. "Some of it mine. Some I used to wish were mine. So I sort of live with the question. Why things happen. I guess this isn't much help."

She liked to hear people tell stories. The saddest ones were the best. She wondered if that meant anything at all. Of course, when people talked about themselves that way, they were usually trying to get you to talk about yourself in the same way. That would be what this preacher wanted. But she and Doll had a secret between them. The old woman who took them in said, "Doll, you know you can go to jail for stealing a child. And I can go to jail for helping you do it." She said, "You're flirting with the worst kind of trouble." So Lila couldn't think of breathing a word, even now. Stealing a child, when Doll had come to her like an angel in the wilderness. The Reverend talked about angels, and the notion helped her to think about certain things. She was swept up and carried away, with that old shawl around her.

He said, "I don't often talk about this. I don't often talk to anyone who doesn't know about it already. You've come here to ask me a question, and I've been going on about myself."

She said, "I liked that story."

He looked away from her and laughed. "It *is* a story, isn't it? I've never really thought of it that way. And I suppose the next time I tell it, it will be a better story. Maybe a little less true. I might not tell it again. I hope I won't. You're right not to talk. It's a sort of higher honesty, I think. Once you start talking, there's no telling what you'll say."

She said, "I wouldn't know about that."

"Apparently not. I do. I've spent my life talking— But you have that question. Maybe you could help me understand it a little better. Tell me how it came to be on your mind. In a few words."

She said, "I got time to myself. I think about things."

"Yes. Clearly you do. Interesting things."

"I spose everybody thinks about 'em."

He laughed. "Right. But that's interesting, too."

"On Sundays you talk about the Good Lord, how He does one thing and another."

"Yes, I do." And he blushed. It was as if he expected that question, too, and was surprised again that the thing he expected for no reason was actually happening. He said, "I know that I am not—adequate to the subject. You have to forgive me."

She nodded. "That's all you going to say."

"No. No, it isn't. I think you are asking me these questions because of some hard things that have happened, the things you won't talk about. If you did tell me about them, I could probably not say more than that life is a very deep mystery, and that finally the grace of God is all that can resolve it. And the grace of God is also a very deep mystery." He said, "You can probably tell I've said these same words too many times. But they're true, I believe." He shrugged, and watched his finger trace the scar on the table.

After a minute she said, "Well, all right. I better go now." She didn't always remember yet to say thank you for the coffee, thank you for your time and your trouble. He walked her to the door and opened it for her, and she forgot to thank him for that. He looked tired, and as though he was sorry the conversation had ended. He said, "Thank you for coming by. It has been interesting. For me." Then he said, "Whatever it is, or was, that you didn't tell me, I regret it. Very much."

Still, she believed she must have turned him against her, when she thought back on it. Showing up at his door like that. But the next few days people she didn't know would stop her on the road and offer her work, even a spare room. One lady invited her for a supper at the church, and she went, hoping the Reverend wouldn't be there. They said they expected him, but he didn't come. That was the lady who told her about the wife and the child, speaking very softly out of respect for the sadness of the story. She said it was something he never talked about to anyone. Reverend Boughton, of course, but no one else. "He forgets things, like he did the supper tonight," she said. "He's always been that way."

If she stayed in Gilead, she could earn some money. She could buy some things at the store. Soap, and thread, and a box of salt. She could be in out of the weather when she wanted. All they asked her to do was a little gardening, a little washing and ironing, and she could do those things as well as anybody. So it wasn't really charity. They didn't bother her with talk. They gave her Sundays to herself. If she left she had nowhere to go especially, except not St. Louis. She decided she might as well stay for a while, putting a little aside to make things easier when she changed her mind. It was one of those Sundays, after church, that she thought to walk up to the cemetery. She found the wife and child there, sure enough. The grass was mowed, but nobody had thought to prune the roses.

He had given a sermon, "'Let your light shine before men; that they may see your good works, and glorify your Father who is in heaven.'" He said it meant that when you did a good thing it should seem to come from God, not from you. It should not feel to other people like your goodness, and it should not feel that way to you, either. Any good thing is less good the more any human being lays claim to it. She thought, All right, that's why he told these other people to help me out. That's why he can't look at me. You'd think he was ashamed of something. Ever since that morning I went to his house and he could see well enough I was on hard times, he's hardly said a word to me.

Well, that's all fine, except it don't seem honest. I spose he wants me to think it's God been putting money in my pocket, when it's just him. It might even be his money they been paying me with. Church money. Doane said they did things in churches to make people believe what they told them.

That was the day she walked out with a pew Bible. They would have been so happy to give her one that she couldn't bear the thought. They'd take it wrong. She wasn't getting religion, she just wanted to know what he was talking about. For her own reasons. And someday, when she had decided to leave, she'd probably bring it back. It made her feel better to be interested in something. That much less time for the thoughts that worried her.

But she wanted him to know she wasn't such a fool as he might have thought she was. Since he did seem to think about her. So she began tending that grave. There was writing on it. *We wept that one so lovely should have a life so brief.* Must be from the Bible. Let's see if he thinks it was God who scraped the moss off the headstone and put the ivy there. Who cut back the yew shrubs so some light could get through. Who would make the roses bloom. And she had noticed that the garden behind his house was running to weeds, so she began tending that, too. Once, he found her working there—looking after her potato plants, though he didn't seem to notice. Picking the beetles off and dropping them in a tin can. He said, "You have done so much. It looks wonderful. I would like to give you something for it." He had his wallet in one hand, his hat in the other.

She said, "I owe you a kindness."

"No," he said. "No. You certainly don't owe me anything."

"I best decide that," she said.

"Yes. Well, if there is ever—anything at all. That you need— If you ever want to talk again, I might do better this time." He shrugged. "I can't promise, but I'll try."

33

She said, "I ain't making any promises," and he laughed. Then she said, "I'm thinking about it. Thank you." He was a beautiful old man. His brow was heavy, but his eyes were kind. Why should he care what she thought, whether she stayed or left, what became of her? She knew what she looked like, with her big hands and her rangy arms, and her face that had been burned a hundred times, more, and her scorched hair and her eyes the sun had faded. In St. Louis they had made a sort of game of it, trying to pretty her up. Everything looked wrong. Just *pretend* you're pretty. Mainly she'd cleaned up around the place, helped the others with their clothes and their hair. When she tried to pretend, they'd laugh. He did have a way of looking at her, when he looked at her at all. She had to admit it. But if she let herself start thinking like that, he would begin to matter to her, and the times she had let that happen, those two or three times, nothing had come of it but trouble. She had a habit now of putting questions to him in her mind. What do you ever tell people in a sermon except that things that happen mean something? Some man dies somewhere a long time ago and that means something. People eat a bit of bread and that means something. Then why won't you say how you know that? Do you just talk that way because you're a preacher? This kind of thinking made a change in her loneliness, made it more tolerable for her. And she knew how dangerous that could be. She had told herself more than once not to call it loneliness, since it wasn't any different from one year to the next, it was just how her body felt, like hungry or tired, except it was always there, always the same. Now and again she had distracted herself from it for a while. And it always came back and felt worse.

But she began to think about getting herself baptized. She thought there might be something about that water on her forehead that would cool her mind. She had to get through her life one way or another. No reason not to take any comfort the world seemed to offer her. If none of it made sense to her now, that might change if she let it. If none of it meant anything, after all, no harm done. Then he told her that they would be having a class, and she would be very welcome to join them. She was still making up her mind, just walking past the church because she thought she might be early or she had come the wrong evening, because she had walked past twice before and had not seen anyone going in. She never really knew the time, and she could lose track of the days. But then there was the preacher coming along the street toward her, so she just stood there where she was and waited. Nothing else to do. He had taken off his hat when he saw her, so he probably meant to speak to her. She had not thought what she might say to him, had not expected to speak to him at all, only to sit in the row farthest from him and listen and keep her questions to herself.

He said, "Good evening. I'm happy to see you here."

And she said, "I figure I better get myself baptized. No one seen to it for me when I was a child." Realizing as she heard herself say the words that after all her thinking she felt almost in the habit of speaking her mind to him. Didn't she know better than to let herself think like that? Hadn't she told herself a hundred times? This is what was bound to come of it. He didn't even look quite the way he looked to her in her thoughts, and still she had spoken to him as if she knew him. That's what came of living the way she did.

"Well," he said. "Yes. We'll take care of that. Certainly."

Everything she said seemed to surprise him a little. No wonder, when it surprised her, too. She thought, How do I know what I'll be saying with all them church people watching me? She said, "I can't come tonight. I got to work." And she turned and walked away, instantly embarrassed to realize how strange she must look, hurrying off for no real reason into the dark of the evening. The lonely dark, where she could only expect to go crazier, in that shack where she still lived because it was hard for her to be with people. It would be truer to say hid than lived, since about the only comfort she had in it was being by herself. If she didn't go back now, before the full ache of shame set in, she knew she would never set foot in that church again. The best thing about church was that when she sat in the last pew there was no one looking at her. She could come a little late and leave a little early, when she wanted to. She could listen to the sermon and the singing. People might wonder why she was there, but they never asked. And it was just interesting to hear the old man talk about being born and dying and the rest of it, things most folks are pretty quiet about. Not much else was keeping her in that town. So she decided she would go back to the church and walk in the door the way she meant to do in the first place. But when she did walk in, he stood up, so she left, and those ladies followed her out into the street. They must have been talking about her. So what? They could have let her go if they'd wanted to. If she felt like a fool, so what? He stood up like he did before, and he smiled and said, "I'm glad you could be here, after all." She said, "Thank you." And after that it was easier. Genesis, Exodus, Leviticus. Abraham, Isaac, Jacob. At least she was beginning to learn a little.

If she thought about the preacher so she wouldn't think about other things, she could just as well be remembering the old times, when she had Doll. No point wondering about that cabin Doll took her from, or who it was that had kept her alive when she was newborn and helpless. She had picked up the Bible and read at the place it fell open, and she found this: *In the day thou wast born thy navel was not cut, neither wast thou washed in water to cleanse thee . . . No eye pitied thee.* And she fell to thinking that somebody had to have pitied her, or any child that lives. *I passed by thee, and saw thee weltering in thy blood.* Lila had seen children born. They were just as naked and strange as some bug you would dig up out of the ground. You would want to wash the child and wrap it up in something to hide it, out of pity. Hard as she tried, all she could remember were skirts brushing against her, hands not so rough as other hands. That might have been the one who made her live. What did it matter. In the evenings when it was too dim to read she wrapped herself in her blanket, huddled up in a corner so that her face and her feet were covered, and thought or dreamed, slept or lay awake. If Doll was her mother she wouldn't have had to steal her, so Lila knew that much. What could matter any less than where she came from? Well, she thought, where I'm going might matter less. Or maybe why I'm here by myself in the dark wondering about it. She didn't mind the dark or the crickets or even the scurry of mice, really, and it pleased her to think that the stars were there, just outside an open window. In the dark of the morning, in her nightdress, with her bar of soap, she walked down to bathe in the river. No one could see her. She could hardly see herself. She liked the smell of the soap. She felt the stones and the silt at her feet, but there was a good sting of cold in the water sliding over her skin. It made her take gasping breaths that left the taste of air in her throat. Doll used to say, "Now you're just as clean as a body can be."

Then she would put on the nightdress again, walk back to the cabin, brush the litter of leaves and sticks off her feet as well as she could, wrap herself in her blanket, and lie awake, her body slowly warming the damp of the dress, and she would think about the way things happened. One night, because she had found those words in the Bible, thinking about how it could have happened that she was born and had lived. Sickly as she was when Doll took her up. Then how to imagine whoever it was that had bothered with her even that much, to keep body and soul together. It was nothing against Doll to think there had to have been someone there before her, someone who held her and fed her. She thought of the preacher's wife, that girl with her newborn baby in her arms. The woman who told her about them said, "She just slipped away, and in a few hours the baby followed her." And the preacher was left all alone.

What had become of Mellie, who was never scared? She could ask him about that. Mellie'd poke a snake with a stick just to get a better look at it. Once, she climbed from a fence railing onto the back of a young bull calf, hanging on with her arms around its neck. Doane saw what she was doing and came over to the fence and climbed up and lifted her off the thing before it could really decide how to get rid of her. It had scraped her leg against a post and left it raw enough that the flies bothered it, but she just said she had a notion that if you rode a bull every day from the time it was young you could ride it when it was growed. Then you could go anywhere and folks would say, Here she comes, riding on that bull. Doane said, "Well, that ain't your bull. Four, five days we'll be gone from here." And she said, "I coulda stayed on that thing if you'd let me. I know that much." He laughed. "You know, if he'd decided to, he'd of broke that leg. For a start. Then, when you're useless, who's sposed to look after you?" She said, "My leg don't even hurt that bad!"

He was always telling her she was going to break her neck sometime and they'd have to just go on and leave her lying beside the road. She never paid any mind to that at all. And she never broke her neck, though sometimes she did seem to be trying to. She saw some town girls skipping rope and found a piece of rope herself and figured out how to do it better than they did, crossing her arms, hopping on one foot. She tried a sort of handspring, but without her hands, since they had to be holding the rope. She'd fall in the road and come right back up again, and she'd say, "I pertinearly done it that time." A skinny, freckled child with her white brows drawn together and her raggedy white hair flying, meaning to make herself the best rope jumper there ever was. If she saw an outhouse she'd go into it, looking for a catalogue, and if she found one she'd come back with a few pages and study them for days, trying to decide what things were and what they were good for. She'd say, "I can't quite make out the words yet. I'm working on it." Doll called it all tomfoolery, and she'd say to Lila, "I'm glad you don't go acting like that," even before Lila was strong enough to have tried to, even though she never showed any sign of wanting to. She was Doll's girl, always at her side if she could be. Mellie had walked the same roads every summer, and she could wander away without getting lost. She would try now and then to make a chum of Lila, telling her she knew where there were huckleberries, or that she would show her how to catch a fish in her bare hands, but Lila always wanted Doll near her, at least in her sight.

What could the old man say about all those people born with more courage than they could find a way to spend, and then there was nothing to do with it but just get by? And that was when the times were decent. She had always been jealous of Mellie because the others took pleasure from her pranks and her notions. She was always making them laugh. Once, Mellie said, "I believe my knees have been skint my whole life. My elbows, too." Doane laughed and said, "Then I guess you must of been born that way. If ever anybody was." And where would a girl like that find any kind of life that asked more of her than just standing up to hardship? Something an animal could do better, a mule. Doll said, Whatever happens, just be quiet and it'll pass, most likely. But those weren't thoughts Lila wanted to have, and when she began to think that way she might as well get up and wait for the dawn to come. She might as well start deciding where she would go for work that day, what house she hadn't gone to for a while. They always gave her work, even if it was only something a child could do, like cutting kindling, and she didn't want to burden anyone by coming there too often.

That morning Mrs. Graham had some clothes for her, a skirt and two blouses that she said her daughter had left when she moved to Des Moines. They'd just been hanging in the closet. Lila might as well have them if she could use them. Lila thought, This is the very worst part of being broke. Everybody can see how broke you are. It seems like this whole town is making a project of knowing every damn thing I don't have. If I left here, I could wear these things and nobody would give it a thought. If I stay, I'm walking around in somebody else's old clothes, somebody's charity. Mrs. Graham was watching her face, a little pleased with herself, and regretful, and embarrassed. She said, "You needn't take them if you don't have any use for them, dear. I just thought they might be your size."

Lila said, "They look about right. I could probly use them. Sure." She should have said thank you, she knew it, but she never asked anybody for anything except work, and if they gave her something else they did it for their own reasons. She wasn't beholden to them, because being beholden was the one thing she could not stand. She wouldn't even look at the clothes, though she knew Mrs. Graham hoped she would. So they must be all right, she thought. Nothing too wore out anyway. And then she did Mrs. Graham's ironing, thinking about those clothes and how she would probably wear them to church, since that would feel better, at least, than wearing the same old dress. Even if the preacher noticed, and that made her feel beholden to him, and they all knew it. So when she was done at Mrs. Graham's house she took the bag of clothes and walked up to the cemetery. There was the grave of the John Ames who died as a boy, with a sister Martha on one side and a sister Margaret on the other. She had never really thought about the way the dead would gather at the edge of a town, all their names spelled out so you'd know whose they were for as long as that family lived in that place. And there was the Reverend John Ames, who would have been the preacher's father, with his wife beside him. It must be strange to know your whole life where you will be buried. To see these stones with your own name on them. Someday the old man would lie down beside his wife. And there she would be, after so many years, waiting in sunlight, all covered in roses.

She couldn't stay in the shack when the weather changed. There would be no way to keep warm. Wind came through the walls and rain came through the roof. That woman had offered her a spare room, but she might have changed her mind since the week or so when everybody in the church was offering her something. If she was going to leave town, she should do it before travel got too hard. She would probably have to decide between a bus ticket and a winter coat. And her shoes were about gone. No point thinking about it. She would decide one way or another for one reason or another, save up what she could while she could, and whatever she did, she'd get by, most likely.

Lila had lived in a real house before. Not the one in St. Louis. A respectable boardinghouse in the town of Tammany, Iowa. Doll took a job there so Lila could go to school for a year, long enough to learn how to read and do some figures. Mrs. Marker, whose house it was, did the cooking, but Doll did the cleaning and laundry and looked after the poultry and the gardens, and Lila helped with all of it. Doll wanted her to know what it was to have a regular life. Not that Doll knew much about it herself, but Mrs. Marker would yell about everything she did wrong, so she got better at it with time, until school was almost out. Then she told Lila, "I'm tired of listening to that woman. She can hang her own damn wash." And they just gathered up what was theirs and walked away.

Lila liked school. She liked sheets and pillowcases. They had a room of their own, with curtains and a dresser. They ate their supper at a table in the kitchen, where Lila did her lessons while Doll washed the dishes. Doll never did complain, so Lila was surprised when she said they were going to leave, but she didn't say a word and she didn't look back, though the house had seemed pretty to her. It was where she had learned to tend roses. But that was their pride, to tolerate whatever they could and not one bit more, to give no sign of wanting or regretting, and for the children to show the grown-ups respect in front of strangers. It was spring, so there would be work, and Doll knew more or less where to look for Doane's people. They were two days finding them and a week waiting to be asked to eat with them again. Things were always different after their year in Tammany. It was as if they had been disloyal and were never quite forgiven for it. When Lila read a sign to Mellie, GENERAL STORE, Mellie would say, "Well, anybody can see that's a general store, so what them words *going* to say? County jail? It don't look like nothing else but a store, does it?" If Lila read DRY GOODS or NOTIONS AND SUN-DRIES, Mellie would say, "Ah, you just making that up. It don't even mean anything."

But Lila could read, and Doll was glad of it, no matter what anybody thought. She said it would come in useful. Maybe it would sometime. Mostly Mellie was right—it told her what she'd have known anyway. NO HELP WANTED HERE. It had been good for knowing the names of towns that were too broke and forgotten to need names, which is why you had to read the sign to find it out. Still, when she was getting a can of beans and a spool of twine at the store, she had bought herself a tablet and a pencil. She was just curious to know what she hadn't forgotten yet. She had turned down the corner of that page, and she copied out those words. *And as for thy nativity, in the day thou wast born thy navel was not cut, neither wast thou washed in water to cleanse thee; thou wast not salted at all, nor swaddled at all. No eye pitied thee, to do any of these things unto thee, to have compassion upon thee; but thou wast cast out in the open field, for that thy person was abhorred, in the day that thou wast born. And when I passed by thee, and saw thee weltering in thy blood, I said unto thee, Though thou art in thy blood, live; yea, I said unto thee, Though thou art in thy blood, live.* She thought, First time I ever heard of salting a baby. She made the letters slowly and carefully, not so easily even as she had made them as a child, but she told herself she would write a little every day. Practice, the teacher said, when her lessons were so clumsy-looking beside all the others that she was shamed almost to tears. You just need a little more practice.

And she began to look forward to morning. As soon as there was light enough, she sat at the door with the tablet on her knee and wrote. She copied words, because she wasn't sure how to spell them, and this was a way to learn. Who would ever know if she spelled them wrong? Nobody ever came around. Still it shamed her to think how ignorant it might look to her if she weren't too ignorant to know any better. So she wrote, *In the beginning God created the heavens and the earth. And the earth was waste and void; and darkness was upon the face of the deep.* Waste and void. Darkness was upon the face of the deep. She would like to ask him about that. She wrote it all again, ten times.

She enjoyed a morning when the heat was coming on and she was still a little cold from washing in the river. At dawn the chant of the crickets and grasshoppers and the tree toads and cicadas was already slow. It was as if the heat and sunlight were taking more than they were meant to take, more damp, more smell, just because they could. They were so strong, and nothing else was really awake yet. There was a feeling of something like injury about the earth smell and the dew smell, the leaf smell. The tansy didn't bother her so much anymore. Doane said deer hate tansy, and maybe that was why they hadn't found the squash growing by the cabin, just a few seeds left lying by the stump other people had used to chop wood and clean fish and gut rabbits. She planted them, and now there were big, tented blooms, yellow as could be, and big vines trailing over the ground. She hoped the old man did not know where she was staying, and she knew he would never come there if he did. But if he ever did come, she hoped it would be in the morning. Those little white moths fluttering over it made that raggedy old meadow seem almost like a garden.

When they were children they used to be glad when they stayed in a workers' camp, shabby as they all were, little rows of cabins with battered tables and chairs and moldy cots inside, and maybe some dishes and spoons. They were dank and they smelled of mice, and Marcelle made everybody sleep outside except when it rained, but they always had a cabin, and they kept everything they carried in it during the daytime. And Lila and Mellie and the boys, when they weren't working, played that it was their house or their fort or their cave. They would search it for anything that might have been left there, and if they found half a bootlace or a piece of a broken cup they would make up stories about what it was and why they were lucky to find it. Once, Arthur's boy Deke found a penny that had been left on a railroad track and squashed flat. He held it up to the door and put a nail through it. Somebody sometime had nailed a horseshoe above the door of a cabin they had for a week, and they felt this must be important. They were wary of the strangers and hostile to their children, except for Mellie, who always wanted to play with the babies and would be just sociable enough to get their mothers or sisters to let her. Mellie playing mumblety-peg and tending a grubby infant between turns, hum-hum-hum, rocking it in her bony arms, playing at mother and child.

They would all be working in the orchards, picking apples or cherries or pears. They would be up in the tops of the trees all day long, and they would never spill a basket or break a branch. It was work children did best. They were given crates of fruit that was too ripe or bruised, and the children ate it till they were sick of it and sick of the souring smell of it and the shiny little black bugs that began to cover it, and then they would start throwing it at each other and get themselves covered with rotten pear and apricot. Flies everywhere. They'd be in trouble for getting their clothes dirtier than they were before. Doane hated those camps. He'd say, "Folks sposed to live like that?" But the children thought they were fine.

She would tell the old man, I didn't use to mind tansy. I still like an apricot now and then. She pretended he knew some of her thoughts, only some of them, the ones she would like to show him. Mellie with her babies. Doll smiling because she had a bit of sugar candy from the store to slip into Lila's hand when the others weren't looking. Any one of them could walk through that field, plucking at the blue stem and the clover, thinking their own thoughts, natural as could be. They had passed through so many other places just like it, a whole world of weedy, sunny, raggedy fields with no names to them. Only that one name, the United States of America. If they could be there the way they were in her mind, before the times got hard, then he could know them. She would want him to know them.

No. Why did she let herself think that way? If he saw this place he would just be embarrassed at how poor she was, how rough she lived. He wouldn't quite look at her, he'd try not to look at anything else, and he wouldn't say much at all. She'd be hating him and hoping he knew it. Then when he was gone she would have all that kindness to deal with. And she hadn't even saved up enough yet for a bus ticket. Maybe that is the one thing she could bring herself to ask them for. A ticket out of town. She'd probably have one in her hand before she finished asking.

So she started copying again. *And the Spirit of God moved upon the face of the waters. And God said, Let there be light: and there was light. And God saw the light, that it was good: and God divided the light from the darkness. And God called the light Day, and the darkness he called Night.* She wrote it out ten times. If she could make herself write smaller, she wouldn't fill up the tablet for a while. She wrote Lila Dahl, Lila Dahl, Lila Dahl. The teacher had misunderstood somehow and made up that name for her. "You're Norwegian! I should have known by the freckles," she said, and wrote the name down on the roll. "My grandmother is Norwegian, too," and she smiled. At supper, when Lila told her what had happened, Doll just said, "Don't matter." That was the first time she ever thought about names. Turns out she was missing one all that time and hadn't even noticed. She said, "Then what's your last name going to be? 'Cause it can't be Dahl, can it?" and Doll said, "That don't matter, either."

She couldn't keep the Bible and the tablet in her suitcase, because that was the first thing anybody would steal. Her bedroll would be the second thing. She had put the money she was saving in a canning jar under a loose floorboard, but it was too dirty down there for anything else. It was really just the clumsiness of the writing she wanted to hide, because she thought, What if he saw it? Then she thought, That's what comes of spending all this time by myself. So she set them on top of the suitcase, thinking a thief would probably just clear them off there and leave them lying on the floor, since they weren't worth anything. And anybody who would steal from her was probably twice as ignorant as she was and wouldn't take any notice of them anyway.

The thought came to her that very morning. Why was she always walking into Gilead? There were farms around. One of them must need help. Anyone who saw her could tell she was used to the work. Those folks in Gilead knew her too well. She was tired of it. And when she asked herself that question and answered it—No good reason—she felt as though she had put a burden down. It used to be when they were with Doane and Marcelle and they had to pass through a town, they'd clean up the best they could first, and then they would walk along together, looking straight ahead, as if there could not be one thing in the whole place that would interest them. Town people thought they were better. They all knew that, and hated them for it. Doane or Marcelle might go into a store to buy a few things they needed and a little bag of candy or a jar of molasses, but the rest of them just kept walking till they were out in the country again. Somehow Mellie would have figured out hopscotch, never seeming to watch the girls that were playing at it in the street, and that would be all she and Lila thought about for days afterward. They left a trail of hopscotch behind them, Mellie always thinking of ways to make it harder. They'd be jumping along in the dust, barefoot, with licorice drops in their mouths, feeling as though they had run off with everything in that town that was worth having.

Walking into Gilead, she felt just the way she had felt in those days, except now she was alone. Doane used to say, We ain't tramps, we ain't Gypsies, we ain't wild Indians, when he wanted the children to behave. She asked Doll one time, What are we, then? and Doll had said, We're just folks. But Lila could tell that wasn't true, that there was more to it anyway. Why this shame? No one had ever really explained it to her, and she could never explain it to herself. *Thou wast cast out in the open field.* All right. That was none of her doing. She had worked herself tough and ugly for nothing more than to stay alive, and she wasn't so sure she saw the point of that. Why did she care what people thought. She was nothing to them, they were nothing to her. There really was not a soul on earth she should be worrying about at all. Especially not that preacher. Doll would be glad to see her no matter what. Ugly old Doll. Who had said to her, Live. Not once, but every time she washed and mended for her, mothered her as if she were a child someone could want. Lila remembered more than she ever let on.

Those thoughts. Still, she would go down the road until she

saw a farmstead, and then she'd just look for someone to talk to and ask. Simple as that. And she'd take some sort of hard work that would wear her out, and then she'd sleep. No dreams and no thinking. No Gilead.

And things did turn out well enough. At the first house she went to there was an old farmer with a sickly wife and a son in the army. There was nothing they didn't need help with. They told her right away that they didn't have much money, and she told them she didn't expect much, so that was all right. It took her most of the day to clean up the kitchen. She would have liked to work outside, but the woman said she'd always taken pride, and now with her health gone bad on her—so Lila scrubbed it clean, every inch of it. And she did some of the wash, in the yard, at a silver metal tub on two sawhorses. She had a big brown block of homemade soap and a washboard, and she had to heat water on the kitchen stove and carry it outside. It did wear her out. She could hardly lift her arms to pin the clothes to the clothesline. The wash would have to stay on the line over-night, but there was no sign of rain and so much wash to do that she had to make a start on it.

She was back the next morning. The farmer had brought in eggs for their breakfast, and there was ham. They told her she had answered their prayers, and what was she supposed to say to that? After a few days they gave her a ten-dollar bill and a plucked chicken and a decent pair of shoes. And they said they were pretty well out of money until they got a check from their son, who was sometimes a little late with it but almost never forgot. And they gave her a carpetbag with some old clothes in it. So that's the end of that, she thought. Well, it ain't the only farm.

There was a red blouse in that carpetbag. It looked almost new. It had long sleeves and a collar and a ruffle down the front. Never in her life before had she worn anything bright red. As soon as she took it out, as soon as she had tried the length of a sleeve against her arm, she decided she might as well take a day off tomorrow and go over to town, maybe with ten dollars in her pocket, just for the feeling of having a little money. Tired as she was, she didn't sleep. She bathed in the river in the morning dark, then she sat in the doorway waiting for enough light to let her do her copying. *And there was evening and there was morning, one day.* She didn't feel like spending much time on it. But she did write it out again and again, as she always did. Lila Dahl, Lila Dahl. Practice. And then she fell asleep. She had been sitting there in the morning sunlight when a sweet weariness came over her, and she had to lie down just for a little while. When she woke up the sun was high, the day half gone. But it is hard to regret sleep like that, even though it was looking forward to the day that had kept her awake all night. She combed out her hair and put on Mrs. Graham's skirt and the red blouse.

At the store she bought some threepenny nails so she'd have a way to hang things up if she wanted to. The one nail someone else had put in a wall had that chicken hanging from it by the twine around its drumsticks. She'd roast it when she got home. She bought a box of matches. A can of milk. Then she thought she might walk past the church. There was a hearse idling there, and just as she was about to go by, the church doors opened and a coffin came out, four men carrying it, easing it down the stairs. Then the preacher came out after it, his black robe fluttering in the breeze, his Bible in his hands, his big, heavy old head bowed down. She knew it must be some friend of his who was dead. He had so many, one of them was always dying. The men slid the coffin into the hearse, but the preacher glanced up and saw her there and stopped where he was, on the step. The mourners stopped behind him, weeping, and not quite sure what to do, since they seemed to think they shouldn't step around him. So they wept and hugged each other, and he just stood there, looking at her. The look was startled. It meant, So you're here, after all! How could you let me think you had left! As if there was something between them that gave him the right to be hurt, the right to be relieved. And she hadn't even missed church lately. So he was aware of her all the other days, knew somehow that she was close by, or that she was not, and it grieved him that she had been gone from Gilead even a little while. The widow or the mother or whoever she was said a word to him, and he nodded and went on. She saw him standing near the hearse, holding the mourners' hands, touching their arms, murmuring to them. What do you say to them, she thought, when they stand around you like that, like they just *need* to hear it, whatever it is? I want to know what you say. She couldn't walk up to them, stand there with them hearing the words he whispered, waiting for him to touch her hand. She didn't even have much to cry about. That woman put her head on his shoulder, sobbing, and he put his arm around her and held her there. He pushed her hair away from her face. Lila blushed to think how good it must have felt to her, to rest her head that way.

Well, Lila thought, can't stand here staring. He ain't going to look my way again. The hearse had to follow the road up to the cemetery, but the old man and most of the mourners took the path. She wanted to wait for him somewhere so she could speak a word to him, but what would she say? I'm back, I ain't going nowhere? That probably wasn't even true. She couldn't just stay around because she thought it might matter to him. Then the cold weather would come and he'd be thinking about something else entirely. Somebody else to feel sorry for. Her stuck in Gilead with no reason to be there and no place to stay, knowing he would never look at her that way again, if he ever really did even once. Staying on anyway because the thought of him was about the best thing she had. Well, she couldn't let *that* happen. Doll said, Men just don't feel like they sposed to stay by you. They ain't never your friends. Seems like you could trust 'em, they act like you could trust 'em, but you can't. Don't matter what they say. I seen it in my life a hundred times. She said, You got to look after your *own* self. When it comes down to it, you're going to be doing that anyway.

Lila had money in her pocket. She went back to the store and bought a pack of Camels. On the way home she stopped and lighted one, cupping her hand around the flame, that old gesture. But it had been a long time, and whatever it is about cigarettes went straight to her head. Like I was a child! she thought. Oh! Well, I just got to do this more often. Here I am walking along the road all alone smoking a cig. They got hard names for women who do that kind of thing. I got to do it more often.

She had a habit of gathering up sticks, firewood, wherever she saw it, and she had a lot of it, so she could make a fire that would be hot enough when it burned down to roast that chicken. It was good of those people to pluck it and gut it before they gave it to her. She could put a stick through it and prop it up somehow, and spend the evening tending it, and eat it in the dark, in the doorway. She might go over to that farm the next morning and do some chores for them, because they gave her too much for the work she'd done. It didn't set right. That would be Sunday morning.

It wasn't the only time she'd felt like this, it surely wasn't. Once, Doll went off by herself for a few days, after things started getting bad. When they were looking anywhere for work they must have wandered into a place Doll knew from before, and she had gone off on some business of her own and left Lila behind with the others. She'd never done that, not once. Lila had never spent an hour out of sight of her, except the time she spent at school, and then she hated to leave her and couldn't wait to get back to her, just to touch her. Doll was always busy with one hand and hugging her against her apron with the other. That time she left Doane's camp she didn't tell any of them where she was going, but she did say she would be back as quick as she could. Lila had never really noticed before that the others didn't talk to her much. She was always with Doll. Once, Marcelle called them the cow and her calf, and Doane smiled. That was after Tammany, when feelings were sore and even Mellie wouldn't have much to do with her. Lila just kept very quiet and helped with whatever she could. By the second day she already felt them hardening against her, and by the third nobody looked at her, but they looked at each other. There was something they all understood and she should understand, too. On the fourth day, early in the morning, Doane said to her, Come along, and Arthur was with him and Mellie, and they walked down the road into some no-name town, right straight to the church. Doane said, Lila, now you sit on them steps and somebody will come along in a while. You stay there. Mellie don't need to stay. You mind and you'll be all right. Hear me, Lila?

She remembered Mellie peering at her the way she did when Lila had gotten a swat or a bee sting, curious to see if she would cry. She remembered them walking away, Arthur and Doane talking between themselves and Mellie tagging along after, and nobody looking back. They took Mellie along to calm her, like you would take an old dog along to quiet a horse or a cow you were going to sell, and Mellie understood, and it made her feel important. So Lila spent a long day in that no-name town, not even sure whether Doane meant they would come back for her, or Doll would, or whether they left her on the church steps because that's where you ended up if you were an orphan. She walked up and down the street, two blocks, so she was always close enough to the church to see if anyone came looking for her. After a while a woman noticed her and brought her a piece of bread and butter. "You waiting for your mama, honey?" she said, and Lila couldn't even look at her, couldn't answer her. After a while the woman came back again. She said, "I got more work than I can do today. I'll give you a dime if you'll sweep up in front of my store." Lila said, "Well, I got to stay by the church. That's what they told me." So the woman went and found the preacher. He was skinny and young. He looked like Arthur's Deke playing at preacher. He bent down to ask her where her mother was, and who she was, and whether she had a mother, maybe a father, any family at all. She and Doll never answered questions like that. She said, "I figure I should just wait, I guess," and the preacher said, "You're welcome to wait here if you want to, and if you get tired of waiting you can let us know. We'll find a place for you to sleep, if you decide you need one. We'll get you some supper." It was Doane who always told them not to trust preachers. This is how you got turned into an orphan. Then they put you in a place with other orphans and you can never leave. High walls around it. That's what Mellie said. So she just shook her head, and he stood up and spoke with that woman about keeping an eye on her. And she could feel them keeping eyes on her, more and more of them, whispering about her and looking at her through their windows. Doane had waked her early that morning, so she was wearing the shabby clothes she slept in and hadn't combed her hair.

When it was evening and again when it was night the preacher came to see how she was doing. The first time he brought a plate of food and set it down next to her, and the second time he brought a blanket. He said, "It can get chilly, sitting out here in the dark. If you'd like, I can spell you for a while. I'd sure like to have a word with these folks you've been waiting for. No? Well, I'll ask again in an hour or so."

And then she was just sitting there on the steps, wrapped up in the blanket, the town all quiet and the moon staring down at her, and there was Doll with her arms around her, saying, "Oh, child, I thought I never *was* going to find you!" Lila couldn't quite wake up from what she had been remembering, and Doll knew what she was remembering, so she kept saying, "Oh, child, oh, child, this never should have happened! I never thought anything like this was going to happen! Four *days* I was gone!" And she kept hugging the child and stroking her face and her hair. Late as it was, the preacher was still keeping an eye on her, because he stepped out the door just then. He said, "You're the mother, I take it?" and Doll said, "None of your damn business." She probably wouldn't have spoke so rough if he hadn't been a preacher.

"Who are you?" he said. "I'd like to know who's carrying off this child."

She said, "I spose you would. Come on, Lila."

But Lila couldn't move. She wanted to rest her head on a bosom more Doll's than Doll herself, to feel trust rise up in her like that sweet old surprise of being carried off in strong arms, wrapped in a gentleness worn all soft and perfect. "No," she said, and drew herself away.

The preacher said, "This better wait till morning. I'd like Lila to have a chance to think this over."

Doll said, "Mister, you ain't nothing to her, and you ain't nothing to me. Lila, you want to stay here?"

So the girl stood up and let herself be hugged, and let herself be guided down the walk. The preacher said, "She can keep the blanket."

And Doll said, "*I* take care of her. She has what she needs."

Lila would not cry. She could see Doll's grief and pity and regret, and she took a bitter, lonely pride in the fact that she could see them and not forgive her and not cry.

She was sitting there remembering those times, and then she thought she heard someone out in the road. Footsteps. The scatter of gravel. She had a knife, but it wasn't much use in the dark, because folks couldn't see it. It was good only for scaring them off. If you cut somebody you were in a world of trouble no matter what the story was. Still, she eased toward it, where it was stuck in the floor behind her bedroll. She didn't hear anything more for a minute or two, and then she heard steps again, whoever it was walking away. She thought, He found out what he wanted to know. I'm here, and I have a fire and supper. That greasy old hen must have smelled like a kind of prosperity. The thought pleased her. Now he'll think I don't need nothing from him. If it was him.

Doane must have decided that if the world was turning mean he might as well go along with it. He wasn't a big fellow. He looked a lot like Hoagy Carmichael, though they didn't know it at the time. But he always could look mean when he wanted, and Arthur would stand right behind him, at his shoulder, looking pretty mean, too, so someone might think if anything started he'd be right there to back him up. Before the times got hard they generally knew who they were dealing with, so they'd act that way only if a stranger came along and they didn't like the look of him, if he showed up after dark, or if he just rubbed Doane the wrong way for no reason anybody needed to know. Doane always kept them safe and they trusted him. They knew he had a knife. Everybody else had one, too, but the way they thought of his knife made them think he probably had a gun. He could be as dangerous as he might ever need to be, they were sure of it. They never saw a gun, and he used his knife to whittle and to cut his meat just like they did. Still. Sometimes Arthur's boys would start scuffling, then they'd get serious about it and they'd start scrapping, trying to do some harm. If Arthur stepped into it they'd just go after Arthur. But Doane would say, "That's enough," and they'd stop. Arthur might cuff them a little because he was their father and he had to teach them respect, but the fight was over when Doane said, "Enough." He'd say, "Someday you're going to hurt yourselves so bad you won't be good for nothing, and then we'll just leave you lying along-side the road."

Lila worked as hard as any of the children. She didn't make them laugh the way Mellie did, but she never complained, she never took more than her share. She knew better than to mention school. But when hard times came they left her behind. There were people Doane just didn't take to.

And now here she was, sitting in the dark, wishing the crickets weren't so damn loud, thinking she might tell that old preacher not to come creeping around her place at night. That would put an end to it, all of it. Then she'd know for sure what he thought of her. She'd say it in church, where all them ladies would hear. Better wait till she could get a bus ticket. There'd be no more work for her after she did something like that. But when folks are down to the one thing that keeps them alive, that one thing can be meanness. It makes you feel like you're there, you're doing something. He is such a beautiful old man. All that kindness would be gone out of his face, and she would see something else, not beautiful, not the face he had worn all the years when he had only good people to deal with. That wife never meant to leave and take the child with her. So he didn't really know much about being left. Lila thought, Maybe I can teach him a new kind of sadness. Maybe he really does care whether I stay or go.

The next morning she didn't dare go to church. The way she'd been thinking, she might say anything. But she began to worry about the little garden she had planted and how the beans would be getting yellow and tough and stringy if she didn't pick them. Sunday morning was the best time to sneak into that garden, because the preacher would be preaching and everybody else would be at one church or another or sleeping in. It was hard to tell just what time it was because the sky was dark with clouds. That meant it might rain, and she'd get caught in it and have to come back when she was halfway there, or get all the

56

way to Gilead and then have to be there looking soaked and pitiful. She grabbed the carpetbag from the nail it was hanging on and smoothed her hair and took off toward town almost running, just to beat the weather, just to make up for a late start. At the preacher's house she let herself in through the gate and went around the side of the house to the corner against the fence, and when she just began picking beans she heard raindrops hitting the leaves. She was going to take the few she had and get home the best she could, but when she reached the gate she looked down the street and saw the preacher coming. She thought, A crazy woman would do something like this. She had known some crazy women, and any one of them would probably have had better sense. There was more shame in life than she could bear.

He took off his hat. He said, "Well, good morning! Or is it afternoon?"

She held out the bag to him. "I thought you might be wanting some beans." Oh, she wished she could die. How many were there in that bag? Eight? Ten?

He said, "That's very kind of you," and he took the bag out of her hand. She couldn't look at him, but she knew he was smiling.

She said, "I got to go now."

"Wait. You'll want your bag." He reached into it and took out the beans, half a handful, and gave the bag back to her. She still could not look at him. He said, "You know, it might be best if you waited out the rain. We could sit here on the porch a little while. It doesn't look like much of a storm. Or I could lend you my umbrella if you really do have to go." Then he said, "I haven't seen much of you lately. I hope I haven't offended you somehow."

His voice was low and kind. After a minute she took a step toward him. Sometimes it just feels good to hug a man, don't much matter which one it is. She'd thought it might be very nice to rest her head on his shoulder. And it was. She'd be leaving that damn town anyway.

"Well," he said. He patted her back.

She said, "I guess I'm tired."

"Yes, well—" and he put his arms around her, very carefully, very gently.

With her head still resting on his shoulder she said, "I just can't trust you at all." He laughed, a soft sound at her ear, a breath. She started to pull away, but he put his hand on her hair so she rested her head again.

He said, "Is there anything I can do about that?"

And she said, "Nothing I can think of. I don't trust nobody."

He said, "No wonder you're tired."

She thought, That's a fact. She said, "You should know I pretty well give up on getting baptized."

"I thought maybe you had. Can you tell me why?"

"I guess it don't make a lot of sense to me."

"That's all right. No hurry about it. Unless you're planning on leaving town."

"That's what I'm planning to do."

He was quiet for a while. Then he said, "I'm sorry to hear that. I am."

She stepped back and looked at him. "I don't see what it would matter."

He shrugged. "We don't have to worry about that now. It looks like we're going to have a decent rain, after all. You could just sit here a while and help me enjoy it. Should I call you Lila?"

"No reason why not."

He brought a sweater and put it over her shoulders. Right away she knew she was going to steal it. It was gray like his jacket and it had the same old wool smell, old wool and a little shaving lotion. She'd find a way to slip it into her bag. She could hardly wait till she got the chance. He'd know what she'd done. That don't matter.

So they sat there and watched the rain, he at one end of the porch swing, she at the other. After a while he said, "I'd like to know what you've been thinking about lately, since the last time we talked. You asked me why things happen the way they do, and I had to say I didn't know. I still don't. But the question is interesting."

"Oh," she said, "you don't want to know what I been thinking."

He nodded. "All right."

"I been wondering why I even bother. There must be a reason, but I don't know what it is." When she sat in the doorway at night with her knees drawn up and her arms around them so there was warmth against her belly and her breasts, she sometimes liked it all well enough, the stars and the crickets and the loneliness. She thought she could unravel the sounds the river made, the flow over the rocks where there was a little drop into a pool, the soft rush of the eddy. Now and then there were noises, some small thing happened and disappeared, no one would ever know what it was. She thought, All right, if that's how it's going to be. If there had not been that time when she mattered to somebody, she could have been at peace with it. Doane was just the world being the world. It was Doll taking her up in her arms that way. Live. Yes. What then?

He said, "I'm glad you do. Bother."

And then she heard herself say, "You come creeping around my house at night? Because I think I heard you out there." And she looked at his face. It was startled and hurt. Shamed. She couldn't look away.

He rubbed his eyes. "Yes. Well, I'm sorry if I worried you. I don't sleep well, and sometimes I walk around the streets at

night, past the houses of people I know. It's an old habit of mine."
He laughed. "I pray for them. So it's harmless at worst."

"You come all the way out there to pray for me? Couldn't you do that at home?"

"I did wonder if you had left town. If you were all right."

"I guess everybody knows I been living in that shack. If you knew where to come to do your praying."

He shrugged. "Some people know. People notice things."

"I hate this town."

"I doubt it's so different from other places."

She laughed. "I hate other places. Worse, probly."

And he laughed. "Well, just so you understand what I was doing out there. So you don't feel uneasy about it."

"I never said I understood. You tell me you was praying. I don't understand that at all."

"Ah!" He shook his head. "It would take me a good while to figure out what to say about that. Days! And I pray all the time." Then he said, "Here is what *I* don't understand. How did you know it was me? It was a dark night, and I didn't come near the house."

She shrugged. "Who else would go to the trouble?"

He nodded. "Thank you. I don't know why. But that's kind of you to say, I believe." Then he said, "You do have other friends here."

"No, I don't. Folks just do what you tell them to do."

He laughed. "Some of them. Sometimes. I suppose."

For a while the rain was heavy, loud on the roof, spattering onto the porch. She gathered the sleeves of the sweater against her.

"Are you warm enough?"

"Plenty warm. But I want to know what you said in that prayer."

"Well." He blushed. "I prayed that you were safe and well. And—not unhappy."

"That's all?"

"And"—he laughed—"I did mention that I hoped you would stay around for a while."

"And get myself baptized."

"I guess I forgot to mention that. Sorry."

"It's nothing to me. I'll be making up my own mind."

"Of course."

"But if you prayed for it, most likely I would make up my mind to do it."

"Maybe. Depending. I don't know."

"If you want me to do something, seems it would be easier just to ask *me*."

"If I did ask you, would you do it?"

She shrugged. "Maybe. I don't know." And he laughed. Then she said, "That all you prayed for?"

"No. No, it isn't." He stood up. "I think I'll make some coffee."

Well, she'd stayed too long and the rain didn't show any sign of ending. So she said, "I'll be going now," after he'd gone into the house, so he might not have heard. And she slipped the sweater into her bag. She was a block away when he caught up with her. He was carrying an umbrella.

He said, "I'm afraid it's too late for this to do you much good. But please take it."

She said, "Don't need it."

"Of course you don't," he said. "Take it anyway." So she did. He said, "I'm glad you came by. I'm always happy to find you creeping around my house." And she almost had to laugh at that. She could put the umbrella over her suitcase and her bedroll. That's how bad the roof leaked. She just might forget to return it for a while. She was going to use that sweater for a pillow. She thought, What would I pray for, if I thought there was any point in it? Well, I guess the first thing would have to be that there was some kind of point in it. The wind was blowing the rain against her and lifting the umbrella almost out of her hands, so she closed it. A little rain never killed anybody.

She thought of a story she would like to tell the old man. Once, when she was still a child, she and the others went to a camp meeting. Doane had been paid mostly in apples for some work they had done. The farmer said it was the best he could do—you can't get blood from a turnip. Doane said it might be interesting to try, and Arthur nodded. But the man just shrugged—hard times—and Doane took the apples, after he had spilled them out on the grass and had the children look them over, so the farmer could take back any that were soft or bruised or too wormy and give them others that were sound. They had to carry the apples in two gunnysacks, since that was after they lost the wagon. They ate apples for breakfast and apples for supper, and still the sacks were a burden to carry, with everything else. So when they found out from people walking along the road that they were going to a camp meeting, Doane decided they would go there to sell what apples they could. The whole business made him disgusted, but he had the children to do the work for him, to talk a few cents out of the old women before they felt the spirit and put anything they had into some damn preacher's pocket. He made them all clean up as well as they could and told them to behave, and then he just leaned against a tree with his arms folded while they chose the prettiest apples and shined them up a little against their pant legs, and took off into the thick of the crowds.

They'd have hung back with Doane and watched those poor fools getting all worked up over nothing if they hadn't had the apples to sell, which obliged them to talk to people and try to act as though they belonged there. Lila followed along after Mellie, who could somehow make those apples seem like something you would want. Lila carried them, her arms full, because

Mellie had already come up with a baby somewhere, a nice baby with a big red bow in its hair. Mellie and the baby handed the apples around as if they were doing a kindness, and people gave Mellie their pennies and nickels, and then she sent Lila back to give the money to Marcelle—Doane was acting like he had nothing to do with any of it—and to get more apples.

Families were pitching tents all over in the woods around the clearing. There were campfires, and people drifting from one to another, laughing and talking, shaking hands and slapping backs, sharing their pickle and crackers and taffy, sometimes singing together a little, since there were banjos and mouth organs and a guitar and a fiddle scattered here and there among the tents. Some of the women and girls were wearing nice dresses. Children in little packs stormed around from one place to another just burning off the excitement of it all. The ground where the meeting would be held was pretty well covered in sawdust, which made it seem strangely clean and gave it a good, pitchy smell. If men spat their tobacco on it you wouldn't notice. There was a stage set up with yellow bunting across the front of it, and there were some wooden chairs on it. And of course they were by a river, and there were people there fishing in it, a little downstream.

Lila and Mellie had seen Arthur's boys feeding their apples to the horses and mules and then sneaking down to the river to skip rocks, so Mellie gave back the baby and they went, too. Arthur was there already, skipping rocks, and when he saw his boys he said he was going to tan their hides if they didn't tell him what they'd been up to. So they started scrapping, without Doane to make them stop. Some of the men tried after a while, when Arthur started bleeding from a cut over his eye, and that got the three of them mad at those men and the fighting went on until an old preacher came tottering down the rocky slope and stepped in among them. He asked what had happened, and then he said that Arthur and his boys seemed not to be in the right spirit for a meeting of this kind and it would be best for them to move along. He was a scrawny old fellow with a croaky voice, but though they dragged their feet about it and glowered past him at the others, they were glad enough to oblige him, since more and more men and boys were coming to take the other side. They walked off into the woods like men who don't forget an insult just because they might have to wait a while to settle up. Then they walked around to the back of the crowd, Arthur with blood down the front of his shirt and Deke with a bloody nose, but other than that as respectable as anybody. None of them wanted to leave, but they knew Doane would want to. They kept moving around because he wouldn't go to the trouble of finding them all. He'd probably ask Mellie to find them, so she was careful to stay out of his sight. Doll and Marcelle had gotten a fire together and were making a supper of their own, which could only be the pone and fatback they'd been eating their whole lives, it seemed like, maybe a little more of it than usual, since those woods smelled like every good thing and people like to have a part in whatever is going on. Mellie had found herself another baby, and its mother brought them sweet bread with blueberry jam in the middle of it and icing on it. People were roasting ears of corn and handing them out to anybody who passed by, even if they passed by more than once. There was hot fry bread with sugar on it.

Evening was coming, a mild, clear evening. Men were hanging lamps in the trees, along the big old oak branches that reached out over the stage, and lighting them, and the banjos and fiddles that had come along in the crowd began to agree on a song, and the people began to sing it—*Yes, we'll gather at the river, The beautiful, the beautiful river.* And then some preachers came up onto the stage and sat down on the chairs, except for one, who came to the front of it and raised up his hands. Everybody got quiet. He shouted, "We are gathered here to praise the Lord, the God of our salvation!" And they shouted back, "Amen!"

For a minute there was just the sound of the crickets and the river and the wind creaking the ropes those lamps were hanging from.

Then, "We are gathered here to confess our sins unto the Lord, who knows the thoughts of our hearts!"

"Amen!"

Quiet again. And then, "We are gathered here to rejoice in the Lord, for His mercy endureth forever!"

"Amen!"

Then all the preachers stood up and began singing the song about the river, and the whole crowd sang with them. Deke found Mellie and said, "He's looking for you," then stepped into the crowd again. Mellie handed back the baby and told Lila, "You don't know where I am," and slipped away. Somewhere she had come up with a kerchief to tie over her hair because it was so white that it would make her easy to see, even when the sun was almost down. So Lila just stayed there watching the lanterns sway and the light and the shadows move and move through the trees, huge shadows and strange light under a blue evening sky. The preachers went on and the crowd shouted their Amens and they all sang. *Bringing in the Sheaves*. She'd heard the song a number of times since then and she didn't yet know what sheaves were. She had some ideas about salvation, and mercy, but the old man never once mentioned sheaves.

"The great gift of baptism which makes us clean and acceptable—" "Amen!"

Doll put her arm around her and said, "You come on now. Doane says so." They were gathering up their things, to get away from the noise, so they could get some sleep and nobody would be tramping around, stepping over them. If Arthur and the boys didn't show up just then, they'd find their camp soon enough. But nobody knew where Mellie was. So the rest of them had to go off down the road while Doane stayed there watching for her. Lila thought those lamps in the trees were the most beautiful things she had ever seen, and that fiddle was the most beautiful thing she had ever heard, and it didn't seem right that Doane, who said he hated it all, should send them away while he stayed behind. But in those days they still minded him, and there was comfort in it.

Mellie turned up finally when the preaching was over. She came walking up the road, tagging after Doane. She was drenched head to foot. Her pant legs were scraping from the wet. She said, "I fell in."

Doane said, "Was it one of them preachers pulled you out?"

"Don't matter. I'm just glad *somebody* did. I coulda drownt."

"Was it one of them preachers told you to step into the river in the first place?"

"Them rocks is slippery. I fell in."

"So I guess you got yourself saved."

"*I* never said that."

"I got a dollar says you're still the same rascal you always been."

"Well," she said, "if you even got a dollar, it's because I sold some of them damn apples."

He laughed. "Sounds like I won my bet already."

She said, "There wasn't no bet. I fell in."

If Lila told the old man that story he would laugh, and then he would probably wonder about it. She would tell him that Mellie always had to try whatever it was she saw other people doing. She was just curious. For the next few days she might have been checking to see if there was any change in her, because she would be mean for no reason, pinching and poking when no one was bothering her at all. Or she might have been letting Doane see that she wasn't saved and didn't want to be, either. Was she baptized or not? Say she walked into the water to be dunked and prayed over like the other people, just to see what it felt like. It was only her nature, poor ignorant child. What would the Good Lord have to say about that? If Lila had gone with her, she would probably have done the same thing, because she generally did what Mellie did, if she could do it. So there would have been the singing, and the lantern light sweeping out over the river, and some man with his hands under her back and her head, lowering her down into the water and lifting her out again, and then wiping the water away from her face as if it were tears, Hallelujah! Lila had seen it done any number of times. There were always meetings and revivals.

Clean and acceptable. It would be something to know what that felt like, even for an hour or two.

Well, she might start going to church again. Then she would feel better about taking her beans and her potatoes, and besides, she had let the weeds get out of hand. It's best to weed after a good rain. The next day was a Monday, and she could always find somebody who wanted help with the wash. And she'd be done by evening, so she could stop by the preacher's and do a little gardening, and have a nice supper afterward. If he walked out along her road, he'd see she was all right.

She read over the page she had been copying from. There were the same words over and over— He saw that it was good, And the evening and the morning. So she turned to the page she had dog-eared, and found the beginning of that book, the Book of Ezekiel. *Now it came to pass in the thirtieth year, in the fourth month, in the fifth day of the month, as I was among the captives by the river Chebar, that the heavens were opened, and I saw visions of God.* She wrote it ten times. Her bedroll had been hanging from a nail, so it wasn't really damp, and she had that sweater for a pillow. People start work early on wash day. She'd be awake in the dark as she always was. She'd practice her writing at dawn and be in Gilead while it was still barely morning.

She had bathed and waked the second time as she warmed herself in her blanket, thinking about things, and when there was light enough she took her tablet into her lap and opened her Bible beside her on the floor. She wrote, *And I looked, and, behold, a stormy wind came out of the north, a great cloud, with a fire infolding itself, and a brightness round about it, and out of the midst thereof as it were glowing metal, out of the midst of the fire.* Well, that could have been a prairie fire in a drought year. She had never seen one, but she had heard stories. *And out of the midst thereof came the likeness of four living creatures. And this was their appearance: they had the likeness of a man. And every one had four faces, and every one of them had four wings.* Well, she didn't know what to make of that. A dream somebody had, and he wrote it down, and it ended up in this book. She copied it ten times, still trying to make her letters smaller and neater. Lila Dahl, Lila Dahl, Lila Dahl. She had four letters in each of her names, and he had four letters in each of his. She had a silent *h* in her last name, and he had one in his first. There were graves in Gilead with his name written out on them, and there was no one anywhere alive or dead with her name, since the first one belonged to the sister she never saw of a woman she barely remembered and the second one was just a mistake. Her name had the likeness of a name. She had the likeness of a woman, with hands but no face at all, since she never let herself see it. She had the likeness of a life, because she was all alone in it. She lived in the likeness of a house, with walls and a roof and a door that kept nothing in and nothing out. And when Doll took her up and swept her away, she had felt a likeness of wings. She thought, Strange as all this is, there might be something to it.

Doll was gone those four days, she told Lila finally, to see how the folks at the old place were getting on. The times were so hard by then that she was having trouble keeping the child fed and keeping clothes on her back, and she had the thought that things might be better where her people were, farther east. She'd expected some of the worst of them might have died off. She said, "Somebody shoulda shot that Hank long since." Who was Hank? "Never you mind." Doll had to be careful, so she asked around the neighborhood—that took a while, since folks don't like to talk to outsiders—and she walked past the old place a few times to see for herself. She said, "It seemed about the same. Nothing you could go back to." Lila said, "If things'd been better, would you a gone back there, too?" And Doll said, "I couldn't. They know I taken you in the first place, so if I come back with you there'd be hell to pay." Doll told her this because Lila wasn't the same to her after what happened while she was gone. She said, "I done it because I wasn't finding no way to look after you." If Doane had ever bothered to explain, he'd have said the same thing. They were just figuring out where to leave her. For her own good. Where to tell her, stay, and wait, and somebody will come along. So after that she couldn't love Doll like she did all those years. For a while she couldn't. She'd never thought she might be sitting on that stoop again, at night probably, watching Doll sneak off into the woods. One way or another, it comes out the same. Can't trust nobody.

They found Doane and the others again. It was evening, after supper, and there was a fat, soft, embery fire in the middle of the clearing. Doll picked up the skillet and tossed it into the fire. Flame roared up and embers flew. "How could you do that!" she said. "Leave my child sitting on the steps of some church! I might never a found her! I *told* you I was coming back!" She was yelling at Doane mainly, but there was no one there she didn't glare at. Only Mellie glared back.

Doane said, "You was gone a while. We sorta gave up on you."

"Now, why would you do that! I keep my word! Has there ever been a time I didn't, in all the years?"

Doane said, "Well, Doll, you can hold your grudge or you can come along. If you're going to be around, I don't want to hear another word about this. None of it."

Marcelle said, "We kept your stuff."

"I just bet you did!" Doll said, and Doane gave her a look.

He said, "We thought about dropping it in the fire. But Marcelle wouldn't stand for it. It mighta been the best thing." He walked over and picked up Lila's bedroll. That shawl was wrapped around it. He pulled it loose, and he smiled, and he went over and sort of dangled it over the fire, and the flames climbed right up it toward his hand. So that was gone. They stayed with Doane's people, Doll having no better idea what to do. They never said another word about what had happened. It was just like before, and everything was different. You best keep to yourself, except you never can.

Mrs. Graham wanted help with her wash. She was a cheerful woman. Friendly. She enjoyed talking. She never seemed to notice that Lila didn't enjoy talking, or listening, and that was all right. They'd worked together times enough that Lila knew how she wanted things done, and that seemed to make the day go faster. Mrs. Graham made them a nice lunch of tuna-fish sandwiches with chocolate cake for dessert. She had a nice house. There were white curtains in the kitchen with strawberries along the hem. Little green stitches to look like seeds. The washing machine was on the back porch. It was a good machine, electric, you didn't even have to crank the wringer. Lila didn't let herself look into the parlor, at the piano and the sofa and the rest, which reminded her a little of St. Louis except that none of it was so big and fine, and the drapes were open.

At the end of the day she had a five-dollar bill and a water-proof coat with a hood. Lila said, "The Reverend told you to give me this," and Mrs. Graham said, "Well, he worries about you, dear. He's a good-hearted man. And it was just hanging in the closet, no use to anybody." She smiled shyly, kindly. Lila didn't ask whose closet it had been hanging in, how many women in the church or in Gilead had been asked if they could spare a coat before this one turned up, or how there could be no one else but her who could use it. Maybe no one was as broke as she was, but there were some people who must come pretty close. He should be worrying about them, too. Well, all right, she thought, so all I got to do now is save up for that bus ticket, save up a little traveling money. I can't wait to get out of this town. She folded the coat and put it into her carpetbag, the five-dollar bill in a pocket, and then she walked up to the cemetery. The roses on the grave were blooming, and the weeds were, too. She said, "Well, I'm sorry, Mrs. Ames. I been staying away too long. I never meant to let this happen." She loved them. The likeness of a woman, and in her arms the likeness of a child.

It was evening when she opened the gate to the preacher's garden. She picked some beans and groped under the plants for some potatoes. There was light from an upstairs window and no other light in the house. Let him be—all right. That seemed like a decent prayer. Let him stop making me feel so damn broke all the time. That was a good one. Better to tell him that one herself. She could do it right now if she wanted. Maybe she hadn't been as quiet as she thought, because he knew she was there. He opened the front door as she was walking to the gate. He said, "I've written you a note. I thought I might give it to you. Well, of course I will give it to you. There wouldn't be much point—" He laughed. "I hope—well, obviously. I mean, if there is anything in it you find disagreeable, that will be despite my best efforts. To the contrary. If you see—" He handed her an envelope. "Good evening. It's a fine evening." He went back into the house. The envelope wasn't sealed, and when she was out of sight of his house she opened it just enough to see that there was no money in it, only the note. She had to laugh at a pinch of something like disappointment. She was close now to having enough money to be able to leave. Maybe it was more than enough. A couple of weeks ago she'd have thought it was. The more you have, the more you want. If he had given her money, there'd have been anger and shame to get her on that bus. She could have stopped thinking about it.

One other time she had been given a note, for Doll from that teacher. Lila read it to her because, Doll said, her hands was all wet and soapy. It said that she was a smart girl and would benefit from further schooling, and that the teacher would be happy to do whatever she could to help make this possible. "Lila is an unusually bright child." Doll said, "Benefit," and Lila told her it meant that it would do her good to stay in school another year. Doll said, "I already knew you was bright. I could've told you that." That was all she said. It was so easy for Lila to forget that Doll had broken the law when she carried her away, and had set off a grudge, too, which was a good deal worse. And for a long time she hadn't realized that the life they lived with Doane was one that would make them hard to find. Because people like them don't talk to outsiders. And they all know that if somebody is on your trail, you can just slip into a cornfield. Once, Doll must have thought she saw somebody from the old place. She'd kept Lila with her a whole day in a hayloft, quiet as could be. That was before the corn was high. But to spend almost a year in a town was dangerous if anyone happened to be looking for them. Doll knew those people and Lila didn't, so if Doll thought they might try to catch her for the sheer devilment of it, Lila guessed they really might have tried. But that was nothing the two of them mentioned even between themselves.

She has made remarkable progress. Lila knew that note by heart. No point reading Doll the parts she wouldn't understand. She was glad that teacher couldn't see her now. What was this old man going to tell her in his note? Don't matter. A letter makes ordinary things seem important. He was wearing a necktie. Expecting her, maybe, because she'd been at Mrs. Graham's and might be wanting to thank him for the coat. Or maybe he waited for her every evening. She found herself sometimes listening for his steps in the road. People talk themselves into these things, and then nothing comes of it. They don't even want to remember there was a time when it mattered to them. They hate you for mentioning it. Those women in St. Louis, the young ones, there was always somebody they were waiting for, or trying to get over. And the older ones would just laugh at them. They'd be laughing at her now. He probably had a meeting at the church, so he was wearing a necktie. You fool, Lila. Whatever it said, it would be kind. And if it wasn't, he'd have found the kindest way to say it.

St. Louis. Much better to be there in the shack by herself. In the evening, with her potatoes roasting outside. Doane used to push a spud out of the fire with a stick, and they'd toss it one to another until one of them could stand to hold on to it, and then it was his. One of Arthur's boys, always. They'd just go to sleep when it got dark. She should buy some candles, maybe even a kerosene lamp, so she could read and practice her writing if she felt like it. But light did draw bugs. And it was better if no one saw the shack at night. Not that people passing by wouldn't notice her fire. But light made you blind in the dark and there might be something you really needed to see out there. The evening was peaceful. But she couldn't stop wondering about that letter. She might just light a cigarette. She might strike another match to read the first few words. They were: *Dear Lila (if I may), You asked me once why things happen the way they do.* Well, she wasn't really expecting that. *I have felt considerable regret over my failure to respond to your question.* She shook out the match. He wasn't asking for his umbrella back anyway.

The next morning she took her tablet and copied, as neatly as she could, *You must have thought that it has never occurred to me to wonder about the deeper things religion is really concerned with, the meaning of existence, of human life. You must have thought I say the things I do out of habit and custom, rather than from experience and reflection. I admit there is some truth in this. It is inevitable, I suppose.* She wrote it ten times. Well, what did old Ezekiel say next? *And their feet were straight feet; and the sole of their feet was like the sole of a calf's foot; and they sparkled like burnished brass.* She wrote this ten times. Salted babies, sparkling calves' feet. Strange as it was, there was something to it. Well, there was the strangeness of it. That old man had no idea. Let us pray, and they all did pray. Let us join in hymn number no matter what, and they all sang. Why did they waste candles on daylight? Him standing there, talking about people dead who knows how long, if the stories about them were even true, and most of the people listening, or trying to listen. There was no need for any of it. The days came and went on their own, without any praying about it. And still, everywhere, meetings and revivals, people seeing the light. Finding comfort where there was no comfort, just an old man saying something he'd said so many times he probably didn't hear it himself. It was about the meaning of existence, he said. All right. She knew a little bit about existence. That was pretty well the only thing she knew about, and she had learned the word for it from him. It was like the United States of America—they had to call it something. The evening and the morning, sleeping and waking. Hunger and loneliness and weariness and still wanting more of it. Existence. Why do I bother? He couldn't tell her that, either. But he knows, she could see it in him. Why does he want more of it, with his house so empty, his wife and child so long in the ground? The evening and the morning, the singing and the praying. The strangeness of it. You couldn't stop looking. He would walk up the hill to that sad place and find them all covered in roses. If he knew, and if he didn't know, who had made them bloom that way, he would think it was strange and right. There was no need for roses.

Marcelle chose that name for herself after she heard some women talking in a beauty parlor. When he started turning mean, Doane began calling her *Marcelle* in a way that let you know it wasn't her real name. When he did that, it made her cry sometimes. She pretended, but she always had, and they had always wanted her to. Lila and Mellie loved to watch when she opened the little box where she kept her powder and rouge and lip rouge, her eyebrow pencil. She almost never opened it, it was so precious. The stale sweet smell of it. Sometimes she let them brush out her hair. They did all think she was pretty. They felt a little pleasure and a little envy at the way Doane favored her. He would take her arm to help her through a muddy place in the road. Once, he bought ribbons at a carnival and tied one in her hair and one in a bow around her neck, and wound one around her wrist and one around her ankle, kneeling right on the ground to do it and setting her foot on his bent knee. Doll said, "They're married people." Lila had no particular notion of what the word "married" meant, except that there was an endless, pleasant joke between them that excluded everybody else and that all the rest of them were welcome to admire. It was that way before times got hard. After that, Doane seemed almost angry at Marcelle because there wasn't much he could spare her. Still, he looked for her and he stood beside her, even when he had no word to say. There are the things people need, and the things people don't need. That might not be true. Maybe they don't need existence. If you took that away, everything else would go with it. So if you don't need to exist, then there is no reason to think about other things you don't need as if they didn't matter. You don't need somebody standing beside you. You don't, but you do. Take away every pleasure—but you couldn't, because there can be pleasure in a sip of water. A thought. There was no reason for Doane to tie a ribbon on Marcelle's wrist, and that was why she laughed when he did it, and loved him for it. Why they all loved them both. There was no reason to let an old man dip his hand in water and touch it to your forehead, as if he loved you the way people do who would touch your face and your hair. You'd have thought those babies were his own. All right, she thought. All right.

I have worried that you might think I did not take your question as seriously as I should have. I realize I have always believed there is a great Providence that, so to speak, waits ahead of us. A father holds out his hands to a child who is learning to walk, and he comforts the child with words and draws it toward him, but he lets the child feel the risk it is taking, and lets it choose its own courage and the certainty of love and comfort when he reaches his father over—I was going to say choose it over safety, but there is no safety. And there is no choice, either, because it is in the nature of the child to walk. As it is to want the attention and encouragement of the father. And the promise of comfort. Which it is in the nature of the father to give. I feel it would be presumptuous of me to describe the ways of God. Those that are all we know of Him, when there is so much we don't know. Though we are told to call Him Father. And I know it would be presumptuous to speak as if the suffer-

ing that people feel as they pass through the world were not grave enough to make your question much more powerful than any answer I could offer. My faith tells me that God shared poverty, suffering, and death with human beings, which can only mean that such things are full of dignity and meaning, even though to believe this makes a great demand on one's faith, and to act as if this were true in any way we understand is to be ridiculous. It is ridiculous also to act as if it were not absolutely and essentially true all the same. Even though we are to do everything we can to put an end to poverty and suffering.

I have struggled with this my whole life.

I still have not answered your question, I know, but thank you for asking it. I may be learning something from the attempt.

Sincerely,

John Ames

Well, he forgot he was writing to an ignorant woman. She'd have hated him for remembering. Still, she'd have to study this a little. A letter written to her. Lila, if I may.

Then what was she supposed to do? Write him a letter? She'd shame herself. Those big, ugly words on a piece of tablet paper, nothing spelled right. But then she'd shamed herself before and he never seemed to mind. Planting her spuds in his flower garden. Knocking at his door before the sun was well up to ask him her one question. Throwing her arms around him. Taking off with his sweater. It should have pained her to remember, but every time she rested her head on that old sweater she was just glad for it all. She had even thought about putting it in the fire, because it worried her how it kept him on her mind. Then maybe she could catch that bus. She certainly did wonder about herself. He should be thinking she's crazy for sure by now.

No sign of it in that letter, though. She thought, How can he forget what I am?

But she hadn't yet put things right with those people who gave her the chicken. She could spend the morning there and then go down to the river and wash out some of her clothes. She'd better get started. Doane used to say that if you start after sunrise, you've wasted the day. The woman was still just as sickly, so Lila cleaned house for a while and then she chopped weeds for a while in the kitchen garden, and then, when no one was looking, she put the hoe in the shed and walked away. Now they were even.

She liked to do her wash. Sometimes fish rose for the bubbles. The smell of the soap was a little sharp, like the smell of the river. In that water you could rinse things clean. It might be a little brown after a good rain, soil from the fields, but the silt washed away or settled out. Her shirts and her dress looked to her like creatures that never wanted to be born, the way they wilted into themselves, sinking under the water as if they only wanted to be left there, maybe to find some deeper, darker pool. And when she lifted them out, held them up by their shoulders, they looked like pure weariness and regret. Like her own flayed skin. But when she hung them over a line and let the water run out, and the sun and the wind dry them, they began to seem like things that could live. At the church once they read the story about how the Queen of Egypt came down to a river and found a baby floating in a basket, and after that it was her baby. Live. The mother was supposed to kill the child, but she couldn't. She put it in the river, and the queen lifted it out. But then it grew up and turned into a man, and he decided he didn't want to be her child. Or maybe she had died, and her father didn't take to him, but that's not in the story. Well, Lila thought, I hope she did die before he could treat her that way. She should have been able to trust him. Here I am thinking that way again. Can't trust nobody. That's what I'm thinking all the time. If I'm ever going to try it, it might as well be now, when I can leave if I have to and I'm still young enough to get by for a while. When it won't much matter if it don't work out.

So.

She'd get herself together as well as she could, walk to the church, to that little room where people came when they wanted to talk to him, and she'd knock on the door. And then she would say to him that she did want to get baptized after all and she was sorry she forgot to come to them classes. Then he'd say something. She would tell him that was a real nice letter. He'd say something else. And what would any of it amount to? She saw them all talking to each other all the time. Laughing. Doll used to say, "No cussing!" and they would laugh because of all the things they knew and nobody else did. But if you're just a stranger to everybody on earth, then that's what you are and there's no end to it. You don't know the words to say.

She went to Mrs. Graham's to see if she needed help with the ironing, and she did. That took the morning and most of the afternoon. She wanted some things from the store, so she had to walk past the church. He was out in front of it, with his hands on his hips, looking up at the roof. But he turned and saw her and said, "Good afternoon." She nodded and kept on walking. He caught up with her and fell into step beside her, a little out of breath. He said, "I'm glad to see you."

"Why?"

He laughed. "Well, that's what people say sometimes. Besides, I *am* glad to see you."

They walked on like that, right past the store. She said, "Why?"

He laughed again. "You ask such interesting questions."

"And you don't answer 'em." He nodded. It felt very good to have him walking beside her. Good like rest and quiet, like

79

something you could live without but you needed anyway. That you had to learn how to miss, and then you'd never stop missing it. "I quit coming to them classes. So I guess I don't get baptized."

"Yes, I've given that some thought. There are things we do hope the person being baptized will understand well enough to affirm."

"Affirm? I don't even know that word. I can't half understand that letter you give me. I'm an ignorant woman. Seems like you can't understand *that*."

He stopped, so she did. He looked into her face. "I think I would understand it if it were true. But I don't believe it is. So I don't see the point in acting as if I do." He shrugged. "Knowing a few words more or less—"

"It ain't that simple."

He nodded. "It isn't the least bit simple. But if you are at church this Sunday and you want to accept baptism, then—I will do it with perfect confidence in the rightness of it. That's all I can say."

She said, "I got to get some things at the store." So they turned and walked back into Gilead.

He said, "I suppose you still don't trust me at all."

"I just don't go around trusting people. Don't see the need." They walked on a while.

"The roses are beautiful. On the grave. It's very kind of you to do that."

She shrugged. "I like roses."

"Yes, but I wish there were some way I could repay you."

She heard herself say, "You ought to marry me." He stopped still, and she hurried away, to the other side of the road, the flush of shame and anger so hot in her that this time surely she could not go on living. When he caught up with her, when he touched her sleeve, she could not look at him.

"Yes," he said, "you're right. I will."

She said, "All right. Then I'll see you tomorrow." Why did she say that? What was she planning on doing tomorrow? He just stood there. She could feel him watching her. Of all the crazy things she had ever done. It was that feeling that she had had walking along beside him that put the notion in her mind. It comes from being alone too much. Things matter that wouldn't if you had a regular life. Just walking along beside that old man, past the edge of town, not even talking most of the time, with the cottonwoods shining and rustling and shading the road. She never really looked at him, but he was beautiful, gentle and solid, his voice so mild when he spoke, his hair so silvery white. If she ever thought of herself marrying anybody, it would have been a man who was young enough not to mind a day's work. Being a preacher was a kind of work, though. And he had that house to live in. Gardens around it. Gone to weed.

What was she thinking about? It was never going to happen. She might be crazy, but he wasn't. She tried to remember that he said those words—You're right. I will—in a way that really meant, That's the strangest thing anybody ever said to me in my whole life. It wasn't hard to hear them that way, except from him. He always seemed to say what he meant. Near enough. But she could see how it might've been different this time. She lifted the loose plank and took out the jar where she kept her money. She had the five dollars Mrs. Graham paid her, since, upset as she was, she didn't trust herself to go into the store and buy the tin of deviled ham she'd had on her mind. So all together it came to about forty-five dollars. If she hadn't been buying things, cigarettes, margarine, there'd have been more. Still, forty-five dollars would take her a long way on a bus. She could go to California, where there wouldn't be winter to worry about. Crops coming in all year long. Doane and Marcelle had always talked about going to California. That was a nice thing to think about. She could do it on her own. Nobody to trust. She knew he wouldn't come to her place, and she couldn't go to his. He might be looking for her, since it was tomorrow, or he might not be looking for her. She would go in to town in the next few days to get her ticket, so if he happened to see her he wouldn't make much of it. She might never know—maybe he meant what he said, but if he didn't, and she saw him again, she wouldn't be able to stand the shame. Or she would, and that would be another, harder shame. It would be best if she could just say, I'm leaving, like I was meaning to do the whole time.

So she spent the next day at the river. She sat down on a rock and dropped a fishing line into the water. She had brought her tablet and pencil and her Bible. Ezekiel said: *And they had the hands of a man under their wings on their four sides; and they four had their faces and their wings thus: their wings were joined one to another; they turned not when they went; they went every one straight forward. As for the likeness of their faces, they had the face of a man; and they four had the face of a lion on the right side; and they four had the face of an ox on the left side; they four had also the face of an eagle.* Doane would be saying, What did I tell you. But it made as much sense as anything else. No sense at all. If you think about a human face, it can be something you don't want to look at, so sad or so hard or so kind. It can be something you want to hide, because it pretty well shows where you've been and what you can expect. And anybody at all can see it, but you can't. It just floats there in front of you. It might as well be your soul, for all you can do to protect it. What isn't strange, when you think about it.

The shadows had moved and the bugs were beginning to bother, so she found a sunnier place. There were huckleberries. If she could only forget why she was there, she'd be fairly pleased with herself. One big old catfish would make it a good day. That letter was in the Bible. She tore it in half and put a rock on it, in a wet enough place that the ink would bleed. *Dear Lila (if I may).*

She thought sometimes that if she decided to do it she could cut off her hand. There was a kind of peace in that. In one way, at least, she could trust herself, crazy or not. She might burn that sweater while she was cooking her catfish. She might burn the Bible, for that matter. Old Ezekiel would nestle down into the flames. He seemed to know all about them. The umbrella would fit in her suitcase, crosswise.

She decided to go to church the next Sunday. If she came late and left early, if she sat in the last pew, he would never be near enough to speak to her or to pay her any notice. She wouldn't mind seeing him one last time, standing there in the pulpit, in the window light, talking to those people about incarnation and resurrection and the rest. She'd hear a little singing. After that she would never step into a church again.

When she came up the bank from the river, she saw him standing in the road, about halfway between her and that damn shack. So there she was, Bible in one hand, catfish jumping on a line in the other, barefoot, and he turned and saw her. He started walking toward her. She couldn't think what else to do, so she waited where she was. He didn't speak until he was close to her, and then he didn't speak, still deciding what to say.

He said, "I know you don't like visitors, but I wanted to talk to you. I wasn't actually coming to your house. But I hoped I might see you. I want to give you something. Of course you are under no obligation to accept it. It belonged to my mother." He was holding it in his hand, a locket on a chain. "I should have found a box for it." Then he said, "We spoke about marriage. I haven't seen you since then. I don't know if you meant what you said. I thought I'd ask. I understand if you've changed your mind. I'm old. An old man. I'm very much aware of that." He shrugged. "But if we're engaged, I want to give you something. And if we're not, I want you to have it anyway."

"Well," she said, "I got my hands full."

He laughed. "So you have! Let me take something. A Bible!"

"I stole it. And don't go looking at my tablet."

"Sorry. Ezekiel." He laughed. "You are always surprising."

"I stole your sweater. Was that a surprise?"

"Not really. But I was glad you wanted it."

"Why?"

He said, "Well, you probably know why."

She felt her face warm. And the fish kept struggling, jumping against her leg. She said, "Damn catfish. Seems like you can never quite kill 'em dead. I'm going to just put it here in the weeds for a minute." And there it was, flopping in the dust. She wiped her hand on her skirt. "I can take that chain now, whatever it is."

He said, "Excellent. I'm—grateful. You should put it on. It's a little difficult to fasten. My mother always asked my father to do it for her."

Lila said, "Is that a fact," and handed it back to him.

He studied her for a moment, and then he said, "You'll have to do something with your hair. If you could lift it up." So she did, and he stepped behind her, and she felt the touch of his fingers at her neck, trembling, and the small weight of the locket falling into place. Then they stood there together in the road, in the chirping, rustling silence and the sound of the river.

He said, "So. Are we getting married, or not?"

And she said, "If you want to, it's all right with me, I suppose. But I can't see how it's going to work."

He nodded. "There could be problems. I've thought about that. Quite a lot."

"What if it turns out I'm crazy? What if I got the law after me? All you know about me is what anybody can tell by looking. And nobody else ever wanted to marry me."

He shrugged. "I guess you don't know me very well, either."

"It ain't the same. Somebody like me might marry somebody like you just because you got a good house and winter's coming. Just because she's tired of the damn loneliness. Somebody like you got no reason at all to marry somebody like me."

He shrugged. "I was getting along with the damn loneliness well enough. I expected to continue with it the rest of my life. Then I saw you that morning. I saw your face."

"Don't talk like that. I know about my face."

"I suspect you don't. You don't know how I see it. No matter. A person like you might not want the kind of life she would have with me. People around. It's not a very private life, compared to what you're used to. You're sort of expected to be agreeable."

"I can't do that."

He nodded. "They're not going to fire me, whatever happens. I'll have my good house, till they carry me out of it."

"I can take care of myself."

"I know that. I meant, if you're not like most pastors' wives, it won't matter. I've been here my whole life. My father and then me. I won't be here so much longer. No one will want to trouble me. Or you." He said, "You have to understand, I have given this a great deal of thought. What an old country preacher might have to give to a young woman like you. Not the things a man her age could give her, a worldlier man. So I would be grateful for anything I *could* give you. Maybe comfort, or peace, or safety. For a while, at least. I am old."

She said, "You're a pretty fine-looking man, old or not."

He laughed. "Well, thank you! Believe me, I would never have spoken to you this way if I didn't think my health was reasonably sound. So far as I can tell."

"You wouldn'ta spoke to me like this if I hadn't mentioned it all in the first place."

"That's true. I'd have thought it would be foolish of me to imagine such a thing. Old as I am."

She thought, I could tell him I don't want to be no preacher's wife. It's only the truth. I don't want to live in some town where people know about me and think I'm like an orphan left on the church steps, waiting for somebody to show some kindness, so they taken me in. I don't want to marry some silvery old man everybody thinks is God. I got St. Louis behind me, and tansy tea, and pretending I'm pretty. Wearing high-heel shoes. Wasn't no good at that life, but I did try. I got shame like a habit, the only thing I feel except when I'm alone.

She said, "I don't think we better do this."

He nodded. His face reddened and he had to steady his voice. "I hope we will be able to talk from time to time. I always enjoy our conversations."

"I can't marry you. I can't even stand up in front of them people and get baptized. I hate it when they're looking at me."

He glanced up, preacherly. "Yes, I hadn't thought of that. I should have realized. I haven't always performed baptisms in the church. If there are special circumstances— All I would need is a basin of some sort. I could take water from the river."

"I can't affirm nothing."

"Then I guess we'll skip that part."

"I got a bucket. No basin."

"That will do fine."

"You wait here. I got to comb my hair."

He laughed. "I'm not going anywhere."

She changed into a cleaner blouse and combed and braided her hair and put on her shoes. She'd do this and think about it afterward. She went out on the stoop and picked up the bucket, which would be clean enough after a rinse. The old man was in the field picking sunflowers. She walked to the road. He brought her his bouquet. "I like flowers at a baptism," he said. "Now we'll fetch a little water." There was a kind of haste in his cheerfulness. She had hurt him, and he couldn't quite hide it. He took the bucket from her and helped her down the bank as if she hadn't gone to the river for water a hundred times by herself, and he sank the bucket into a pool and brought it up, brimming, and poured half of it back. The crouching was a little stiff, and the standing, and he smiled at her—I am old. "I don't need much at all," he said. "A few waterskeeters won't do any harm." He was dressed in his preacher clothes, and he was careful of them, but he liked being by the river, she could tell. "What do you think? Up there in the sunshine or down here by the water?" Then he said, "Oh, I left the Bible lying on the grass. I could do it from memory. But I like to have a Bible, you know, the cloud of witnesses." She didn't know. "Since there aren't any others." She still didn't know. No matter. He was glad to be doing this, and not just so he could put aside that talk they'd had. So it must mean something.

She said, "I like the sunshine." He helped her up the bank, and he found the Bible, and he opened it and read, " 'Then cometh Jesus from Galilee to the Jordan unto John, to be baptized of him . . . And Jesus, when he was baptized, went up straightway from the water: and lo, the heavens were opened unto him, and he saw the Spirit of God descending as a dove, and coming upon him; and lo, a voice out of the heavens, saying, This is my beloved Son, in whom I am well pleased.' These are the words of John, who baptized for the remission of sins, and who baptized Our Lord: 'I indeed baptize you in water unto repentance: but he that cometh after me is mightier than I, whose shoes I am not worthy to bear: he shall baptize you in the Holy Spirit and in fire.' The sacrament is an outward and visible sign of an inward and spiritual grace. Dying in Christ we rise in Him, rejoicing in the sweetness of our hope. Lila Dahl, I—"

"But that ain't my name."

"What is your name?"

"Nobody ever said."

"All right. It's a good name. If I christen you with it, then it *is* your name."

"Christen?"

"Baptize."

"All right."

"Lila Dahl, I baptize you—" His voice broke. "I baptize you in the name of the Father. And of the Son. And of the Holy Spirit." Resting his hand three times on her hair. That was what made her cry. Just the touch of his hand. He watched her with surprise and tenderness, and she cried some more. He gave her his handkerchief. After a while he said, "When I was a boy, we used to come out along this road to pick black raspberries. I think I still know where to look for them."

She said, "I know where," and the two of them walked across the meadow, through the daisies and sunflowers, through an ash grove and into another fallow field. There were brambles along the farther side, weighed down with berries. She said, "We don't have nothing to put them in," and he said, "I guess we'll just have to eat them." He picked one and gave it to her, as if she couldn't do it for herself. He said, "We could put them in my handkerchief. I'll hold it."

"You'll get stains all over it."

He laughed. "Good."

She spread it across his open hands and filled them, and then she tied the corners together. Fragrance and purple bled through the cloth. He said, "I'll carry it so it doesn't stain your clothes, but it's for you, if you want it. You can steal my handkerchief. If you want to remember. The day you became Lila Dahl."

She said, "Thanks. I figure I'll remember anyway."

They walked up to the road. "Well," he said. "It's almost evening. And we forgot all about your catfish, didn't we. And your Bible, and your tablet. I'll help you gather them up. It might rain. And then I'll be going."

"Wait," she said. "I was wondering. Can you still get married to somebody you baptized?"

He raised his eyebrows. "No law against it. Why do you ask?"

"I don't know. Seems like I just want to rest my head—"

He said, "I'd like that, too, Lila. But I think we made a decision."

"No. No." She wasn't crying. She couldn't look at him. "I want this so damn bad. And I hate to want anything."

" 'This'?"

"I want you to marry me! I wish I didn't. It's just a misery for me."

"For me, too, as it happens."

"I can't trust you!"

"I guess that's why I can't trust you."

"Oh," she said, "that's a fact. I don't trust nobody. I can't stay nowhere. I can't get a minute of rest."

"Well, if that's how it is, I guess you'd better put your head on my shoulder, after all."

She did. And he put his arms around her. She said, "The second you walk off down that road I'll start telling myself you're gone for good, and why wouldn't you be, and I'll start trying to hate you for it. I *will* hate you for it. I might even leave here entirely."

He said, "I expect I'll be having a few sleepless nights myself. A few more, that is. I was thinking, if you moved into town we could sort of keep an eye on each other. Talk now and then. That should make things better. Boughton will marry us. I'll talk to him about it. We'll do it soon. To put an end to the worrying."

"But don't you wonder why I don't even know my own name?"

"You'll tell me sometime, if you feel like it."

"I worked in a whorehouse in St. Louis. A whorehouse. You probably don't even know what that is. Oh! Why did I say that."

She stepped away from him, and he gathered her back and pressed her head against his shoulder.

He said, "Lila Dahl, I just washed you in the waters of regeneration. As far as I'm concerned, you're a newborn babe. And yes, I do know what a whorehouse is. Though not from personal experience. You're making sure you can trust me, which is wise. Much better for both of us."

"I done other things."

"I get the idea." He stroked her hair, and her cheek. Then he said, "I really better go home. If I find a place for you, will you move into town? Yes? And I'll talk to Boughton. Promise you won't be out here trying to hate me. If that's something you can promise." He went off and came back with her Bible and tablet and that muddy catfish, which he had dropped into the bucket, along with the bouquet of sunflowers. He said, "With a catfish you just never know." He looked at her. "Sleep well," he said gently, like benediction, as if he meant grace and peace. So now she was going to marry this old preacher. She couldn't see any way around it that would not shock all the sweetness right out of him.

The hotel belonged to an old friend of Boughton's, and Lila had a room there free of charge. Such a dead little town, half the rooms were empty. Reverend Ames came by most nights for supper on the veranda under the big ceiling fans, bringing Boughton along often enough. Mrs. Graham brought clothes, from the Boughtons' attic, she said. He had four daughters. They were very good quality clothes, they might as well get some use. The mothball smell will air out. Lila hated the hotel, the drapes and sofas and the great big pink and purple flowers on the wallpaper and the rugs. Dressing nice for the evening.

Sometimes she would walk out to that farm to help, to sweat

and get her hands dirty. So she could sleep at night. They might give her a little money, depending. But she was back before supper and washed up before the old men came. And smelling like mothballs. She learned about propriety without anybody ever telling her there was a word for it. "He's very protective of you," Mrs. Graham said, which meant she sat next to him but not close to him, that he touched her elbow but did not take her hand. That she was about as lonely as she had ever been.

On her way to the farm she might look in on the shack. Nobody there but the mice and the spiders. She'd sit on the stoop and light a cigarette. Her money was still in the jar under the loose plank. She'd stuffed that handkerchief into it, too, because it reminded her of a wound and trying to blot it up or bind it. The field was turning brown and the milkweed pods were dry and prying themselves open. Everything in that shack she had not hidden was gone, every useless thing. He had come there and gathered it all up, she was sure, to save it for her. Some visiting Boughton had brought him out there in his father's car, no doubt, since the odds and ends, the pot and bucket and bedroll and suitcase and the rest, would be far too much to carry. So much that she would have left it behind when the winter drove her out. Maybe the Boughtons helped take her things to the car. She hated to think they had been there. If he had asked, she'd have said don't do it, so he didn't ask. She never thought of emptying the shack, even though the winter would ruin whatever was left in it. If a farmer decided to plant the field, he would probably knock it down or burn it. Still, she had thought of it as hers. Her things had been her claim on it. The money wasn't safe—only the Reverend would not think to look under a loose board—but it was hers while it was there. Her knife was gone. What did the old man think about that knife? Why did she wonder? Everybody needs a knife. Fish don't clean themselves.

And she went up to the cemetery to look after Mrs. Ames

and her child. She meant to ask the old man sometime what would happen when they were all resurrected and he had two wives. He had preached about that, which probably meant he had been wondering, too—they won't be male or female, they won't marry or be given in marriage. Jesus said that. So the old man wouldn't have a wife at all, not even one. This girl and her child, after so many years, would be like anyone else to him. He might be as young as he was when she left him. Lila could see sometimes what he'd been like when he was young. The girl would still be holding that baby he had hardly even had a chance to hold. And there would be no change in her, and no change in him, as if dying had never happened. It would be a strange kind of heaven, after all they'd been through, and all the waiting, if he did not feel a different peace when he stood beside them. Lila could watch them, and love them, because old Doll would be there to say, "It don't matter." Don't want what you don't need and you'll be fine. Don't want what you can't have. Doll would be there, ugly with all the trouble of her life. Lila might not know her otherwise.

A month in that hotel, and then the wedding. Mrs. Graham told her the Reverend probably wanted people to understand that the marriage was a considered decision, since men his age could sometimes be a little foolish. Lila said, "Well, it seems pretty foolish anyway," meaning that if she was as good as married, she might as well have some of the comforts of it. Mrs. Graham smiled and nodded and said, "He's just trying to make the best of things. For your sake, too." Lila hated Boughton. Once or twice she saw him taking a long look at the old man as if he was wondering about him, as if he might say, Are you really sure about this? Damn knives and forks. And he was always talking about foreign policy. Then the old man would say something just to remind him gently that Lila might not have an interest in foreign policy, which was true enough, since she'd never even known there was such a thing, and Boughton would start talking about theology. Then it would be something about somebody they had both known forever. They would be laughing at the thought of something that had happened when they were boys, and then the old man would turn to her and say, "Are you comfortable here? Is your room comfortable?" because he couldn't think of anything to say to her, either. He couldn't go up to her room to see for himself because of propriety. He blushed when she said she'd be happy to take him upstairs, and she had to laugh at herself, which made it worse. Boughton tried to change the subject. Mrs. Graham and her husband were there, too, ready to talk foreign policy out of the plain goodness of their hearts. They had dinner at the hotel a few times so that Mr. Graham would know her well enough to give her away. That was the strangest thing she'd heard of yet. But she had her days to herself.

They were married in the parlor of Reverend Boughton's house, with the Boughton children there except for the one. They even brought Mrs. Boughton downstairs in a pretty dress and put her in her chair. The girls bent down to tell her it was a wedding, John's wedding, and wasn't that nice? Then they left her to her smiling quiet, since it always upset her to feel that more was wanted of her.

They went to the old man's house after the wedding and the dinner Boughton's daughters had made for them. Lila had never understood the whole business of knives and forks, that there was a way you were supposed to use them. But he sat beside her, close to her, her husband, all their kind feelings toward him now owed to her, too. There was a big white cake with frosting roses on it, and the sisters laughed about how many they had made and how few of them turned out to look at all like the pictures in the magazine. Or anything else. Cauliflowers. Mushroom clouds. Gracie knocked one on the floor and got so frustrated she washed her hands of the whole thing and went for a walk, but Faith got the trick of it, just in time, before people began to arrive. Then there she was with frosting in her hair. There was frosting all over the kitchen. Teddy said he caught Glory licking her fingers. They were all laughing, all so used to each other, so fine-looking, the brothers, too. Lila could hardly wait to leave.

Then there they were in that quiet house. Everything of hers, everything she had been given, had been brought from the hotel and hung in the front closet. There was food in the icebox and the pantry and on the kitchen table, and there were little gifts on the counters, embroidered tea towels and pillowcases and aprons, and a needlework picture of apples and pears and grapes with the words *Bless This House*. There were flowers in every room. The windows were all opened to let the day in. Everything that could be polished shone. "The church," he said, and smiled as if to say, I did warn you. She stepped out on the back porch, just to look. They had weeded the garden.

She'd thought, I'll do this first and think about it afterward. Now afterward had come and she had no idea what to think. I am baptized, I am married, I am Lila Dahl, and Lila Ames. I don't know what else I should want. Except for the shame to be gone, and it ain't. I'm in a strange house with a man who can't even figure out how to talk to me. Anything I could do around here has been done already. If I say something ignorant or crazy he'll start thinking, Old men can be foolish. He's thought it already. He'll ask me to leave and no one will blame him. I won't blame him. Marriage was supposed to put an end to these miseries. But now whatever happens everybody will know. She saw him standing in the parlor with his beautiful old head bowed down on his beautiful old chest. She thought, He sure better be praying. And then she thought, Praying looks just like grief. Like shame. Like regret.

He showed her the house, where things were to be found. There was a room upstairs he said would be her study if she liked. The carpetbag with the tablet and Bible in it was there on a table by the window, beside a bowl of zinnias. Or she could have another room if there was one she liked better. The house had been built for a big family. The rooms weren't large, but there were several of them. His own study was just down the hall. If there was anything at all she wanted to change, she should certainly feel free. The house was as it had always been, more or less, at least since his father and mother lived in it. But there was no reason to keep it that way. He said, "It is so wonderful to have you here, in this house. I hope you'll be very happy. Of course."

She said, "I expect I will be. Happy enough. It's yourself I'd be worried about."

He laughed. "I think I'll be fine," he said.

"I seen you praying."

"A habit of mine. No cause for concern."

"Well," she said, "if you decide sometime I'm a bother, you can just tell me."

He laughed. "Dear Lila, we're married! For better and for worse!"

"I spose so. We'll see about that."

He took her hands and studied them, her big, hard hands. He said, "If you say so, I guess we will."

She had probably said a mean thing to him. For weeks she wished she could take it back. All it meant was that she still didn't trust him and he'd be a fool to trust her. And that was only the truth. He might as well know it was her nature to feel that way, nothing she could change. She was just as lonely as she had ever been. The only difference was that now this kind old man was sad and embarrassed about it, still not even sure how to talk to her. If she was quiet for a while he would come down from his study to look for her in the kitchen or the garden—to get a drink of water or to enjoy the weather, he said. If she had walked out to the farm, to the shack, the sight of her coming in the door stung his eyes. It was to comfort him, and herself, that she slipped into his bed that first dark night.

Lila thought once, when she was out walking, what if she saw someone ahead of her on the road and it was Doll. What if she called out her name, and the woman stopped and turned and laughed and held out her arms to her, wrapped her into her shawl. She would tell her, I have married a fine old man. I live in a good house that has plenty of room in it for you, too. You can stay forever, and we'll work in the garden together. And Doll would laugh and squeeze her hand—"It come out right, after all! I ain't dead and you ain't in some shack just struggling to get by! I had to leave for a time, but I'm back now, I'm resurrected! I been looking everywhere for you, child!" She could tell herself what she would tell Doll, things that would help her stay in that life. A married woman with a good husband! It was worth all the trouble, every bit of it.

Doll's eyes would shine the way they never did when anyone but Lila was there to see. Just that little room in the house in Tammany made her happy for all she was giving her child, her own dresser drawer and a lamp with a ruffled shade and school besides. Then she must have seen someone, or heard that some-one was asking after them, and they left as soon as Doll could dry her hands and change her apron. She said she had wearied of Mrs. Marker's hollering, but they ate the lunch she had made for Lila to take to school as they walked away from Tammany, through the woods, not along the road. Doll had a red stain, like a birthmark, on one side of her brow and on her cheek, and people who saw her didn't forget her. That was why they couldn't stay in one place. She never explained any of this to Lila. It was a part of everything they never spoke of. But it was clear enough when she thought back on it. They managed to stay in that town for months, almost a school year, Doll taking the risk so Lila could learn to read. Well, the old man's house was full of books. She would work on her reading. Doll would want her to.

When she thought this way, she could almost begin to enjoy her life. She was stealing it, almost, to give it to Doll. People might think she liked the old man's house and the Boughtons' clothes and all the proprieties and the courtesies. They might think she liked the old man, too. But she just imagined how all of it would seem to Doll—a very good life, a comfortable life that she had because Doll had stolen her, and had taken care of her all those years. She lived for Doll to see. Lila made the old man smile for the pleasure in his eyes, because Doll would have been so happy to see it. When she put her arms around him, when she slipped into his bed, Doll would have smoothed the pillow and whispered to her, "He's such a kind old man!"

Lila went along with him to Boughton's house to drink iced tea on the porch and listen while they talked, and one afternoon as she listened she understood that Doll was not, as Boughton said, among the elect. Like most people who lived on earth, she did not believe and was not baptized. None of Doane's people were among the elect, so far as she knew, except herself, if she could believe it. Maybe their lives had gone on, and some revival preacher somewhere had taken them in hand. But Doll's life ended, and no one had rested his hand on her head, and no one had said a word to her about the waters of regeneration. If there was a stone on her grave, there was no name on it. A real name might have made her easier to find, or have added another crime to child-stealing, so she never even told *Lila* what it was. When Doll gave Lila her knife she said, "It's only for scaring folks with. If you go cutting somebody it's going to be trouble no matter what the story is." So Doll might have been hiding already when Lila first knew her, sleeping in that miserable, crowded old cabin, coming and going in the night the way she did. Calling herself by that one name. Maybe she died with dark sins on her soul. Lila had heard the preachers talk that way. Or maybe the other crime was just some desperate kindness, like stealing a sickly child. And maybe it made no difference to the Lord, one way or the other.

The old man said, "We'll be going home now. It must be close to suppertime." He could tell when she was bothered, and Boughton could tell when he was concerned about her, so they said good evening without any of the usual joking and lingering and clearing away of glasses and spoons. He walked along beside her, silent in the way he was when he could not be sure what to say, or to ask. He opened the door for her. That house, so plain and orderly and safe. He said, "Boughton likes to talk about the thornier side of things. You don't want to take him too seriously."

She went into the parlor and sat down, and rested her head in her hands. He stood near her chair, keeping a respectful, patient distance as he always did when he hoped she would tell him what she had on her mind.

She said, "I just never thought about all them other people. Practically everybody I ever knew. Some of them been kind to me."

He said, "I'm so glad they were kind to you. I'm very grateful for that."

"But they never gave one thought to the Sabbath. You never heard such cussing and coveting. They stole sometimes, if they had to. I knew a woman who maybe killed somebody with a knife. She's dead now, so I guess there's nothing to be done about that." She said, "Them women in St. Louis, I believe adultery is about the only thing they was ever up to. And there was no one to help them with any of it. Their sins. So I guess they're all just lost? What happens to you if you're lost?"

He said, "Lila, you always do ask the hardest questions." There was a gentleness in his voice that made her think he wouldn't tell her painful things in words that really let her understand them.

"I knew a man once who said churches tell folks things like that to scare them."

"Some do."

"So they'll give them their money."

He nodded. "That happens."

"You never say nothing about any of it."

"I don't really know what to say about it."

"But it's true, then?"

"There are other things I believe in. God loves the world. God is gracious. I can't reconcile, you know, hell and the rest of it to things I do believe. And feel I understand, in a way. So I don't talk about it very much."

"That's the only time I ever heard you say that word, 'hell.'"

He shrugged. "Interesting."

"Does Jesus talk about it?"

"Yes, He does. Not a lot. Still."

She said, "I don't know. For a preacher you ain't much at explaining things."

"I'm sorry about that. Sorry if you're disappointed. Again. But if I tried to explain I wouldn't believe what I was saying to you. That's lying, isn't it? I'm probably more afraid of that than of anything else. I really don't think preachers ought to lie. Especially about religion."

She said, "I just wish I'd known a little more about what I was getting into. My own fault. I should've gone to them damn classes."

He sat down on the sofa. "My fault, too. My fault entirely." They were quiet for a while.

Then she said, "I know you didn't mean no harm."

He shook his head. "I didn't do you any harm. I'm sure of that."

Well, he didn't know Doll and the rest of them. The loneliness that settled over her at the thought that they were lost to her. He buried his face in his hands, praying most likely. So she went into the kitchen and made sandwiches.

He'd wanted to get her baptized before she could take off and lose herself in some rough life and then be lost in whatever came after it. That was kind of him. Dipping his hand in that bucket, river water running up his sleeve while he blessed her with it. Bees buzzing, her catfish flopping in the weeds. He surely did look like he meant every word he said. The heavens torn asunder. A dove descending. There was no sign of all that except the look on his face and the touch of his hand. It wasn't often in her life that anyone had been so set on doing her good as he was, after she had said she wouldn't marry him, too. A preacher doing what preachers do to give you what safety they can. But it might not be a kind of safety you want, once you think about it. For a while Lila had liked the thought of resurrection because it would mean seeing Doll. The old man might have his wife and his child. She would have Doll, so that would be all right. There would be such crowds of people, but she would look for her until she found her if it took a hundred years. She understood the word "resurrection" to mean just what she wanted it to mean. The idea was precious to her. Doll just the way she used to be, but with death behind her, and all the peace that would come with that. A few blisters ain't going to kill you. A little dust ain't going to kill you. Nothing going to kill you ever again! Hanging couldn't kill you! Doll would laugh at the surprise of it all, because she'd probably never heard of such a thing.

But Boughton mentioned a Last Judgment. Souls just out of their graves having to answer for lives most of them never understood in the first place. Such hard lives. And there Doll would be, whatever guilt or shame she had hidden from all her life laid out for her, no bit of it forgotten. Or forgiven. But that wasn't possible. The old man always said that God is kind. Doll was so tough and weary, with that stain on her face, and the patient way she had when people looked at her—I never see it, but I know what you see. Whatever it was she did with that knife, who could want to cause her more sorrow? Lila hated the thought of resurrection as much as she had ever hated anything. Better Doll should stay in her grave, if she had one. Better nothing the old men said should be true at all.

He came into the kitchen and sat down at the table. "I must seem like a fool to you," he said. "You must think I've never given a moment's thought to anything."

She was always surprised when he spoke to her that way, answering to her, when she had never read more than a child's schoolbook. "I'd never think you was a fool," she said.

"Well," he said, "maybe. But I do want to say one more thing. Thinking about hell doesn't help me live the way I should. I believe this is true for most people. And thinking that other people might go to hell just feels evil to me, like a very grave sin. So I don't want to encourage anyone else to think that way. Even if you don't assume that you can know in individual cases, it's still a problem to think about people in general as if they might go to hell. You can't see the world the way you ought to if you let yourself do that. Any judgment of the kind is a great presumption. And presumption is a very grave sin. I believe this is sound theology, in its way."

She said, "I don't know nothing about it." Then she said, "I don't understand theology. I don't think I like it. Lots of folks live and die and never worry themselves about it."

"Ah, of course!" He laughed. "You don't like theology! I should have thought of that. Too many years alone, I suppose. Talking to Boughton. Or to myself. Preaching. I *am* a fool."

"Well now, I didn't say I won't start to like it sometime." She said this because she could hear sadness in his voice.

He laughed. "That's kind of you. I suppose it's a little late to ask, but what do you like?"

"I don't know. Working."

He nodded. "Work is a fine thing." And he put his hands to his face. "Listen to me! Every word I say is just pure preacher! I could cite text!"

She said, "I expect you'd be used to it by now."

That night, lying against the warmth of him, she said, "Maybe you don't have to think about hell because probly nobody you know going to end up there."

After a moment, he said, "I suppose there's an element of truth in that."

"Except me."

"Lila," he said, "I have to preach tomorrow. If you put more thoughts like this in my head, how am I supposed to get any sleep?" He drew her closer to him, stroked her cheek. "I'm going to keep you safe. And you're going to keep me honest." Maybe he couldn't think she would go to hell, because he loved her. She thought, He'd have as good reason, or better, to love any one of the whole world of people who might have turned up on his doorstep. The thought of them made her wish it was morning, Doane and Mellie and the others. That long time when she had no notion of what time was. Lying down to sleep in the dew and darkness, being roused again in the dew and darkness, a fire for supper, a fire for breakfast, if Doane could get it started soon enough, a pot of beans, or ashy potatoes in their husks, and that bitter, urgent smell that comes in the wind, as if the world were scared to sleep and then sorry that the morning had to come. Waking up with her hair in tangles. They always said no whimpering, the grown-ups, and she would try to stop and then stop and sit there with Doll's arm around her, the two of them eating from the same dish.

The next morning, before it was morning, she had gone to the river, and he had waked to an empty house. She put on her old dress, and she went to the river and washed herself in the water of death and loss and whatever else was not regeneration. But there was a child, she was almost sure of it, and what else could she expect, with that way she had of creeping into the old man's bed when he never even asked her to. She had seen women bearing their children in a shed, at the side of a field, babies that the light of day shouldn't have seen for a month or two but the women's bodies just gave them up out of weariness. She and Mellie had found a woman like that once, alone in a cabin at a little distance from a huckleberry patch. They heard her crying, and Mellie said they'd better look in the door. Then Lila ran to find Doll, and when they came back Mellie was crying, too, because the woman had taken hold of her hands and wouldn't let go of them. She said, "I was trying to help, now I guess I nearly got some busted fingers." Doll talked to the woman so that she'd know there was someone there besides children, so she calmed a little and let Mellie go. Lila and Mellie drew some water from the well, and they gathered an armful of starwort and spread it on the grass to dry. Then they sat on the stoop and listened, because they couldn't help it, and Doll talked to the woman, trying to comfort her. The woman knew the baby shouldn't be coming yet. It was just a long, bloody struggle and at the end of it a little body to wash. Doll could be so gentle. They couldn't help watching her. She swaddled it up in a flour sack. And then she walked the woman out to the porch and washed the blood and the sweat off her, and they couldn't help watching that, either. The woman was so thin, except for the pouch of her belly. Her bare legs trembling. She kept saying, "My husband will be back soon. He went for help. He'll be back." But that's the kind of lie people tell sometimes when they got only strangers to rely on. There's shame in that, so people lie. They helped Doll clean up around the place as well as they could, and did the milking, and fed the chickens, and she and Mellie found some meal and cooked it, and told her the starwort would help if she burned a little of it, and they left her their huckleberries. That poor baby just lay there on a bench, waiting for its father to see it, the woman said. Walking along in the dark, looking for their camp, they didn't say a word. Well, Doll did say, "That's how it is."

So what she had to do was stay in that house and let the old man look after her, and when the time came, the church women who would be so glad to put a living child into his arms. They could bring all the cakes and casseroles they wanted for as long as they wanted, and he would be happy to have something he could talk to her about. Lila thought of herself as old, nearly safe from childbearing. She might not have given in so easily, other-wise, to the comfort of him, the feeling of him next to her, so much better than resting her head on that old sweater she stole from him. No point in worrying about that now. There would probably be a child, and that would probably be a good thing. But only if she stayed. At least now she knew he would let her stay, however crazy she might be, or ignorant, or lost. If there was going to be a child. So she went back to his house and put on her new dress and waited for him on the porch.

The thought of a child made him older. He never slept much or well, but now he hardly seemed to sleep at all. She wore her ring and tried to stay near the house, but if it helped at all it just worried her to think how sad he would be if she did a wrong thing and upset him. The more she might seem like a wife to him, the more he would fear the loss of her. One morning she found him in the kitchen before the sun was up, looking stooped and rumpled, stirring oatmeal. She touched his shoulder in a way he took as a question, and he said, "I don't know about myself, Lila. Such a night. I'm almost afraid to pray. I find myself praying now that I'd be able to accept"—he shook his head—"things I can't bear to think about. It's against my religion to say it would be too hard. But I'm afraid it would be." He shook the oatmeal off the spoon into two bowls and set them on the table. "I cooked it too long. It's pretty sticky. But it's good for you. Here's some milk." He gave her a spoon and a napkin, sat down across from her, clasped his hands, and prayed briefly over his oatmeal. "And much the worst of it is that all the real hardship falls to you. I'm sorry. I shouldn't talk this way."

She said, "Women have babies. All the time. I figure I can." To comfort him she could have said it might all turn out just fine, it usually did, but she was as much afraid as he was to think that way. She couldn't tell him she had unbaptized herself for fear he thought it would harm the child. Why did she do it that morning? She could just as well have done it after the baby came. Then if something went wrong she wouldn't have to wonder whether she was to blame for it. It was dread at the thought that made her ask him right then if once you been baptized you could ever just wash it off you, and he smiled and said no.

"Even if you wanted to?"

"Well, that's probably about as close as you could ever come. But no. You don't have to worry about that." She was relieved, in a way.

She'd heard people say that a sad woman will have a sad child. A bitter woman will have an angry child. She used to think that if she could decide what it was she felt, as far back as she remembered, she could know that much, at least, about the woman who bore her. Loneliness. She pitied the woman for her loneliness. She didn't want this child of hers to feel afraid with no real reason. The good house, the kind old man. I got us out of the rain, didn't I? We're warm, ain't we? In that letter he had said there's no such thing as safety. Existence can be fierce, she did know that. A storm can blow up out of a quiet day, wind that takes your life out of your hands, your soul out of your body. *The fire went up and down among the living creatures; and the fire was bright, and out of the fire went forth lightning. And the living creatures ran and returned as the appearance of a flash of lightning.* She had copied this fifteen times. It reminded her of the wildness of things. In that quiet house she was afraid she might forget.

She thought, An unborn child lives the life of a woman it might never know, hearing her laugh or cry, feeling the scare that makes her catch her breath, tighten her belly. For months its whole life would be all dreams and no waking. The steps in the road, the thought of the knife, then the dread sinks away for a while, and how is a child to know why? She could only guess what all it was that Doll was afraid of, or ashamed of, but she lived her fear and her shame with her, taking off through the woods with an apple thumping in her lunch bucket and Doll wearing a big straw hat she must have hoped would shade her face enough to hide it a little. More than once Doll took her hand to hurry her along and wouldn't let her catch her breath and never told her why. She always stayed back from the fire-light even when the night was cold and even when there were no strangers there to see. Doane and the others saw, of course, but Lila was the only one she ever really trusted to look into her face. Well, child, Lila thought, I will see you weltering in your blood. And mine. Lonely, frightened, my own child. If the wildness doesn't carry us both away. And if it does.

She looked after the gardens. She walked up to the cemetery to see to Mrs. Ames and the child, and now the boy John Ames and his sisters. No need to go out looking for ironing to do, the Reverend told her. There was a woman who had taken in his laundry for years, so there was no need for Lila to do that kind of thing at all. She should take care of herself. That was the best thing she could do. Everything would be seen to.

She had that room he called her study. The Bible was there, and her tablet, and a drawer of new pencils and erasers and pens and tablets. There were books with pictures of other countries in them, China, France, some of them from the library. Most evenings the Reverend walked with her after supper, her arm in his, pausing to speak to everyone he knew, however slightly, to say, This is my wife Lila. Every courtesy owed to him was owed to her also, now that she was his wife, and he wanted to be sure they, and she, understood this. When anyone spoke to her, she nodded and said nothing. Whoever it was always changed the subject to the weather, the corn crop. If they walked out past the edge of town he would put his arm around her waist, still shy of her and pleased to be alone with her, knowing she was relieved to be alone with him. She knew he was thinking and praying about how to make her feel at home. She had never been at home in all the years of her life. She wouldn't know how to begin. But the shade of the cottonwoods and the shimmer of their leaves and the trill of the cicadas were comfort for her. The pasture smell. Elderberries grew in the ditches by the road, and they picked them and ate them as they walked. Sometimes it was dark when they turned back toward Gilead. Once, he noticed a bush glimmering with fireflies. He stepped into the ditch and touched it, and fireflies rose out of it in a cloud of light.

When he was in the house she kept the door to her room open. She sat at the table and did her copying and paged through the books he had given her, since she knew he might look in from the hall. *And over the head of the living creature there was the likeness of a firmament, like the terrible crystal to look upon, stretched forth over their heads above . . . And when they went, I heard the noise of their wings like the noise of great waters, like the voice of the Almighty, a noise of tumult like the noise of a host: when they stood, they let down their wings.* She shut the door and locked it when the Reverend left the house, and then she sat in the corner on the floor and hugged her knees to her chest and closed her eyes and thought.

There were other people on the road Doane knew, who would share the fire and add whatever they could to supper and talk with him about where work was needed and where there had been flood or hail or grasshoppers or foreclosure. They would scratch out maps on the ground—the bridge is out here so you'd best take this road south of it—and they'd tell stories about the farms they'd worked, stinginess or meanness or stupidity they'd seen or heard about, and who was fair or more than fair. This was after the dust began to blow to the south and west, and the people who would have been working those farms began to drift into the parts Doane knew, and Doane's people were obliged to wander a little to find work. Doane said those folks would work for just about nothing. How was a man supposed to make a living? And finally he said, Hell, if they're so set on Nebraska they can have it, and Kansas to boot. He was going back to Iowa and east from there. He was tired of eating sand anyway.

Even before the worst of the dusters there was grit drifting around everywhere. They slept with damp cloths over their faces, and when they woke up they had to shake sand out of their hair and their blankets and clothes. People who lived in houses said they had begun stuffing wet rags into every crack they could find and sweeping their floors five times a day. But there was no living outside when the dust began drifting north. Doane had waited a little too long for things to get better, so when they started east there were other people on the road who had the same idea, and others ahead of them, already taking any kind of work there was. Doane said he had seen hard times, but this just did beat all. Arthur said they should have started east sooner, as if the thought had just come to him, and Doane said he didn't want to hear it. What use was there in saying something like that. A couple of good rains and they'd have been right where they'd have wanted to be. And don't say nothing if you got nothing useful to say.

It wasn't like Doane to speak to Arthur that way, or it hadn't been up till then. But Doane had never before had much trouble keeping everybody fed, and it weighed on him. Things got worse, and pretty soon he was cross as a snake. Arthur and his boys took off, thinking they could do better on their own. It would have been hard for them to do worse, and at least they wouldn't have Doane bossing them around when nobody ever said they were working for him anyway. But they were back with him in a few days. They got lonely and they were fighting all the time. Doane didn't say a word to them about it, except that they were more than welcome to their share of nothing. That was when he began to sort of hate Marcelle. She'd gone out into a bottomy field where she knew there would be nettles, and somebody else had already gathered them all. Doane told her she was ugly when she cried and he didn't want to look at her. That was when Doll went off on her own and was gone for four days.

Doane and Arthur got work clearing some young trees and brush off a field that had been abandoned and was going to be turned to pasture. They all helped, limbing the trees and stacking and burning the brush, and they were paid in potatoes and dried beans, which is how things were then. So when Doll came back there was a fire and supper, people fed and tired, and her child gone. They said they didn't know the name of the place where they left her, some shabby little town down the road a few miles. She probably didn't even wait long enough to let herself cuss. She just ran and walked and ran and walked down the road the way they would have come, through one shabby little town, so closed up for the night that no one answered the doors she pounded on, and then on to the next town. And there the child was, sitting on the church steps. Doll might not have seen her except that the church door was open and there was a light from inside because that preacher was watching out for her. Lila was so sure he had wanted to make an orphan of her that only years later did she think he might have been a kind man. An orphan is what she was, and she knew it then, and she thought that preacher must somehow know it, too, and be ready with the frightening word that would take her life away from her if only he chose to say it. *And there was a voice above the firmament that was over their heads; when they stood, they let down their wings.* She didn't want to know what the verse meant, what the creatures were. She knew there were words so terrible you heard them with your whole body. *Guilty.* And there were voices to say them. She knew there were people you might almost trust who would hear them, too, and be amazed, and still not really hear them because they knew they were not the ones the words were spoken to.

She had never heard anyone talk this way about existence, about the great storms that rise in it. But when she saw these words, she understood them. A time came when Doane couldn't figure a way to keep them fed. His good name meant nothing because along these new roads he was just one more dirty, weary man with dirty, weary women and children straggling after him. He couldn't very well keep his pride when he couldn't even ask for work without seeming to ask for pity. Those years of saying, if he had to, Be fair to me and I'll be fair to you, and being twice as careful to live up to his side of the deal as he was to make sure the other fellow lived up to his, all that was gone, and still they trailed after him, trusting him because they always had. They got work once pulling the tassels off corn, miserable work at best, out in the field with all the dust and heat and the grasshoppers getting on you and the itchiness of the silk and the edges of the corn leaves rasping against you. But by that time they almost weren't up to it. They went so slow they didn't finish the rows they were supposed to do, even though they worked until dark, till they could hardly lift their arms. And then they weren't paid but half what had been agreed on, because they didn't finish. Mellie cussed and cried where the man could hear and Doane slapped her. That was the first time he ever did any such thing. What does it matter if some ignorant man nobody would even notice loses the pride he has been so careful of all his life? If somebody said to him, No work here, mister—that's just how it was, no harm intended. But it was also a great voice they heard everywhere, saying, Now, those half-grown children will be hungry and you'll have the shame of it and there's nothing you can do but wish at least you didn't have to look at them. And he did seem to begin hating the sight of them. But they were bitterly loyal to him for the insult he suffered because his pride had been their pride for so many years.

When he finally took to stealing, it was a big dog that caught him at it. So he went to jail with his pant leg slit open to make room for the bandage and the swelling, and no stick to help him walk because it would have been a weapon. They scattered after that. Marcelle stayed as near to the jail as she could manage to, and so did Mellie, and Em, who was never good for much and by that time needed Mellie to look after her. Arthur and his boys had been stealing a little, and meant to do a little more stealing, so they took off. People remembered Doll for her face, and that made it a problem for them to travel together. It was the same whether the boys were recognized or she was and they were seen with her. So then it was just Lila and Doll. Arthur and his boys had no sense at all, and still it was a lonely thing to have them gone, too.

How could it be that none of it mattered? It was most of what happened. But if it did matter, how could the world go on the way it did when there were so many people living the same and worse? Poor was nothing, tired and hungry were nothing. But people only trying to get by, and no respect for them at all, even the wind soiling them. No matter how proud and hard they were, the wind making their faces run with tears. That was existence, and why didn't it roar and wrench itself apart like the storm it must be, if so much of existence is all that bitterness and fear? Even now, thinking of the man who called himself her husband, what if he turned away from her? It would be nothing. What if the child was no child? There would be an evening and a morning. The quiet of the world was terrible to her, like mockery. She had hoped to put an end to these thoughts, but they returned to her, and she returned to them.

Every Sunday after that one she went to church, her hand at the crook of the Reverend's arm. Every Sunday she had swelled a little more, and people could think what they liked about it. He was fairly pleased with what he had planted, and shy as well. An old fellow like him, he said, had to expect a few remarks of one sort and another. He was kind to her in every way he could think of, always trying to find out what she liked and disliked and ready to spare her any annoyance, even though that meant seeing a little less of Boughton. Did she feel annoyance before she knew the name for it? Would she have felt she had the right to it? He did say that why things happen the way they do is essentially a theological question, at least a philosophical question, and she said she supposed he was right, since he would know.

Once, when they were out walking, he asked her what was on her mind, because she had been so quiet, and she said, "Nothing, really. Existence," which made him laugh with surprise and then apologize for laughing. He said, "I'd be interested to know your thoughts on it."

"I just don't know what to think about it at all sometimes."

He nodded. "It's remarkable, whatever else." He picked up a few rocks from the road and tossed them at fence posts, hitting them sometimes.

"Remarkable," she said, considering the word. *She has made remarkable progress.* It had begun to seem to her that if she had more words she might understand things better. And it would take up the time. "You should be teaching me."

"I suppose. If you like."

The corn was head high, rustling its heavy, dusty leaves, and for a while anyway it had nothing to do with her. He would hardly let her clear the dishes.

"I never meant to be ignorant my whole life. But there was never much I could do about it." That was true enough. And they might have something to talk about besides how she was feeling from one day to the next. She was about to start making things up, just for the sake of conversation.

He said, "I guess I should have realized. But I've never for a moment thought of you as ignorant, Lila. I couldn't if I tried."

"Well, once you start teaching me you're going to find out."

"We'll see."

She said, "I had to learn that word 'existence.' You was talking about it all the time. It took me a while to figure out what you even meant by it."

He nodded.

She said, "There's a lot I haven't figured out. Pretty well everything."

He took her hand and swung it as they walked, a happy

man. "I feel exactly the same way. I really do. So this will be very interesting," he said. "You'll talk to me. I'll find out what you think."

She shrugged. "Maybe." And they laughed. If there was one thing she wished she could save from it all, it was the way it felt to walk along beside him.

He said, "You know, there are things I believe, things I could never prove, and I believe them all day, every day. It seems to me that my mind would stop dead without them. And here, when I have tangible proof"—he patted her hand—"when I'm walking along this road I've known all my life, every stone and stump where it has always been, I can't quite believe it. That I'm here with you."

She thought, Well, that's another way of saying it ain't the sort of thing people expect. She had heard the word "unseemly." Mrs. Graham talking to someone else about something else. No one said her belly was unseemly, no one said a word about how the old man kept on courting her, like a boy, when she was hard and wary and mainly just glad there was a time in her life when she could rest up for whatever was going to happen to her next. She felt like asking why he couldn't see what everybody else had seen her whole life. But what if that made him begin to see it? First she had to get this baby born. After that she might ask him some questions.

She might tell him some things, too. Why she maybe thought of marrying him. Once, Doll wanted her to marry another old man. What would he think of that? Doll heard somewhere about a widower who might be looking for a wife. She sent Lila to his house, with ribbons in her hair. The times were so bad then, and Doll wouldn't stay anywhere long, so she couldn't marry him herself. He had new overalls on, and his hair combed to the side, and he was sitting there on the porch waiting for her. The shanks of his legs were just two white bones with hair on them, and his boots were big and worn and one not quite like the other. They made her think of two very old dogs from the same litter. He told her his wife was dead and his children were gone, that he owned his house and a few acres outright, and that he would enjoy a little help around the place and a little company. She couldn't say a thing. Then his voice rose and he said, "None of this was my idea. I'm a decent man. Have been all my life. You can ask anybody. That woman with the mark on her face, she knows it, too. She's been talking to the neighbors. She said she couldn't take care of you anymore. I should have just told her in the first place it was ridiculous. Well, you wait here a minute." He went into the house and came back with a silver dollar. He held it out to her and she took it. "Now, goodbye," he said. Then she went to find Doll. She said, "He give me this." She wasn't crying. Doll said, "You shouldn'ta took it." And then she said, "He would've been good to you. That's what matters. You got to do the best you can, and be grateful for whatever comes of it." And, after looking at her for a moment, mildly and sadly, she said, "If there was just something about you."

By then she was helping Doll, not being taken care of by her, and that was one of the reasons Doll wanted to be rid of her. Poor child, she would say. She had to lean on Lila's arm just to walk up a rise in the road. She couldn't do any heavy work at all. There was no strength left in her. So she was anxious to get the girl settled somehow, before the things could happen that did happen.

I'm a decent man. The Reverend could have said the same thing to her. Not because she was young anymore but because she was rough and ignorant. And then what would she have done? What could have made her take such a chance? Sometimes she thought she wanted the worst thing to come finally, a shame that would kill her. Why else did she say, You ought to marry me? Did she think he would laugh? Maybe she didn't want him to say, I will. She never thought he would. She didn't believe him when he did. Maybe she meant to go back to that leaky old cabin and feel ache and sting down to her bones and nothing else. To put everything else away from her, because that ache was, first and last, where she came from and what waited for her. Maybe she slipped into his bed to see if she really was the wife of this decent man, not just a stray he had taken in out of pity. And now she had this belly, and he was always at her elbow saying, This is my wife, this is Lila, my wife. You see, Doll, I did what you said. So many times she had thought, if she had just said a word to that old man, if she hadn't stood there staring at his boots, Doll could have stayed somewhere nearby, and Lila would have taken food to her and made sure she was warm, sneaking out at night to find her. They'd have laughed with the pleasure of the secret.

The Reverend let her think her thoughts, waiting until she looked up from them to speak. He said, "You still don't trust me at all."

And she said, "No. Can't really say that I do. No reason you should trust me, either. There are things I ain't told you."

He nodded. "I know. Maybe you should just tell me those things, whatever they are, and you'd see that I didn't care about them, and then you could trust me."

She said, "Not till I get this baby born."

He laughed and put his arm around her. "Well, isn't it a beautiful evening? Hardly a cloud. Are you warm enough?" He took off his jacket and put it over her shoulders. "We might not be having many more warm nights." Then he said, " 'The heavens declare the glory of God; and the firmament showeth his handiwork. Day unto day uttereth speech, and night unto night showeth knowledge.' "

"I guess that's the Bible." When he was happy he was always saying something from the Bible.

"Psalm 19. 'There is no speech nor language; their voice is not heard.'"

"That's another thing I don't understand."

"Maybe nobody does, entirely. But it's beautiful."

Pretty nearly anybody must understand more than she did. She said, "What is the firmament?" It was easier to ask questions, walking along in the dark like that, her arm in his, in the warmth of his old black coat, his preacher coat.

"The sky the way it looks to us. As if there were something like a dome over us, like a glass bowl turned over—"

She thought, Then I guess there ain't. He told her that the moon is much closer than the sun, falling stars aren't really stars. She and Mellie had wondered about those things, why some stars came unstuck and the others didn't, where they landed when they fell, whether all of them would fall down sometime, even the moon. It was nice to be talking about the stars. She could hardly think of them apart from the sound of cicadas and the smell of damp and clover, whispering with Mellie because they should have been asleep. Children come up with these notions, and then after a while they forget to wonder about it all, because what does it matter, what does it have to do with them, things are what they are. So the only ideas she had were a child's ideas, and she knew how they would sound to him. He'd try not to smile, and his voice would be very kind. But he seemed to know she had to be told everything, that she wouldn't know what to ask. The earth goes around the sun. It spins and it tips. All right.

Once, when she was new at the school in Tammany, the teacher asked her what country they lived in. The corn was tall, the sun was hot, the river was high for that time of year, so she said, "Looks to me like pretty decent country." That is what Doane would have said about it. And the children laughed, and some of them leaned out of their desks to wave their arms, and they whispered the answer loud enough that the teacher would hear even if she didn't call on them. "The United States of America!" Yes, the teacher said, the United States. What state? What county? And Tammany was an Indian chief who was kind to William Penn. Every day Lila stood off by herself during recess and lunch, but that day the teacher asked her to stay in to help her clean the blackboards, so she wouldn't be teased, probably. She said, "You mustn't be sad over a little thing like that, Lila. You'll catch up soon enough."

Lila said, "Don't seem like it. Maybe I won't. Maybe I don't even want to."

And the teacher said, "Well, I want you to. And I'm going to see to it."

The teacher was just a girl herself, a gentle girl. She helped Lila read and write, add and subtract, the things she would most need to be able to do, because Lila was the kind of child who would leave school the minute she could, or the minute her mother decided she had to. The teacher let Lila stay in the classroom working on her spelling and numbers when the other children played outside. She was glad to be by herself with something to do. She hated the other children because they had laughed at her, because they were town children, because she would never stay there anyway and they knew it. The teacher said she was a bright girl, and called on her to spell words or do sums in front of the class as soon as she knew Lila would probably get the right answers. That was all that made her bother learning them, but it made her like learning them because she was good at it. At the front of the room there was a map of the United States of America. A painting of George Washington. A flag with forty-eight stars and thirteen stripes. These things had a kind of importance about them that Lila had never even heard of before. She'd thought the world was just hayfields and cornfields and bean fields and apple orchards. The people who owned them and the people who didn't. And towns. Doll wanted to give her another kind of life. She didn't know how to go about it, rough and ignorant as she was, but she did try.

She heard herself say, "There was a woman who took care of me. She wanted me to marry an old man. But I couldn't. A young girl just has other ideas. She told me there wasn't no more for me to expect."

He said nothing. They walked the rest of the way home, neither speaking a word. She felt the old loneliness seize on her from one heartbeat to the next, the old, hard awkwardness of her body. How could a child stay alive in a body that felt so dead? Best that it shouldn't. There was no place for her to be alone now except in his house. She would leave the next morning, before he was awake, before it was light. There was nothing left in that cabin. She'd take a blanket off her bed, and a kitchen knife. Maybe her money was still out there where she hid it.

He opened the door for her and switched on the light. His face was slack and his lips were pale. He took the coat from her shoulders and hung it up. Then he just stood and looked at her. He said, "I'm at a loss. But you're right." His voice broke, so he cleared his throat. "You should stay here until the baby comes. After that, of course, you can do whatever you think is best."

What could she say? She said, "You know how I stole that sweater? I done it because it had your smell on it."

He laughed. "Why, thank you, Lila. I mean, I guess that's a sort of compliment."

"Then I was sleeping with it for a pillow."

"I'm honored."

"I used to make believe you was there and I was talking to you. I was thinking about you all the time. Seemed like I was going crazy."

"And I was thinking about you. And wondering about my-self. So what do we do now?"

She shrugged. "Just what we been doing, I'd say."

"So maybe I'm not just any old man?"

She said, "You surely ain't."

"Well. That's a relief." Then he said, "Do you still pretend you talk to me? Now that I'm here and all? Do you ever think of telling me the things you used to imagine you were telling me?"

"Asking, more like. And you just seen what happens. Whenever I talk."

He said, "I liked the part about the sweater. That was worth all the rest of it."

So she put her arms around him. So she put her head on his chest. "You're a good-hearted man," she said, enjoying the feel of his shirt. Of him stroking her hair.

"I believe that's true enough, most of the time. And very trustworthy. So there's no need to cry."

She said, "Yes, there is. I just now come near scaring myself to death."

"Hmm. We can't let that happen. We're supposed to be taking care of you." He kissed her forehead and touched tears off her cheeks, and then he said he had to go to his study to finish a little work. She thought, You mean, to do a little praying. Because I come near scaring you to death, too. So you have to talk me over with the Lord. Better Him than Boughton, I suppose.

But she had told him the truth about something, and it had turned out well enough. Now all she had to do was give up the other thought, that if she had minded and married the first old man, maybe Doll would be alive. He was probably about as ignorant as they were. At least he might not have known any more about the Judgment than they did. Then even if Doll had died, Lila wouldn't have to think of her standing there all astonished and ashamed, in the same raggedy clothes she was probably buried in, if she was buried, because why would they even bother to straighten her back and take the weariness out of her

120

face if they was just going to say "Guilty" anyway? That voice above the firmament. Doane was nothing but an ignorant little thief, his clothes all filthy with his own blood. The judge said, "I guess that dog got the better of you, fella. Looks like he took a pretty good bite. You got anything to say for yourself?" And what could he say? It was all the pride he had left just to say nothing. Doll had her pride, too, ugly as she was. She cared for a child. Yes, she stole it—away from death, probably. Away from loneliness. And she brought it up to be a fairly decent woman who wasn't afraid of a day's work. The way they used to laugh together! It was better than anything. But all that wouldn't count, because Doll cut somebody. Maybe more than once. So there was nothing she could say for herself, not a thing. When Lila pictured it in her mind, it was a preacher looking down from the firmament, judging. That would be hell enough for Doane, no matter what came after it.

Always the same thoughts. The Reverend was still in his study, but she believed there might be comfort for her in lying down in his bed, and there was. She took his pillow and gave him the other one, and that felt better. When he came in he must have thought she was asleep, because he whispered, Bless your heart. He lay down with his arm across her waist, and she touched his hand to her lips. If he took it for a kiss, that was his business. He settled closer against her, and that felt very nice.

It was October when the child began stirring. Lila had pinched off some sprigs of ivy and put them in water glasses to sprout roots, and when they did she had taken them up to the cemetery for the boy John Ames and his sisters. She was clearing away leaves from them when she felt the child move. She said, "Well, child! I been waiting on you." The sun was brightly mild. There was the crisp sound of maple leaves just ripe enough to fall, and leathery oak leaves that would cling until a wind took them, and the smell from the fields of all the life that had burned through all those crops until it spent itself down like a fire. It was almost the smell of smoke. She said, "This town's called Gilead, child. That's a Bible name. We going to stay here till you're born. I figure we're safe here. We'll see what happens." She said, "I'm going to be a little bit more careful about what I say, that's one thing." The old man would have liked to be told that she felt the child moving, but she wouldn't tell him yet. It lived in her and knew her, and if her thoughts were dread or regret or anger or anything that stirred her heart, it knew her thoughts.

She had forgotten how it felt not to be by herself, as she was still, till that very moment, no matter what the old man said or did. Kind as he was. She put her hand on her belly and she said, "You got a pa who is a preacher. His brother and sisters are here, and his mother and father, and his wife and her baby. The whole family lying here together. We come up now and then to see to them because who else do we have? Just Doll, and I don't know where to look for her. I might figure it out sometime. I'm going to get me some crocus bulbs. There's folks who bring in the best corn crop you could imagine, but they're just useless when it comes to a flower garden. You can see that, looking around up here. Irises would be nice, too." Three women came up the path. Lila said, "I spose they'll think I'm talking to myself." She nodded to them, and then she walked down the hill and through the quiet evening streets to the preacher's house. Gilead was the kind of town where dogs slept in the road for the sun and the warmth that lingered after the sun was gone, and the few cars that there were had to stop and honk until the dogs decided to get up and let them pass by. They'd go limping off to the side, lamed by the comfort they'd had to give up, and then they'd settle down again right where they were before. It really wasn't much of a town. You could hear the cornfields rustling almost anywhere in it, they were so close and it was so quiet. She said, "You'll like it here well enough, child. For a while."

The old man came out on the front porch and smiled at her with his head to one side, the way he did when there was something he wasn't going to ask her, so she said, "We been up to the graveyard, looking after things a little." She said *we* and he didn't ask about it, so she said, "Me and the child. Seems like there's two of us, now it's moving around a little."

"Two of you," he said. "That makes three of us, I believe. The three of us should probably have our supper." And he held the door for her.

Doll would have loved that kitchen. It was all painted white, and the curtains were white. Sunlight came in in the morning. Lila polished it every day, the way Doll did that kitchen in Tammany. It was strange, but if Lila pretended she was just there to do the cleaning it made things easier. She knew how to do it, and she could stop thinking about what else might be expected of her. Like cooking. She took cuttings from some red geraniums she saw at the cemetery. "The frost going to kill them anyway. No reason they should go to waste. You never want to waste things," she told the child. She put them in glasses on the windowsill to root, and they looked so beautiful that she brought her Bible and her tablet downstairs so she could work at the kitchen table.

The old man was always making them toasted cheese sandwiches and canned soup, and then worrying over whether she was eating what she ought to. Ladies from the church brought in supper from time to time, so he probably mentioned his worries. Somebody had left a cookbook on the counter, most likely Mrs. Graham, since she was the one who was a close enough friend to Lila to help out in ways that might offend her if someone else tried them. Well, she knew she wasn't really Lila's friend, but somebody did have to help her sometimes, and Mrs. Graham took it on herself, which was kind. Just as well not to chew your fingernails, dear. This is what they call an emery board, it's really just a piece of sandpaper. It'll keep your nails from snagging on things.

Well, who thought of that? And little tiny scissors. One of the girls in St. Louis had trimmed her nails and painted them, what there was of them, while another put her hair up in rags to curl it. They plucked her eyebrows almost down to nothing, and then drew them back in with a pencil. They got the idea to pierce her ears with a darning needle right then, when they were thinking about it. Laughing the whole time. They put powder on her face to try to hide the freckles, and purple lipstick, and pink rouge. She just sat there and let them do whatever they liked because she was so young and such a fool. And because they were playing the Victrola. They enjoyed the Victrola. Best forget all that.

It was strange to wonder what she had really forgotten. Never you mind. Doll must have said that to her hundreds of times, and all it did was make her wonder and remember and keep it to herself. Where did you go that time you left me? How long did it take you to get there? Never you mind. Lila would have asked who was there at that house, still there after so many years. Her mother? Was she born there? Were there other children born after her? But she knew what Doll would say. Lila knew how desperate she must have been even to think of taking her back there. Maybe she'd begun to doubt that she was right to carry her off in the first place, since she was having such trouble finding any way to live. So it was best to forget all that, too. Not to wonder. Why should she wonder? When she felt the baby stir she remembered sleeping on Doll's lap, restless in her arms with the warmth and damp, and dreaming.

The old man had said, "Why Ezekiel? That's a pretty sad

book, I think. I mean, there's a lot of sadness in it. It's a difficult place to begin."

She said, "It's interesting. It talks about why things happen." Well, the old man said, and cleared his throat. That was a special situation. God had a particular relationship with Israel, certain expectations. *Moreover I will make thee a desolation and a reproach among the nations that are round about thee, in the sight of all that pass by. So it shall be a reproach and a taunt, an instruction and an astonishment, unto the nations that are round about thee, when I shall execute judgments on thee in anger and in wrath, and in wrathful rebukes.* She copied the verses ten times. Her writing was getting smaller and neater. Lila Ames. The old man worried over her reading in the Bible just at that place. So she told him she had looked at Jeremiah and Lamentations and thought she probably liked Ezekiel better. He nodded. "Also very difficult." Then he told her that it is always important to understand that God loved Israel, the people in these books. He punished them when they were unfaithful because their faithfulness was important to the whole history of the world. Everything depended on it, he said.

All right. She was mainly just interested in reading that the people were a desolation and a reproach. She knew what those words meant without asking. In the sight of all that pass by. She hated those people, the ones that look at you as if they want to say, Why don't you get your raggedy self out of my sight. Ain't one thing going right for you. Existence don't want you. Doll couldn't hide her poor face anymore, the way she did when they were all together and Doane did their talking for them. People would try to figure out that mark. A wound, maybe a scar? It was an astonishment to them. They would stare at it before they realized what they were doing, and Doll would just stand there waiting till they were done, till they looked past her and spoke past her. And then she would try to sell them what little she had in the way of strength. Or they could just swap something for it, if that was easier. In those days it seemed to Lila that they were nothing at all, the two of them, but here they were, right here in the Bible. Don't matter if it's sad. At least Ezekiel knows what certain things feel like. That voice above the firmament. He knows the sound of it. *There is no speech nor language.* But it was asking a hard question all the same, something to do with the trouble it was for them to hold up their heads, and where the strength came from that made them do it no matter what.

The old man said to her one evening that he would like to know a little bit about the woman who looked after her. He'd been telling her stories about his family. His grandfather used to talk to Jesus in the parlor, and they all had to be very quiet until they heard him at the front door saying, "Lord, I do truly thank You for Your time!" He was trying to get her to talk to him a little more, probably wanting company. He said, "My grandfather was a pretty wild old fellow. He shot a man. One that I know of. Then he was in the war, so there might have been others. He enlisted as a chaplain, but he had a gun, and he took it along with him." People do want company, in the evening.

So she said, "The woman who took care of me, she called herself Doll. You know, like something a child would play with. I never knew no other name for her. A teacher gave me Dahl for a last name, but that was just a mistake. Doll used a knife on somebody, cut him. I believe she regretted it on account of the trouble it caused her. She was sort of looking over her shoulder all the time I knew her. It wasn't so much the law that caught her. She ended up having to do it again, cut somebody. Nothing else to say. She was good to me." That was more than she meant to tell him. "She give me that knife I had out at the shack." Why did she say that? "I wouldn't mind having it back." That was just the truth. It was a pretty good knife.

"Well, yes," he said. "Everything you had out at the cabin is in a couple of boxes in the attic. I'm sorry I forgot to tell you that. I'll bring them down for you."

"Just the knife is the only thing I been missing." She said, "Since I've got that Bible." She didn't mind if he remembered who she was for a minute, but she didn't want to scare him too much, either. He did look a little concerned.

"Yes," he said, "Ezekiel. Are you planning to copy that whole book?"

"Only the parts I like."

He nodded. "Sometime I'd like to know which parts you like." He said, "I don't want to intrude, of course. It would be interesting to me. From the point of view of interpretation. I'd like to know your thoughts."

She said, "I'm still thinking. Maybe I'll tell you when I'm done."

He laughed. "I'll look forward to it. But you might never get done, you know. Thinking is endless."

"It's true I been taking my time about it."

"There's no hurry. Boughton and I have been worrying the same old thoughts our whole lives, more or less. There's been a lot of pleasure in it, too."

"Well, I been trying to work something out. Trying to make up my mind about something. So I'm going to want to finish with it."

After a minute he said, "I'm trying not to ask what it is. You have every right to keep your thoughts to yourself. It's clear enough that that's what you want to do. So I'm not going to ask." He laughed. "This is a real test of my character."

She shrugged. "It's just old Doll. That's what it comes down to."

"I see."

She said, "You know that part where it says, 'I saw you weltering in your blood'? Who is that talking?"

127

"It's the Lord. It's God. And the baby is Israel. Well, Jerusalem. It's figurative, of course. Ezekiel is full of poetry. Even more than the rest of the Bible. Poetry and parables and visions."

She knew he'd been wanting to help her with Ezekiel, so much that it made him downright restless. He'd been reading it over, just waiting for this chance to tell her it was poetry. Hardly a man is now alive who remembers that famous day and year. That was practically the only poem she'd ever heard of, so she didn't really know what to make of the help he wanted to give her. The rude bridge that spanned the flood. "Well, it's true what he says there. It's something I know about."

"Yes. You're absolutely right. I didn't mean that it wasn't true in a deeper sense. Or that it wasn't describing something real. I didn't mean that." He shook his head and laughed. "Oh, Lila, please tell me more."

She looked at him. "You ask me to talk. Now you're laughing at me."

"I'm not! I promise!" He took her hand in both his hands. "I know you have things to tell me, maybe hundreds of things, that I would never have known. Things I would never have understood. Maybe you don't realize how important it is to me—not to be—well, a fool, I suppose. I've struggled with that my whole life. I know it's what I am and what I will be, but when I see some way to understand—"

"Is that why you married me?"

He laughed. "That might have been part of it. Would that bother you?"

"Well, I just don't know what I'd have to tell you."

"Neither do I. Everything you tell me surprises me. It's always interesting."

"Like that I been missing that knife?"

"I'll find it for you. First thing tomorrow."

"That was Doll's knife."

He nodded, and he laughed. "Sentimental value."

She said, "I spose so."

"Well," he said, "before I give it back to you, promise me one thing. Promise me you know I would never laugh at you."

She said, "You laughing at me now."

"Only in a certain sense."

"'A certain sense,' now what's that sposed to mean? The way you talk!"

"I only meant—" He looked at her. "Lila Dahl, you're deviling me!"

She laughed. "Yes, I am."

"Just sitting there watching me struggle!"

"I do enjoy it."

"Hmm. That's good! Because you'll see a lot of it."

They laughed.

"But I did mean to ask you something," she said. "There's a baby cast out in a field, just thrown away. And it's God that picks her up. But why would God let somebody throw her out like that in the first place?"

"Oh. That's difficult. You see, the story is a sort of parable. You know how in the Bible the Lord is spoken of as a shepherd, or the owner of a vineyard, or a father. Here He is just some kindly man who happens to pass by and find this child. In the parable He isn't God in the sense of having all the power of God."

"But if God really has all that power, why does He let children get treated so bad? Because they are sometimes. That's true."

"I know. I've seen it. I've wondered about it myself a thousand times. People are always asking me that question. Versions of it. I usually find something to say to them. But I want to do better by you, so you'll have to give me a little more time. A few days. I don't really know why I think that will help, but it might." He touched her hand. "'Because I love you more than I

129

can say, If I could tell you, I would let you know.' That's poetry, but it's also true. It is."

"That's a nice poem."

" 'The winds must come from somewhere when they blow, There must be reasons why the leaves decay.' It's kind of sad, really."

"I was never one to mind that."

"Me either, I suppose." He said, "In my tradition we don't pray for the dead. But I pray for that woman all the time. Doll. And now I have a name for her. Not that it matters. Except to me."

"There was a girl named Mellie. She's probly still alive. And Doane. I don't know about him."

"I'll remember them, too."

"But it's Doll I mainly worry about."

"Yes."

"Well," she said, "you keep on praying. It might ease my mind a little."

And he said, "Thank you, Lila. I'll do that."

He sat beside her until the room was dark. She was wondering what he might want to say, and what she might say if she began talking. She was sitting there with her hands folded in the lap of her dress, the Sears dress with flowers on it. There was a little mirror on the wall across from them, bright blue with the evening sky, and there were lace curtains behind them, and the chill of the window, and beyond that trees and fields and the wind. To have a man sitting beside her still felt strange, one she liked and pretty well trusted, but a man just the same, in those plain dark man clothes he never gave a thought to and smelling a little of shaving lotion. There was warmth around him that she could feel though she didn't touch him. His ring on her hand and his child in her belly. You never do know.

She said, "Now, why would they want to salt a baby?"

"Hmm? I looked that up in the Commentary. It said they did it to make the baby's flesh firm. Too much salt would make it too firm. That's Calvin. The way he talks about it, they must still have been doing it in the sixteenth century. Four hundred years ago."

"I didn't even know he was dead. Calvin. The way you and Boughton talk about him."

He laughed. "Well, maybe the old preachers need to reflect on that. But Calvin can be very useful. About salting babies and so on."

"Does he say anything about why a child would be treated so bad in the first place?"

"Well, he says, basically, that people have to suffer to really recognize grace when it comes. I don't know quite what to think about that."

"What about them children nobody ever finds?"

"My question exactly. In fairness to Calvin, he had only one child, and it died in infancy. A little boy. It was a terrible sorrow to him. He knew a lot about sorrow."

"A baby like that one in the Bible, just born, it wouldn't feel what it was to have somebody take it up. Or it wouldn't remember well enough to know the difference. So there wouldn't be no point in the suffering."

"That's true. But this is a parable. God had rescued Israel out of slavery in Egypt, so *they* would know the difference. Between suffering and grace. Ezekiel talks a good deal about the captivity. In fact, he was writing from the captivity in Babylon, another one. So I see Calvin's point, if I look at it that way. I mean, the Old Testament does pretty well depend on the idea that Israel would know the meaning of grace, because they had suffered."

"So God let them suffer in Egypt. And they go on suffering afterward."

He shrugged. "That seems to have been the case. You know, I wouldn't mind if you were reading Matthew, along with Eze-kiel. Just a suggestion."

She said, "I'm interested in what I been reading. He talks a lot about whoring. Maybe I'll read Matthew next."

He laughed. "Oh, Lila! I could explain about that." He put his head in his hands. "Not that it's so easy to explain. I just hope it doesn't upset you."

"Don't worry about it. I got my own thoughts." Then she said, "By the way, I don't use that word in front of folks. I know it's practically cussing. Worse. I tell you, I surely didn't expect to find it in the Bible. That's interesting. There's a lot in there I didn't expect."

He said, "It is interesting. I guess I'll have to read the whole thing over again. It is amazing how I always seem to be think-ing about the parts I like best. And there are a lot of them. But there *is* all the rest of it." There in the darkness they were quiet for a while, and then he said, "I guess I've had my time of suf-fering. Not so much by Ezekiel's standards. And there might be more to come. At my age, I'm sure there is. But at least I've had enough of it by now to know that this is grace." His arm was across the back of the couch behind her, and he touched her hair. He was still so shy of her.

She said, "Well, that's interesting." She had to wonder what Mrs. Ames would think about it. Poor girl just trying to give him a baby. "I'll reflect on it."

Now that her belly was getting round she sat at the table in her room to do her thinking, but she still locked the door when he left the house, for the loneliness of it. He never came into her room, he never preached from Ezekiel, and he never asked her another question about Doll, even when he gave her back

132

that knife. The morning after she mentioned it, it was just lying there on the breakfast table between the cream pitcher and the sugar bowl, the blade closed into the handle, looking harmless enough. She'd left it there. Seemed like he might want to know where it was, until he knew her a little better. Doll had whetted the blade till it was sharp as a razor and a little worn down, the polish gone off the edge of it. When Lila was alone, she opened it. Doll's patience and her dread were all worked into that blade. She would be spitting on the whetstone and then there would be that raspy, whispery sound, Doll thinking her thoughts, working away at her knife, making it sharp as it could be. Never you mind. Then that one night she said, "Better you take it. Wash it down good, and hide it when you get a chance. Don't you never use it unless you just have to."

It was the only thing Doll had to give her, too good to be thrown away and much too risky to keep, but what else could she do? It had a handle made of antler, shaped just enough to feel right in her hand, smooth and stained with all the hands that had held it. Doll never was the first one to own anything, and she wasn't the last, either, if she could help it. There was always something to trade for, even if it was only a favor of some kind, and everything came with a story about the woman who got it from a fellow who stole it from somebody else, which wasn't really stealing, since she never used it, and he knew she took it from a cousin's house when he was dead, and he had brothers, so she had no right to it, but he felt bad anyway, so he was selling it cheap.

Everything was as stained and worn by use and accident as a hand or a face. There were things you just had to respect, and that knife was one of them. Sometimes a stranger would settle himself at the fire, sitting on his heels the way folks do when they might want to move quick, and they'd study him to see what was at his back, what he carried with him, which was nothing at all and could be anything at all, like a shifting of the wind. And sometimes he had that Heck, I wouldn't harm a fly! look that made Doane glance at Arthur, and then there would be the long, careful business of sending him on his way, meaning no offense, since he looked like the kind who might want to take offense, given the slightest chance. Snakes, knives, strangers, darkening in the sky—you felt some things with your whole body. What they might mean. It could be they were on their way to do harm elsewhere and you just saw them pass by, but how could you know? Maybe twenty people had owned that knife and only one or two had done any hurt with it. A wound can't scar a knife. A knife can't weary with the use that's been made of it. Still.

She was sorry there was nothing left of that shawl. It would have been a different thing entirely to tell the old man Doll had left that to her. When Doane held it over the fire it burned so fast it was like a magic trick. It was gone before the heat could touch his hand. It was so worn then, threads that stayed together somehow, you could see right through it. Gray with enough pink here and there to show where the roses used to be. He didn't know what it was, why they kept it. It was useless, except for the use they made of it, remembering together. There wasn't much that felt worse than losing that shawl. *There is no speech nor language; their voice is not heard.* That's true about things. It's true about people. It's just true. So the knife was lying there where the old man had put it, on the kitchen table next to the sugar bowl, which was missing its cover and a handle because one of the children broke it, the boy John Ames. His mother and father remembered the day. The children were at home and inside because of a blizzard, and they were all in the kitchen because it was the warmest room in the house. There was bread baking. Days like that make children rambunctious, eager to be out in the snow. The old man said he always wished he remembered that day, too. Not that there weren't always more blizzards, more days in the kitchen. But they made his father serious and his mother sad, so there wasn't much pleasure in them. Lila told the child, "The world has been here so long, seems like everything means something. You'll want to be careful. You practically never know what you're taking in your hand." She thought, If we stay here, soon enough it will be you sitting at the table, and me, I don't know, cooking something, and the snow flying, and the old man so glad we're here he'll be off in his study praying about it. And geraniums in the window. Red ones.

Don't go wanting things. She said that to herself. Doll hated snow.

She was still thinking about Ezekiel, as much as anything. The man takes up the baby that's been thrown out in the field. *Then washed I thee with water; yea, I thoroughly washed away thy blood from thee, and I anointed thee with oil.* The blood is just the shame of having no one who takes any care of you. Why should that be shame? A child is just a child. It can't help what happens to it, or doesn't happen. The woman's voice calling after them from the cabin, Lila probably made that up. She could never ask. Doll said, Nobody going to come looking for her. And for a while nobody did. There must have been someone Lila hoped would call after them, someone a little sorry she'd be gone.

Why did it matter? Doll had washed away her shame, some part of it, when she took her as a child. And then that night, when she hadn't even seen her for a month, didn't even know she was in the same town, Doll came to her all bloody. The scrawnier Doll got, the more time she'd spent on that knife, whetting it long after it was as sharp as it ever would be. Sometimes Lila would hear that sound, be waked by it, when Doll had trouble sleeping. Doll carried it open, tied to her leg, so there wouldn't be any problem in using it fast if she had to. When

Doll came to her finally, white and trembling, it took Lila a lot of washing even to find her wounds, because she had been hiding all day until it was dark, with her dress loosened so the blood wouldn't dry the cloth onto the cuts. And the blood wasn't all hers, either. Probably most of it wasn't. The poor old woman seemed positively ashamed she hadn't died. She said, "I do hate to trouble you, child." She said, "When him and me went to it, I thought that would be the end of me for sure. I expected I might die this morning, or die on the way over here. I don't know." So Lila tried to be gentle and Doll tried to be brave, and there was just blood all over everything. The sheriff came the next morning. He said, "I never thought I'd see a woman your age mixed up in a knife fight," and Doll mustered the strength to say, "He wasn't no spring chicken hisself." He laughed. "Looks like you won for sure. He lost, no doubt about that. Too bad for the both of you." He was amusing himself with the strangeness of it all, and Doll knew it. But her face and hands were washed and her hair was brushed, and the rags were hidden away under the bed so some of the awfulness was put out of sight. Lila had slit Doll's dress open with that filthy knife, and then pinned it closed again over the bandage, so she was covered, at least. They brought a stretcher for her.

The sheriff said, "This your mother?"

Lila said, "No, just trying to help. She come to my door." And Doll was watching her. Maybe Lila'd just gotten tired, but by then she'd started saying the first damn thing that came to mind, even if it was true.

"You have her knife?"

"I didn't see no knife. I guess she wasn't carrying it with her."

"Well," he said, "we'll want to be sure about that. That thing must be sharp as the very devil."

It would have been just like Lila to say, I got the nasty thing here in my stocking, right against my leg, the first place any girl in Missouri would have hid it. The first place I'd expect you to look. She might even have said, If you don't mind, I'd be glad to be rid of it. But she took the trouble to lie because Doll was looking right at her. When the sheriff said, "Somebody go get the stretcher, I guess we got to get her over to the jail," Doll closed her eyes and set her lips and folded her hands and was satisfied. She didn't even turn her head to the side to hide the mark. She said, "If ever a man had it coming." All the time she spent sharpening that blade she was probably thinking where it would be best to cut, just one or two strokes to get him bleeding. It all worked out the way she wanted, except he didn't kill her, too. At least not right away. When they took her off to jail, Lila stayed behind to take the knife out of her stocking. She dropped it behind a rain barrel in an alley Doll must have passed through coming to find her. Anyone looking for it would have seen it. But it was there three weeks later, when Doll was gone and people had stopped talking much about her. So Lila slipped it back into her stocking.

Doll was very frail, not fit to stand trial, they said. After she'd healed a little, the sheriff put a rocking chair out on the sidewalk in front of his office and she sat there in the sun in the afternoons with a blanket across her lap, wearing a huge brown dress somebody had found for her. People came to look at her and she looked at them, calm as could be, a proud old savage, that mark like a bloodstain she chose not to wash away. They kept their distance, even though they were fairly sure her ankle was cuffed to the chair. Lila came as often as she could, and Doll turned that same look on her. And all she said to her was "I don't know you." Then somebody forgot to fasten the chain, or somebody wanted her to know that the law just couldn't bring itself to deal with her, so she walked away one evening after supper, leaning on the cane they had given her, and lost herself in the woods or in the cornfields. They said she couldn't have lasted long or made it far, but they didn't find her, and Lila didn't find her, and finally the snow fell.

I don't know you! Why did she say that? They'd talked the whole night. Doll was still expecting to die, so she told her things. Then why did she turn that cold look on her? Sitting there, rocking on the porch, the molasses cookie Lila brought for her just there in her hands like she didn't really notice what it was. She wished she could ask the old man about it all, but she'd have to tell him the whole story or he wouldn't understand. And what would he understand if she did tell him? That Doll was wild when she was cornered, like some old badger. Nothing the least bit Christian about her when she was cornered. She'd better tell him other things first, maybe even how she stole Lila off that stoop. Why be loyal to a secret? What did it matter to anybody now? Talking to the old man about it would just be her giving in to the idea that it would feel better to say a few things out loud to somebody. Maybe she would even have to tell him that her first regret, when she found out Doll was gone, was that she hadn't thought of some way to get that knife back to her. Off on her own like that, she'd need it so damn bad. Well, Lila thought, I am going to see him at the church, so I can put my head on his shoulder. He won't ask me why. He'll just stroke my hair.

That was the first time she walked down to meet him in the evening. And there he was, in his gray not-preaching coat and the white shirt she had ironed all over again since she did that better than anybody. When he saw her at the door, she could tell he was moved, almost saddened. She thought, A man this old knows there won't be so many more evenings. Can't go thinking about that. She decided then she would always come to find him and walk home with him. Not that the word "always" ever did mean much. He was surprised to see her there, concerned at first. Those thoughts of hers. He could see them in her face. She said, "I been missing you." And he said, "Oh. Well then." And he put his arms around her, just the way she knew he would, just the way she meant for him to do. She was like all the others who came to him with their grief, and that was all right. She didn't mind. He was blessing her. He was doing that to people all the time. He rested his cheek against hers, too, and that was different. She felt his breath against her ear. She was his wife.

She'd had one dream a hundred times, and she had it again that night. It was still there after it woke her up. The hair as stiff as the cloth of the dress, all of it weightless and crumpled in on itself, the way anything is that lies out in a field through a winter. And there would be too little of it, because winter does that, parches things down to their husks. Maybe critters been at it. You wouldn't dare touch it, it would fall to pieces. She was afraid to see the face, and the face was hidden, from shame at just lying out in a field like that, or because it was turned away from her, "I don't know you." Once, Mellie found a dog, what was left of it. She never could let anything be. She pushed at the carcass with a stick, and there were teeth lying there. Lila thought, What would it be like to have different dreams. Or no dreams at all. Well, he was praying for Doll. Lila would say, I got a real preacher speaking for you, speaking to the Almighty. And what would Doll say then? Child, why'd you want to do a thing like that! Best He forget all about me. Lying there with her cheek in the mud, stubborn as ever. Lila would say, Ain't much else I can do, is there. You never let me find you. And Doll would say, I'm hiding real good here. That Almighty of yours can't even find me. She'd be sort of laughing.

Lila thought, The dream, again. Seems like I can't even close my eyes. Well, but she had this old man now, lying here beside her, and he didn't give any sign at all that he was getting tired of having her around. And men don't last so well. A woman said once that when men get a few years on them they're harder to keep than a child. She said, They can look all right and then one day they'll just drop in their tracks. Lila had seen it herself, out harvesting. And wouldn't she feel like a fool if all she'd been thinking about was Doll, when here she was with this warm, breathing man beside her, for now at least. He was always worrying that she might be tired or cold. Or sad. He brought her a dictionary, and it was very interesting. She'd never even have known to want it. She could put her hand on his chest right now and feel his heart beating. Hair on his chest, all soft and silvery. She was going to put some thought to being kinder to him. He liked seeing them geraniums. "The woman's touch," he said. Well, she thought, I guess so. She didn't know much about that.

That money of hers was still out there at the shack, most likely. She could buy him something with it. Wouldn't have to spend it all. She'd just want the money in her hand to make sure somebody hadn't come along and settled into the place and found where she hid it. It would be a hard life now with the cold coming on, but you never knew. If they'd found the money, they'd think it was theirs for sure and they might not want to give it up. She thought she could bring that knife along, and then she thought no. If he saw it was gone, he'd start wondering. Just showing a knife can be trouble, and here she was pregnant. What was she thinking about. She had no business at all carrying a knife. She wasn't even supposed to be biting her nails. But the money was so much on her mind that she couldn't go back to sleep. She remembered that the Sears catalogue was on the shelf in the kitchen, and then she had to get up and look through it. There was everything you could think of in there.

When she heard him stirring the way he did when he was waking up, she put the catalogue back on the shelf and set the table. Ham and eggs and a pot of coffee. Nothing hard about that. Toast and jam. He came downstairs whistling, scrubbed and shaved and combed. "Ah," he said, "wonderful! And how are you two this morning?"

She said, "I guess this child of yours don't want me to sleep. Maybe he don't like my dreams or something."

He helped her with her chair. "You're having bad dreams? Here, I'll get the coffee." He poured her a cup. "Do you want to tell me about them?"

"They're just dreams. You must have bad dreams sometimes. Maybe you don't, being a preacher."

He laughed. "I have had more than my share, it seems to me." And he said, in that low, gentle voice he used to speak to widows, and knew that he did, "Sometimes it does feel better to talk about them."

"Who you been talking to about them all these years? Old Boughton, I suppose."

He nodded. "Boughton."

"Jesus, I suppose."

"Jesus."

"You never told me nothing about your dreams. Anything."

"I guess it's been a while since I had any dreams worth talking about. Something's chasing me and I don't know which way to run. Then I wake up. That's all most of them amount to. I'm just running like the devil. I haven't really run like that since I was ten years old. And then I wake up with my heart pounding."

"And that's what you tell Jesus."

He laughed. "The Lord is very patient. Something I learned from my grandfather. Well, from watching my grandfather. I used to wonder when I was a boy how the Lord could just listen to him going on the way he did. I suspected sooner or later He might stop coming around. I sort of hoped He would. I was a little scared of Him."

"Maybe He's what you was running away from. In your dream." Now, why did she say that?

He shrugged. "What a thought. Now, wouldn't that be something." He toyed with his fork, considering.

She said, "I'll tell you the truth, I'm scared of Him. I'm always dreaming that Doll's trying to hide from Him. That's why she don't want no grave, so He can't find her."

"Well," he said, "that's a very sad dream. I'm sorry about it. You probably never would have dreamed such a thing before you came here and started listening to me. And Boughton."

"Don't worry about it. My dreams was already bad enough. It would have just been something else. There's nothing good about her dying the way she did, Lord or no Lord."

He looked at her, and he nodded.

"I didn't mean nothing by that. No offense."

"No, no, I'm just thinking."

It seemed she was going to say any damn thing. "You're kind of like your grandfather. You think the Lord is living here, in this house. It's Him I might be offending. It don't scare me, though, to have you thinking that. Couple of dreams is all."

"Well, my thinking about these things isn't really the same as my grandfather's. I suppose I should say my experience is different from his."

"But I know you still think you might offend Him. Jesus."

He nodded. "True enough."

She said, "I don't know what started me talking like this. I don't want to go on with it, I truly don't."

"That's fine. I just want to say one thing, though. If the Lord is more gracious than any of us can begin to imagine, and I'm sure He is, then your Doll and a whole lot of people are safe, and warm, and very happy. And probably a little bit surprised. If there is no Lord, then things are just the way they look to us. Which is really much harder to accept. I mean, it doesn't feel right. There has to be more to it all, I believe."

"Well, but that's what you want to believe, ain't it."

"That doesn't mean it isn't true."

She thought, Don't go hoping. Let's see what comes of this child. Let's see how long I keep this old man. What a body might hope for just ain't in the way of things, most of the time. Never for long. She said, "I might try thinking about that. It's a nice idea." And he said his grace, and she bowed her head. Why did she talk to him that way? So that she could say when it ended she always knew it would. Not very long after he kissed her cheek and left for the church she put on her coat and walked down to the store as if a wedge of cheese and a box of crackers were all she had in mind, and then strolled along down the road, on past the edge of town, past the fields of dry cornstalks. It was a good coat, new and heavy and too warm for the weather, since the winter was a little late coming on, but she told herself it would be a kind of waste not to get all the use of it she could. It was a nice dark blue.

You could see pelicans by the hundreds sometimes. It was late in the season for them, but winter was late, so she might still see some. There was a wide place in the river where people went to look at them, so that's what she'd say if anyone asked her where she was going. She'd seen those birds all her life and never had a name for them, because they had nothing to do with getting by. She'd never once heard of anybody eating one. Ducks, for sure, but never pelicans. They were white as anything could be, flying up off the water together and spreading their wings so wide you couldn't believe it, and then settling together on the water again, sliding along. They just came when the weather started to change, and then they were gone till the next year. It was the old man who told her what they were called. There was one of them carved into Mrs. Ames's gravestone. After Lila stopped at the shack she'd go on down to the river so she could tell him where she'd been without lying.

She'd never thought before how strange a cornfield can look so late in the year, all the stalks dead where they stand. The country had always just been work waiting to be done. Now she saw the dim shine of sunlight on the leaves, and how the stalks were all bent one way, the tops of them. The wind had bent them and then left them rigid, with their old tattered leaves hanging off them. But it was as if they had all heard one sound and they all knew what it meant, or were afraid they did, and every one of them waited to hear it again, to be sure, every one of them still with waiting. She said, "It don't mean nothing," speaking to the child. "It's the wind."

The shack was there, the field in front of it filled with the same old weeds, blanched and beaten down or poking up this way and that. The path she had worn from the road was pretty well overgrown. Somebody had been there, had come and gone just enough to bruise the grass. Somebody might still be there. She knew it wasn't smart to look in the door. You can get in a set-to so fast you don't even know what happened. Nobody harder to deal with than a thief, once he decides you're trying to steal from him. She had this baby now to think about. So she stood a way off and picked up a rock and threw it against the wall. It made a good, solid thunk. Nobody looked out the window or the door. She found two more rocks and threw them. Nobody. So she decided it would be safe to look inside.

She could see from the stoop that there was a blanket in the corner. That was about it. A few empty tin cans. Her canning jar, empty. Well, she should have known. She would look under that loose plank, to be sure. One jar does look just like the next one. But there was nothing there except the Reverend's handkerchief with the raspberry stains on it. She shook off the dirt and cobwebs and put it in the pocket of her coat. She said to the child, "What a day that was." Him out there in the field picking sunflowers for her. After she told him she wouldn't marry him. Maybe someday she'd be saying, Once, back in Iowa, your papa gathered flowers for me, from a field that was all gone to weeds. Before you was even born. She never thought a preacher would act that way. Every morning when he left for the church she stood on the porch and watched him walk down the road. He'd turn around to wave at her. If she kissed her fingers and held up her hand—she had seen women do that—he would clutch his hat to his chest and tilt his head to the side like a lovestruck boy in a movie. And she'd hear herself laughing. It would have been nice to give him a present. He wouldn't expect that.

She was sitting on the stoop in the sun, just for a minute, thinking about things. How good the sunlight felt on a chilly morning, and how familiar that old parched wood smell was, and how strange it seemed to be at peace where she had been so lonesome before, to be more at peace than in the old man's house, kind as he always was. She opened her coat to the sun so the baby could feel it warming her lap. She might even have fallen asleep, because there was a boy standing at a distance watching her, there for a while at least without her noticing him, she could tell by the way he was shifting his weight from one foot to the other, shifting a little bundle he had from one hand to the other. When she saw him he looked away. She said, "Morning."

He said, "That there's my shack. I been using it. Got my stuff in it." He was small, but he had hair on his face. He looked like something that came up in a drought and bloomed the best it could and never got its growth. There was a crack of sadness in his voice, or worry, and that made it seem like a boy's voice, younger than the rest of him. Still, you never know. He looked pretty desperate. Best let him have the money.

She said, "I was just sitting here for a minute, catching my breath. I was going down to the river to look at them birds." She stood up and found her little bag of groceries. "I'll be going. Didn't mean to trouble you."

He said, "Mainly folks don't come here."

"I know. I was using this shack most of the summer."

"Oh. You was using it. Why'd you come back? Maybe you left something here?"

"This," she said. She took the handkerchief out of her pocket. "I know it don't look like much. But since I was walking by."

He glanced at the shape of her now that she was standing, and then he looked away. "Maybe you ain't done resting. Don't matter to me. Nothing here I need. I was going to be doing something else anyways." He took a few steps back.

"Well, I was tired a little while ago, so I rested. And now I'm hungry. I got some cheese and crackers here. Plenty for both of us, if you'd like to join me."

"No," he said, "I best not."

Maybe he thought it was all she had. She said, "I'm real hungry, and I never could eat in front of folks. So I guess you're just going to let me starve."

He laughed, and he came a few steps closer to her. She could tell he hoped she would persuade him.

She said, "Sit here on the stoop. The sun is nice." No point saying he looked cold. She flattened out the paper bag and put the cheese on it and unwrapped it and opened a packet of crackers. She broke off a piece of cheese, and he came close enough to take it from her fingers. His hands were as dirty as could be, too big for him and brown with callus. His pants didn't reach his ankles and his shoes were all broken down. He was the kind of people Doane used to tell them they were not, the kind that didn't wash. Doll was after her with a wet rag all the time so she wouldn't slip away into that tribe, the ones who never touched a comb to their hair and who always had shadows of grime on their necks and wore unmended clothes till they were falling off them. They probably were her tribe, and that was why Doll kept such a close eye on her and never even told her where she came from. They ain't people you want hanging around. That's what she'd have said about a boy like this. No matter. Here he was licking his grimy fingers. She said, "Take some more."

And he said, "Don't mind if I do." He was happier than he wanted to be, with the food and the kindness. He sat down on the lowest step and put his little bundle on the ground beside him.

He had wandered there from somewhere south, probably Missouri, maybe Kansas. "I guess I'm heading the wrong way, this time of year. I shoulda thought about that, I guess." He laughed and glanced at her, shy of her. "I don't want to go back the way I come, that's for sure. So, I don't know. I'll do something." He laughed. He said, "There was some trouble down there, so I guess I won't be going back." He shook his head, but he looked up at her as if he wouldn't entirely mind her asking him about it. Maybe he was just surprised by it, lonely with it, not used to the idea that any important thing could be true of him. She thought, He should be careful. She was a stranger, and in his mind she was like someone who would listen and not blame him too much. His mother, maybe.

She said, "Well, sounds like you better keep it to yourself, whatever it was."

"Yeah," he said, and laughed. "I better." After a minute he said, "You ever had a dog? I did once. Then he took off after a rabbit or something and he never come back. So how you come to be living here?"

"Same as you. Drifting." She said, "Then this man wanted to marry me. So I said all right."

"Sounds like you making that up."

"I spose it does. And he's a preacher."

The boy laughed. He could tell things by looking at her, too. "I ain't joking. He's a big old preacher."

"Well," he said, "maybe so. That his child you got there?"

"You bet it is."

"So you're all right."

"Yes, I am."

"Because," he said, "I was thinking you was maybe back here looking for that money I found. Was you the one hid it there?"

"That was my money."

"Then how much was it?"

"It was almost forty-five dollars. Three fives, a lot of ones, and change. I had it in that canning jar, with the handkerchief. You can keep it."

He nodded. "That's about the most money I ever seen in my life."

"I was saving up. Thinking about California."

"If I give you half, that would still mean I had about twenty bucks."

"That's all right. You can keep it all. I was just going to buy some kind of a present for my old preacher. But he don't need nothing. He'd be the first to say. Better you keep it."

"I got it hid away in a good spot."

"Figured you might."

"Well, it would be safe there, if somebody was meaning to steal it." He looked up at her. Kindness was something he didn't even know he wanted, and here it was. It made him teary and restless, and he was trying to seem to repay it by pretending he'd hid the money partly for her sake.

She said, "Can't be too careful."

"First thing I done when I seen that board was loose was I looked under it. First thing anybody's going to do." She thought,

It comes with the whiskers, that idea that they know how things are. They get a lot of happiness out of it.

He was looking out over the field, as if there were something to see out there. "Yeah," he said. "I knew a fellow had a hunting dog. It'd do any damn thing he said. A hundred things."

She said, "You planning on getting a dog?" He had never cut that beard, never shaved. It was reddish and curly at the edges, and then it was straight and brown, what there was of it. And his hair was reddish, matted like sheep's wool. He'd scratch at it. And his skin was milky white. She'd seen that before. Like the sun just didn't shine on him the way it did on most people. His big hands were lying on his knees, palms up, and he was looking at them as if he'd never really gotten used to them.

He glanced up at her. He might have been about to say, The way I am ain't your business. It was you told me to sit down here. And that was true enough. So she looked away. He shrugged. "Thought about getting one." Then he said, "I been thinking I might give that money to my pa. He'd be glad to see me then, that's for sure." He laughed. "He was always telling me I was too puny to be worth keeping. Well, he'd think I stole it, anyhow. He'd tan me for it, too. Like he never done any stealing. But he'd be glad to have the money."

She said, "Then you'll be going back where you come from, I guess."

He said, "Probly not. My pa and me was fighting, and I hit him with a piece of firewood. I don't know. I think I killed him. If I didn't, he would have killed me, soon as he woke up. So I just took off." He looked at her. That dirty, weary child face with a beard stuck on it like a mean joke. "I don't know where I'll go. I don't even know where I am now!" He laughed.

She said, "Well, you're in Iowa. And the winter here is even worse than it is everyplace else. So you better not try staying on in this shack. You must be freezing already. For sure you won't last till the spring."

He shrugged. "Might not anyway. Might not want to. I hated my pa about half the time, but I sure never thought I'd end up killing him."

"Maybe he ain't dead."

"I sure did mean to kill him. I hit him three or four times. Hard as I could. Him laying there." Tears were running down his cheeks. "I think back on how it was, and I figure I must have killed him. I remember the sound it made when I hit him." He rested his head on his folded arms and wept.

After a while she said, "Well, you got to get some warm clothes and some good shoes. The preacher keeps things like that in a box somewhere. I can bring them out here tomorrow. Then you spend that money on a bus ticket."

He said, "After what I done to him, I know he wouldn't let me come back anyways."

"Then you figure out where else you want to go."

"This is the first time I ever been away from home," he said. "First time. I can't hardly even sleep nights."

"I guess you better get used to it."

He laughed. "Don't think I will." He looked at her. His face was a mess of grief, so she gave him the handkerchief.

"You have folks?"

"My pa. That's all. So." He shrugged and gazed out at the field again, calm for no reason except that he was done crying. "You ever talk to a killer before?"

"One. That I know of. She really did kill somebody, too. No doubt about it."

"Why'd she do it?"

"He'd have killed her. That's as much as I know. She got the jump on him, so they said she murdered him. I keep the knife she used right there on the old man's kitchen table."

"Why?"

"She was a friend of mine. About the only one I had. She give it to me."

"The preacher know about that knife?"

"I told him."

He nodded. "So you never turned against her after what she done."

"I did regret it."

He was quiet for a while, and then he said, "I tell you what happened. My pa was drunk, and he was yelling at me about nothing, some little thing I done, so I said I was going to run off and leave him. He followed me out to the road, and he was saying 'Git!' and throwing sticks and rocks at me, the way you'd chase off a dog. I come back to the house later and he was laying there asleep, and I took a piece of firewood, about yay big." He made a circle with his hands. "It just come over me."

"I can see how it might."

He looked at her. "So now I don't know *what* I'm going to do."

"Well," she said, "you stay here tonight, and then tomorrow I bring you some clothes, and you get yourself a ticket somewhere. And you better start telling yourself you don't know if you killed him, 'cause you don't. No point making it worse than it has to be. And you sure better stop talking to strangers about it."

He shook his head, and he said, very softly, calmly, "I think I'll just go back there. Tell 'em what I done." He said, "I'd like to take that money, if you're sure you don't mind. Some of it, anyways. At least I'd have something to give him. If he's still alive. I'd have that." Then he said, "They hang that friend of yours?"

"No. They might've been thinking about it, but she got away."

"You know, I'm kind of hoping they hang me. Then I'd just be done with it."

She said, "You shouldn't be talking that way. You ain't half grown. That's no way for you to talk." She put her hand on his shoulder.

He smiled up at her. "I figure, if my own pa got no use for me—" Then he said, "I'm growed. This is all there's going to be. Nothing much."

"I don't know about that. You look like you been working. I bet you been doing your share."

He shrugged. "I guess I tried." He smiled at her kindness, and looked at his hands again. "You know, I just wish I'd stayed there with him. Maybe I could've helped him somehow. I don't even know why I bothered running off. Didn't have no place to go. I knew that right along. I was always thinking about leaving, all them years. Never did. Sure wisht I had now. Scared to, I guess."

The wind was coming up, bringing cold with it. That would happen for good one day soon. The cold would set in, and there it would be for months and months. The boy crouched over his folded arms. The coat he was wearing was no use at all, and his poor, filthy ankles were bare.

She said, "How long you been here?"

"I come here, to this place, a couple days ago."

"Well, it ain't sposed to be this warm. It might change any time. It could snow tomorrow."

He nodded. "I feel it at night."

She said, "That's probably why you ain't sleeping."

"It's a fair part of it."

"Well then, I think you best come to my old man's house. Just for the night. He'll find some clothes for you and get you some breakfast. He's got a couple spare rooms."

He shook his head. "He ain't going to want me in his house. You know that."

"He does whatever I ask him. Hasn't said no to me yet anyway."

"What you ever ask him for?"

"You're right. Nothing much." She laughed. "I did ask him to marry me."

"'Cause you got that baby?"

"Nope. I wasn't even thinking about no baby. At the time."

"Well," he said, and he glanced up, hoping he wouldn't have to offend her, "I guess I just rather stay here."

That's how it is, she thought. Keep to yourself. So long as you can do that, you're all right. Then somebody finds you in a corner somewhere, and you ain't even there to hear them say, What a pity. And that seems better than asking for help. She said, "I understand that. I do. I know how you feel around strangers. I feel the same way. So you can trust me."

"No," he said. "I mean, I trust you. Still."

"Then I guess you better keep my coat."

He looked at her, startled and hurt, and laughing. "What? I can't wear no woman's coat!"

She said, "I don't mean you should wear it. I mean you should use it like a blanket. Sleep under it. Nobody's going to see."

He shook his head. "Nah. I'd probly spoil it. You going to need it yourself anyways."

"I'll get it tomorrow."

He picked up the little bundle. "You best be going along now. It's getting cold. And I best get out of this wind."

She said, "That's where you keep the money. Tied up in a rag."

"I like to keep it by me."

"That's fine."

"You sure you don't want some of it?"

"I'm sure." He stood there, waiting for her to be gone, skinny and dirty, and a good child all the same. Nobody's good child. "I don't want the rest of them crackers, either," she said.

"All right. Well, good talking with you." He nodded and stepped away from her, and then he watched her out to the road.

She buttoned her coat and turned up the collar, because by now the wind was bitter, and she walked about halfway to Gilead. Then she said, "This won't do." So she went back to the cabin. It was barely warmer in there than the weather outside. The boy was curled up in the corner where she had slept, the one that was intact enough to give some shelter, and he was wrapped in that sad old scrap of a blanket, the little bundle under his head. He looked at her, but he didn't move. She took off her coat and draped it over him. "Just for tonight," she said. "So maybe you can get some sleep." He didn't say anything, he just settled himself under it. She pulled the collar up around his ears. She said, "Feels good, don't it?" And he laughed.

And then there was the walk back to Gilead, through the bright day and the sharp wind. The stiff leaves of the cornstalks rustled and stirred, and a few pelicans were sailing and turning overhead, though she could hardly bear to look up at them, with that wind at her throat. She wondered if she might get so cold even the child would feel it. She felt it stir. She said, "Don't worry about it. You ain't going to have this kind of life. Once we're home we'll be fine." But she thought to herself, This might not be the smartest thing anybody ever did. Best think of something else. But not that. Not looking for Doll in the snow. Not getting lost in that cornfield. She had followed footprints into it, so why couldn't she just follow them back out again? But they ended where the snow ended, at the edge of the field, and farther in, there was just frozen ground. Anybody knew how lost you could get in a cornfield, and there she was, thrashing around, scared to death, the stalks so close and so high over her head that she couldn't tell where she was, and it was only luck that she got back to the road finally. Covered in dust and sweat. She couldn't have been in her right mind then, while she was looking for Doll. And what did she mean to do if she found her? She had some thought of covering her up, to keep her warm. As if anything could keep her warm. And then the next day there was real snow, hours of it, and no point trying to find her after that.

There was the time they were sitting by the fire, their faces hot and their backs freezing and the fire sizzling and popping and smoking because it was damp, sappy pine branches mostly. Lila had a bowl of fried mush, scraps of it, dark the way she liked them, because when Doll was doing the cooking she kept the crispy pieces for her. Mellie was right there beside her, close as she could get, watching that mush, and Lila was eating it a bit at a time. Mellie said, "I seen something go crawling into that bowl. I did. Its legs was all"—and she did a spidery thing with her fingers that made gooseflesh pass over Lila's arms and across her scalp. Lila said, "Wasn't no spider," and Mellie said, "Not saying it was. Just saying what I seen," and she did the thing with her fingers again.

Lila said, "I'm telling Doane."

"Why? What you going to tell him?"

"That you trying to get me to throw my supper in the fire."

Mellie said, "No need for that. I never mind a spider. You can always spit it out. They taste funny, so you'll know to do it. And you feel them little legs. I swallowed one once and I ain't dead. I'll eat that mush for you if you don't want it."

So Lila just sat there with the bowl in her lap, thinking about spiders, and Mellie sat there beside her, watching, breathing on her. Doll saw that Lila hadn't eaten her supper and told her she would thrash her if she didn't, which was just to let

Mellie know there was no use trying to talk her out of it. Lila felt Doll's hand on her shoulder. That meant, Mellie's the clever one, but you've got me here looking out for you.

Mellie whispered, "She always saying she going to thrash somebody. She ain't going to, though."

And Doll said, "Most likely I'm going to thrash *you*." But it was true, she never would do it. She was a kind, quiet woman as far as anybody ever knew. That knife was a secret she kept, not easily, not always, like the mark on her face. She just forgot to hide them both from Lila because she knew the girl loved her. One time Doane saw her cutting Lila's hair with that knife, and he stopped and watched the strands fall, whiff whiff whiff, and he said, "Well, I'll be danged."

Lila was halfway to Gilead by now. The sky was gray and the wind was acting like it owned the place, tossing the trees, and the trees all moaning. Somehow there was always the notion that one day would lead to the next, mild today meant mild tomorrow, a sunny morning meant a decent afternoon. And then winter would take over everything before you knew what was happening. It would be there like the world after sleep, a surprise and no surprise. Whatever happened to Mellie? She could be anywhere doing anything. She could be in jail. Lila had heard there were women who flew bombers across the ocean so they could be used in the war, and she had thought of Mellie. Wherever she was, even in jail, she'd be better at it than anybody ever had been, and all wrapped up in herself, twice as interested as anybody else in whatever notion she had just come up with. She was probably all right. But Lila had seen plenty of times how a bird will hatch or a calf will be born, and pretty soon they know things they couldn't be taught, they're up on their legs scratching or suckling, and their eyes are all bright with it. The world is so fine. That's when children can play with them, because their eyes are bright, too, and they're finding out how

clever *they* are. Then pretty soon the critters are just critters, live-
stock. And the children are just folks trying to get by. Could
be even Mellie is just some woman somewhere, with that look
in her eyes that says, I don't want to talk about it. Lila told the
child, "Don't worry yourself. I'm going to do the best I can. Just
like Doll done for me," she said, and she laughed. Poor old Doll.
Then she was thinking about that man-boy, crouching under
her woman's coat and sure to be wretched with cold anyway.
He'd have frozen right to death before he'd let anyone see him
wearing it. She should have made him come with her. Somehow. No. His pride was going to kill him. Well, she thought,
worse things can happen.

If she had some of that money she'd get a ticket to the matinee, and maybe a box of popcorn. She could warm up there in
the dark, watching *The Treasure of the Sierra Madre* again, but
warm, at least. Then she could go on home. She didn't want to
walk into his office at the church looking as miserable as she was,
knowing it would worry the old man. She'd seen that movie
with him. He'd read the book, and he'd read about the movie in
one of his magazines, so he'd been waiting for it. In the theater,
in the dark, he'd held her hand. That was the best part about it.
She was thinking, I don't need to watch raggedy-looking men
eating beans. I seen that plenty of times. Nice as it was to be sitting there with him, she was sort of glad when the men started
shooting each other, so the movie would have to end. She liked
movies where people wore nice clothes and tap-danced, but they
were never the ones he'd read about in his magazines.

If she had some of that money, she'd go into the diner and
have a cup of coffee and a piece of apple pie. If she had some of
that money, she'd go into the dime store and look at dress pat-
terns or something. She could do that anyway, but she thought
people had begun to notice her, out in the cold that way, when
anybody in her right mind would at least have a coat on. She had

almost forgotten the dread that someone might speak to her, and here it was again. She wouldn't let that happen if she could help it. It was like old times. No money and nothing to do about it, and people watching her. But there was the church. That was like old times, too. Stepping in out of the weather. She could just sit in a pew and wait till she stopped shivering and her fingers stopped aching. Then she'd find him in his office, and he'd say, Oh, my dear, and put his coat over her shoulders, and they'd walk to the house, and make some supper, and she would tell him she was fine, fine. She'd just gone for a walk.

She was too cold to stop trembling yet, so she put her hands between her knees and waited. Her toes ached. No point thinking about it. It always was quiet in there. You could hear any shift or creak anywhere in the building, and when the wind was blowing the way it was then, the church strained against itself like some old barn. You could practically hear nails pulling loose. And still it was quiet somehow. It was drafty, too, but that boy could have stretched out on a pew under a blanket or two and slept right through the storm, and who would have minded. If she'd had any idea how bad it was going to be, she'd have made him come with her.

It took her that long to realize the old man could ask somebody with a car to drive out there and bring him to town. She never got used to that. He could just say a word and whatever needed to be done got done, most of the time anyway. Even if it meant Boughton starting up his DeSoto. But when she did go to his office he wasn't there. Of course he wouldn't be hiding from her, but that was the first thought she had. The room just felt like he should be in it. The whole church felt that way. People who live in rooms and houses don't know about that. It seems natural to them. You might pick up something belonging to somebody and feel for a minute how theirs it is, particularly if you hate them enough. But a whole roomful of somebody's days and thoughts and breath, things that are faded and they don't see it, ugly and they don't care, things worn by their habits, it seems strange to walk in on that when you're almost nothing more than a cold wind. She did wish she could at least find a way to tell him how hard it was, the ache you feel walking out of a cold day into a warm room. And here she was angry at him for being somewhere else, almost crying about it. Because here was his whole long life and it had nothing to do with her unless he was there with her to say, This is Lila, Lila Ames, my wife.

Well, she thought, standing here worrying about it doesn't make much sense. He'll be at the house. And the thought she wouldn't let herself have was How long has it been since I felt the child stirring? Every woman she ever knew had stories about some child that was lost or didn't come out right because its mother ate too much of something, or took a fright, or took a chill. But there was nothing else to do but go on to the house. She said, "It's just a few blocks. Then we're home."

He wasn't there, either. The house was empty. Probably someone had died, or was about to die. Plenty of times he was called away to do what he could where comforting was needed. The last time it happened he came in the door after midnight, grumbling to himself. He said, "Asking a man to apologize on his deathbed for the abject and total disappointment he was in life! That does beat all." He took off his hat. "So I took them aside, the family. And I said, If you're not Christian people, then what am I doing here? And if you are, you'd better start acting like it. Words to that effect." He looked at her. "I know I was harsh. But the poor old devil could hardly get his breath, let alone give his side of things. There were tears in his eyes!" He hung up his coat. "I've known him my whole life. He wasn't worse than average. Wouldn't matter if he was." And then he said, "You shouldn't have waited up for me, Lila. The two of you need your sleep," and he kissed her cheek and went up to his study to pray over the regret he felt because he'd lost his temper. Anger was his besetting sin, he said. He was always praying about it. She had thought, If that's the worst of it, I'll be all right.

She wasn't warm yet, so she decided to go upstairs and lie down in his bed until she heard him at the door. She'd just slip off her shoes and pull up the covers and wait. She thought it would comfort the child. But the cold of her body filled the space it made under the blankets, a hollow of cold. Maybe that's how she felt to the child. Winter nights Doll would pull her against her, into her own shape, and she would pull the quilt up over her, and her arm would be around her, and Lila would only feel warmer for the cold that was everywhere else in the world. She was probably thinking of this when she gave that boy her coat, tucked him in. And then he laughed just the way she might have laughed all those years ago, for pleasure that seemed like a piece of luck, a trick played on misery and trouble. Now here she had this child of her own, and maybe it felt the cold. Maybe it feared it was being born to a woman who couldn't be trusted to give it comfort. Maybe it would have the look that boy had, as if the life in him had decided to cut its losses when it had just begun to make him a man's body. She thought, Then I'll steal you, and I'll take you away where nobody knows us, and I'll make up all the difference between what you are and what you could have been by loving you so much. Mellie said, "Her legs is all rickety," and Doll just kept her closer and seen to her all the more. Even Doll said, "If there was just something about you," looking at her the way other people did because she couldn't go on protecting her from other people. But Doll always made up the difference the best she could. Lila would, too. And there'd be no old man to say, I see what you've done to my child. No old man. It would happen sometime anyway. She pulled up her knees and hugged her belly, and she felt it moving.

The sound of the front door woke her. Boughton was talking with him, and she could hear worry in their voices. Boughton always came along when there might be something difficult to deal with, on a cane now half the time, but still as willing as could be to help out a little. He was there when Mrs. Ames died and the Reverend was off somewhere doing something. Once, after Boughton had gone on through a long evening about the Rural Electrification Act and its implications, the old man said, "He prayed with her. He closed her eyes." We wept that one so lovely should have a life so brief. *We* because Boughton was there, just trying to help out. She heard him saying, "I'll wait down here a minute, John," and the old man starting up the stairs alone. What did they think had happened? No, better ask what *had* happened. She'd done something she shouldn't. She knew half of it and he would probably tell her the rest. She stood up and slipped on her shoes and smoothed her hair and her dress.

When he came into the room, she felt a surge of relief at the sight of him that made it harder for her to do what she meant to do, which was nothing. Stand there and hear him out. She couldn't leave, now that she'd given her money to that boy. Well, she'd figure a way if she had to. She was thinking, I'm gone the minute he talks down to me, no matter what. And just that morning she'd been feeling so safe.

He spoke down the stairs, "She's here. She's fine," and Boughton said, "Tomorrow, then," and let himself out. Then the old man said, "That's true, isn't it? You are fine?"

She said, "Far as I know."

He nodded. "Me, too. Far as I know." He sat down on the edge of the bed. "A little winded, maybe." He covered his face with his hands. A moment passed, and then he patted the bed beside him and said, "Come, sit down." He cleared his throat to steady his voice. He said, "So. I'll tell you about my day, if you'll tell me about yours."

She shrugged and sat down beside him. "I been out walking."

"So I gather." A longer moment passed, and then he said, "Someone came by my office and told me he'd seen you at the cabin. He mentioned it because the weather was turning bad. So I got Boughton to drive me out there so I could spare you the walk home. But we missed you somehow."

She said, "Who told you?"

"George Peterson. He's not in the church. They all know better by now."

They all knew better than to tell him about her comings and goings. She'd have to think about that.

He said, "You weren't there, but your coat was, and there was a fellow underneath it. When I saw it, I thought it was probably you under it. I said your name and there was no answer, so I turned it back, and this fellow jumped up with a knife in his hand." He laughed and rubbed his eyes. "I never had such a scare. Or felt so relieved. I thought Boughton might die on the spot. Then he pushed past us and ran off, and we were just too floored to do anything much but look at each other. We started worrying about where you were and how he got your coat. We couldn't very well ask him. So we came back here." He laughed. "Boughton must have been doing forty the whole way. He's so scared of that car he's always got two wheels in the ditch, but he was Barney Oldfield this evening."

She said, "Well, I was just here resting."

"So I see. But perhaps you could clarify things a little. I'm curious. And I feel as though I owe Boughton the rest of the story. Nothing urgent about it, of course."

"Part of the time I was sitting in the church, trying to warm up a little."

He nodded. "I guess that's how we missed you."

"And I give him that coat. The use of it. Just for the night. I never thought you'd be out there."

He nodded. "That was very generous."

"Well, I didn't know it would turn so cold."

"I'm sure he was glad to have it. The use of it. So you walked home in the cold without a coat."

"I felt sorry for him. A boy like that. He was so miserable he wasn't even sleeping nights. He thought it was because he'd killed somebody, but I thought it might be that he just wasn't comfortable. Partly, anyway."

"Well," he said. "He'd killed somebody."

"He thought he probably did. Sounded to me like he did and he didn't want to be sure of it. It was just his pa. I mean, he wasn't out looking for somebody to kill. He lost his temper, I guess."

He laughed. "That happens."

"He wasn't going to hurt anybody. All he wanted to do was go back where he come from. So they could hang him."

"I see. Of course I had no way of knowing that, did I. You can imagine what I thought, finding your coat there. And he was a pretty rough-looking individual, from what I saw of him." He said, "I have a lot of memories these days. And I have some pretty bad dreams. I talked to Boughton about it, and he said he has them, too. So we couldn't be very sensible in the circumstances, I suppose. Maybe we could have talked to him if we hadn't brought so much dread into the situation. Lila, I haven't wanted to bring this up, but I would appreciate it a great deal if you were very careful with yourself. Just to spare two old men a little wear and tear."

She said, "I will give it some thought."

He laughed. "Yes. Do it for my sake. Oh, what a shock I had." And he lay back on the bed with his arms across his face.

After a while she said, "He had a little sort of bundle with him. Did he take that when he run off?"

"There was something like that lying on the floor. We left it there. Why?"

"Well, it's just that he'll likely come back for it." Maybe she shouldn't have said that. "If he seen that you wasn't chasing him, he's probly already come and gone."

"I take it you don't want to talk to the sheriff about this."

"Wouldn't be much point."

He laughed. "If you say so."

She said, "I'm not much for talking to a sheriff. That's a fact. But if he turns himself in, they might not hang him. If some law catches him, for sure they will. But he'll need that money to get home. He don't have a decent pair of shoes."

He said, "Now you're crying."

"I'm tired is all." She said, "I was thinking we might bring him here and let him sleep the night at the church. That was before he run off."

He handed her his handkerchief. "Well, Lila, I'll talk to Boughton again. I guess we could go back out there. Maybe talk to him this time. You can stay home." He sat up and stood up like the weariest man in the world, steadying himself against the bedpost. She knew she should tell him not to trouble himself.

She said, "I better go along. He won't be scared of me. He'll never come with us. He'd never get in the car with us now. But we could take him some things. If we hurry."

"All right. Then you put some things together and I'll go get Boughton."

So she put socks and long underwear and a flannel shirt in a pillowcase, and a pair of the preacher's old shoes. None of it would fit the boy, but it was better than nothing. She bundled a piece of ham in wax paper and put it with the rest, and some apples, and took two wool blankets out of the cupboard. She put on the blue coat, which she found draped on the newel post, and went out to the DeSoto. Boughton said, somberly, "I believe they call this aiding and abetting. I know they do." He said, "Nobody will have to get out of the car. I'll honk the horn. We'll just pull up to the stoop and drop it all out the window. I'm going to keep the car running."

When they stopped in front of the cabin, Lila stepped out. She called, "Hey. You there? We brought you some clothes and some blankets. I'll just set them inside here in case it snows." The Reverend stepped out, too, and gave her a flashlight, and took the parcel, and took her arm. He said, "I'll go in."

"No, I will. He's touchy, all right, but he ain't scared of me." She said, "We don't want to corner him. He'll get himself in worse trouble."

He laughed. "We can't have that, can we. Whatever you say. Let's just be quick about it."

She set the things inside the door, and then she swept the flashlight across the room. She said, "It's still there. His money. He ain't come back for it."

"Well, he won't come back as long as we're here. It's good that he hasn't come back already. This way he'll find what you've left for him."

"Oh, maybe," she said. "I don't know, I don't." The old man's voice was so low and so weary. Then all the way home they were silent. She could feel thoughts passing between the two men, who had grown old in their friendship. She's going to be a world of trouble, John. And: Let's see what she has to say before we judge. And: Old men can make foolish decisions. And: Let's leave that to another time. And: No matter what happens, I'm on your side. And: You are, you always are, even when I'm not. Still, the longer he thought about it, the graver he was. That night she lay beside him, wondering if he ever would sleep. He didn't take her hand, and she didn't dare take his. But the child was there. She could feel what must be the press of its head below her rib, the press of its foot against her hip. She thought, Seems like you're about as strong as you ought to be.

The next morning the Reverend came downstairs dressed for Sunday. She still forgot to pay attention to the days of the week sometimes, but she was pretty sure it was Thursday. He told her once that his preacher clothes helped him remember himself, helped with that worry of his about anger. So here he was, remembering himself before he'd even had breakfast. He said, "Good morning."

She said, "Morning." There was nothing to do but wait for him to say what was on his mind. She poured coffee into his cup, so he sat down.

Then there was a knock at the door, and he went to answer it. She heard him talking with someone. When he came back to the kitchen he said, "That was Boughton's boy Teddy. He's been out to the cabin already, to leave some things that might have a better chance of being the right size. Boughton is too stove up in the mornings to do much himself, and Teddy wanted a look at things anyway, since he's almost a doctor. He thought the fellow might be needing his help. No sign of him, though. Everything is the way we left it." He said, "I'm sorry about that. Sorry we scared him off."

She said, "Nobody's fault."

He was standing there with his hands on the back of his chair, looking at her, tired and serious. She could almost see what he had been like as a young man. He said, "There are people you seem to know the first time you see them. And other people you might spend your whole life with and never really know. That first day you walked into the church, that rainy

Sunday, I felt as though I recognized you somehow. It was a re- remarkable experience. It was."

"But you don't really know nothing about me," she said, since he couldn't bring himself to say it. She was about to hear those words again: I don't know you.

He said, "Well, in one sense that may be true."

"I'd say it's true." She wasn't going to be standing there wait- ing for it.

"Not in a way I thought would matter. And it doesn't matter now, Lila. Not really."

"I guess that's good, because there ain't much to tell. I don't know who my folks were, I don't know my own last name."

He said, "I understand that. It makes no difference to me. None at all."

"Well," she said, "if there's something else you want to ask me about, you might as well do it."

He said, "Yes." And then he said, "It makes me uncomfort- able, you can see that. But I feel as though I need to know—how things stand. I can't help wondering why you went back there. What you were doing there."

"I was just going to look at the pelicans on the river, and see- ing the shack reminded me that I left some money hidden under a plank in the floor. I could see the place was empty. I looked for the money and it was gone. I thought it would feel good to rest a little anyway, so I sat there on the stoop in the sunshine and I guess I fell asleep. Then I woke up and that boy was standing there looking at me."

"You didn't know him at all."

"Never seen him in my life before. That's the truth."

"Yes, of course. Of course." Then he said, "I hate to seem to be questioning you, Lila. But when I heard you had gone out there, I thought it might mean you weren't happy. You know, here, with me. I knew from the beginning that things might be difficult, and I thought I could accept whatever happened. But it never crossed my mind there might be a child. I thought I had learned not to set my heart on anything. But I find myself thinking about that child—much of the time. So the idea that you might want to leave—it would be extremely difficult for me to live with that."

She said, "I ain't leaving. Farthest thing from my mind." If this was not entirely true, it was true enough. "I just go off to look at pelicans and everything goes haywire. I don't know. I thought I might as well get some use out of that money. Took me all summer to save it up."

"I only asked because, if there was anything I could do to make you want to stay—"

She said, "My child is going to have a big old preacher for its papa, and live in a good, warm house, and eat ham and eggs three times a week. And it's going to know all them hymns by heart. You'll see."

"Well," he said, "that will be wonderful. Wonderful." Then he sat down to his breakfast. He said his grace to himself, behind his trembling hands, and she thought it would be good if she could tell him she had meant to buy him a present with her money, but that would sound like a lie, and then he wouldn't trust her the way he wanted to.

She said, "That boy out at the shack, he was just an ugly, dirty, lonely little cuss, half scared to death. And I was thinking he could've been any child that had nobody to take him up and see to him."

He looked at her. Then he said softly, "I *did* know you. I *do* know you," and his eyes filled with tears.

"That's good, I guess." She shrugged and turned away. "Maybe I ain't so hard to know as some people. No reason why I should be. More coffee?" She couldn't talk to him the way he was talking to her. That boy out at the cabin, he knew her. Married? To a preacher? Sounds like you making that up. That his child you got there? Meaning no harm, knowing no better. It seemed almost as if she had lied to the preacher when she said she didn't know that boy. He had been at the edge of her sight all those years, orphaned, his whole life just that terrible little ember of pride, meanness and kindness all that he had to shelter it with, and the injured fearfulness that comes when anybody at all might do you the worst kind of harm, just by the way they look at you. This old man is beautiful and kind and very patient, she thought, and if he looked at me that way I might just die of it. Well, but for now he is mine to touch if I want to. So when she brought his coffee she put her arms around his neck and she kissed his hair. Might as well take pleasure where you can.

He stroked her hands. Then he said, "I've been thinking, Lila—at my age I can't really hope for a call to another church, but maybe we could move to another house, at least. The church could rent this one, to cover the cost. It would give us a fresh start. We could get rid of some things around here that I've been looking at for too long and just start over."

She said, "Well, I tell you one thing. That's the last time I'm going out looking for pelicans."

"So you're all right here?"

"I'm just fine."

"You don't mind all the scars and scratches? All the departed souls who left them behind? You don't mind if the Lord's in the parlor?"

"I believe I'd be lonesome without them."

He said, "I think you're being kind. I'm going to let you do it, though. I'm pretty sure I'd miss them."

" 'Course you would." She rested her cheek against his hair. She thought, The child knows about this, too. Not just the dread I feel sometimes. Not just the cold.

It was probably Mrs. Ames he was thinking about. He never said her name. One so lovely. There was a wedding picture in his study he never showed to her and never hid from her. Him with his collar standing up, beside him a pretty girl in an old-fashioned dress, one hand in the bend of his elbow, the other holding a bunch of roses. The big front bedroom he kept for guests who never came, that would be where they made the child, and where Boughton in his unimaginable youth had stood weeping while he prayed, touching water to the tiny head. Two young men in that room, one of them Jesus. One of them hardly knowing what to think, the other knowing, leaving it to Boughton to find words if he could. Well, that was a thing she did not understand. But Boughton had taken up that child while it was still in its blood, held it and blessed it from his very heart, and she did understand that. She wished she could have done the same for that boy at the shack, done right by him, filthy thing that he was, all trembling at the thought of what he was. Teddy had gone out looking for him, walking the empty woods alone so the boy wouldn't be afraid to be found. One day was all Teddy had to give to him, because he was studying to be a doctor, just home to check on his mother and old Boughton. Lila couldn't go off wandering in the cold, what with the child she was carrying. So the boy would be on his own.

She went up to that bedroom with her Bible and sat in the rocking chair by the window. There was just the faintest shadow of dust on the dresser, but once she noticed it, it bothered her, so she found a cloth and wiped it off. Now that winter had come and there wasn't much to do outside, she had started tending to the house a little, even though women from the church came in every week or two to take care of things, as they had done for years because he was alone, and as they still did because now they were looking after his wife and his child, doing all the heavy work, hoping to protect him. But there was always more dust, drifting down from somewhere.

When she told the old man that she thought she might start reading the Book of Job, saying it "job," which is exactly the way it is spelled, he had all he could do to keep from laughing. He had to wipe tears from his eyes. He told her it was a man's name, so it was pronounced differently, and this made her a good deal less interested in it. But she had to read it so he could pretend she wasn't just making an ignorant mistake in the first place, though he knew perfectly well that she was. He said, "You really do have a way of finding the very hardest parts—for somebody starting out. For anybody. That's fine. They're Scripture, too." And then he could let himself laugh a little, which must have been a relief.

So she meant to sit in the rocking chair by the window with Job open in her lap and see what she could make of it. She did wonder why dust fell so evenly, more like rain than like snow, since the wind pushed snow into drifts. Well, the air in a good house is so still. There was the clock ticking, steady as could be, and time passing, and no sign of anything else happening at all, but then in two days there would be the shadow of dust again, anywhere you happened to look for it. She wiped it away, the room was perfect for a little while, and then she fell to thinking. Rocking for the sound it made, and thinking.

The clock struck eleven. He always came home for lunch. If she met him at the door he put his arms around her. If there was rain on him he still might not even wait to take his coat off first before he kissed her forehead or her cheek, and she liked the coldness and the good smell. He never asked her how she had spent the morning, but she told him sometimes. Reading a little. Thinking about things. She felt good, and the baby was moving around more than ever, elbows and knees. The old man would look into her face for sadness or weariness, and she would turn her face away, since there was no telling what he might see in it, her thoughts being what they were. She'd been thinking that folks are their bodies. And bodies can't be trusted at all. Her own body was so strong with working, for what that was worth. She'd known from her childhood there was no use being scared of pain. She was always telling the old man, women have babies, no reason I can't do it. But they both knew things can go wrong. That's how it is. Then there'd be poor old Boughton again, if he could even make it up the stairs this time, and there'd be Jesus, still keeping His thoughts to Himself. And she'd be thinking, Here's my body, dying on me, when I almost promised him I wouldn't let it happen. It might make her believe she was something besides her body, but what was the good of that when she'd be gone anyway and there'd be nothing in the world that could comfort him. She guessed she really was married to him, the way she hated the thought of him grieving for her. It might even make him give up praying. Then he'd hardly be himself anymore.

Well. *There was a man in the land of Uz, whose name was Job; and that man was perfect and upright, and one that feared God, and turned away from evil.* All right. *And there were born unto him seven sons and three daughters.* But she kept thinking, What happens when somebody isn't herself anymore? I seem to be getting used to things I never even knew about just a few months ago. Not wondering what in the world I'm going to do next, for one thing. Maybe it'll be something the old man liked about me that will be gone sometime, and I won't even know what it was. She found herself thinking she might stay around anyway. She thought she'd always like the feel of him, she'd probably always like to creep into bed beside him. He didn't seemed to mind it.

That boy, never meaning to kill his father, looking at his hands, almost wishing he could be rid of them. Rid of himself. She'd felt that way, too, plenty of times. That night or morning when she was trying to clean away all the blood, and Doll, who probably wasn't in her right mind, saying, "He wasn't your pa. I'm pretty sure. Maybe a cousin or something. An uncle, maybe." And here was his blood all over Lila's hands and her clothes, some in her hair. She had brushed a strand away from her eyes, and it fell back, wet and heavy. So much blood she knew he was dead, whoever he was. So, whoever he was, he took it with him. It died in his body. Doll said, "A grudge was all it come down to. They should've let me be. After all these years."

Lila said, "What was his name?"

"Which one? There's just so damn many of 'em." And she gave Lila a look, puzzled and scared and tired of it all. Rolling her eyes, too old and spent to lift her head, still trying to settle on any sort of plan, what to do next.

The name of the man she was fighting with.

"You expect me to know? There must be a dozen of 'em. One meaner than the next." She said, "I'm the only ma you ever had. You could've just died entirely, for all they was doing for you."

Lila knew. She remembered. But what was their name?

"There was that one—I cut his hamstring. Years ago. I thought that might put an end to all the trouble he was causing me. But it give him a dreadful limp and his brothers got all riled up about it, so I just had more to worry me. His cousins. They thought they could catch me easy enough, a scar-faced woman with a child in hand." She laughed. "I guess it weren't so easy after all."

The folks at that cabin?

"Don't matter. They wasn't your folks. You was just boarded out there." She said, "Your pa got the idea he should take you back from me, after he'd left you behind like that. Then the whole bunch of 'em was looking for me, whenever any of 'em could spare a little time. Where was they when you was just scrawny and naked? Folks like a grudge. That's all it comes to."

Lila said she wouldn't mind knowing a name, though.

"What? You going to go looking for 'em?"

No. No point in it.

"That's the truth. I think they pretty well forgot about you anyway. Me laming that fellow was what mattered to 'em. Because he was so young, I suppose. Well, they shouldn'ta sent him after me. It was just the revenge they was after. This last one never asked me where you was. Not that I give him much chance."

So he might have been her pa.

"He wasn't your pa. He didn't look like him, far as I could tell. It'd been a while. It was pretty dark." So Lila had that blood all over her, and it was the first time she had heard a word about her father. And here was Doll, probably dying. For months Lila had had a decent room and a job clerking in a store, and she'd been thinking just that day how good it was of Doll to make sure she could read and figure. Now all that was done with. The more she tried to wash the blood away, the more of it there was. Blood had soaked into the rug and stained the floor. She wished everything was done with, every damn thing. That she could be rid of herself. Somebody was going to find her like this. But there was Doll to see to. She'd ripped her other dress into rags before she even thought how fouled the one she was wearing was. Oh, what to do next. How to live through the next damned hour. That has to be the worst feeling there is. She hated the way she could stand just anything. It was her body going on. Her body, her hands remembering how Doll used to comfort her.

She shouldn't be thinking about any of this. Here I go, scaring the child. She said, "Your papa's going to be coming home pretty soon. He just loves you so much." When she hugged her belly the child might feel her holding it in her arms. It might feel safe. She said, "Now, you going to go kicking that book off my

174

lap? What's your papa going to say about that?" She had a child now, this morning, whatever happened. She had a husband. Maybe loneliness was something she'd get over, sooner or later, if things went well enough. That night on the stoop was the first time Doll ever took her up in her arms, and she still remembered how good it felt. Those shy little presents, made of nothing. The rag baby. That shawl she could have used to keep herself warm at night, but she put it over Lila when she came in and only took it away again just before she went out the door in the dark of the morning. Maybe she never would have been so fierce if she hadn't been set on keeping the child she'd stolen. She could probably feel the life coming into the child, sleeping in her arms day and night. And the child could feel it, too. Now motherhood was forcing itself into Lila's breasts. They ached with it.

Here she was thinking again. Well, this Job was a good man and he had a good life and then he lost it all. *And, behold, there came a great wind from the wilderness, and smote the four corners of the house, and it fell upon the young men, and they are dead.* She'd heard of that happening, plenty of times. A wind could hit a town like Gilead and leave nothing behind but sticks and stumps. You'd think a man as careful as this Job might have had a storm cellar. It used to be that when the sky filled up with greenish light Doane would start looking around for a low place where they could lie down on the ground if the wind started getting strong. A barn was nothing but flying planks and nails if the wind hit it. The house fell upon the young men, and they are dead. Any tree could fall. The limbs would just fly off, even the biggest ones. There was that one time the wind came with thunder and rain and scared them half to death. The ground shook. There was lightning everywhere. Leaves and shingles and window curtains sailed over them, falling around them. Mellie lay on her back to watch, so Lila did, too, wiping filthy rain out of her eyes. There were things never meant to fly, books and shoes and chickens and washboards, caught up in the wind as if they were escaping at last, at last, from having to be whatever they were. The rain was too heavy sometimes to let her see much, and they all complained a little afterward about the cold and the mud. Doane combing leaves and mud out of Marcelle's hair with his fingers, and both of them laughing the way they always did in those days, whenever things could have been worse. But for the next few days they heard that farms had been swept away, children and all, and for a while they minded Doane more than they usually did. Nobody knew what to say about sorrow like that. *And the living creatures ran and returned as the appearance of a flash of lightning.* She never expected to find so many things she already knew about written down in a book.

So Job gets all covered with sores. Dogs licking them. That could happen. Dogs have that notion of tending to you sometimes. Maybe flies do, too, for all anybody knows. Strange the story don't mention flies, when the man is sitting on a dung heap. She'd seen maggots in raw places on a horse's hide, and Doane said they were good for healing. Just the sight of them makes your skin crawl, though. Horses spend their whole lives trying to keep the flies off, flicking their tails and shivering their hides. Squinting their eyes. You'd think a horse would know if they were good for anything.

There were flies bothering her that day, after Doll came to her all bloody. You'd think the cold might have killed them, even houseflies, but there they were. That mess had roused them, and they were nuzzling at the stains on the rug, clinging to her skirt. She'd brush them away and they'd come right back. She had a coat that was long enough to cover the worst of it, so she put it on and put what money she had in her pocket and went off to a secondhand shop in a back street where a woman sold clothes cheap. The sheriff had already taken Doll away. The men that had come with him were a while finding a stretcher, so he said, Hell with it, and picked her up in his arms and carried her. "She don't weigh no more than a cat," he said, and the old woman folded her hands and seemed a little pleased with it all, looking at the sky.

It was still early enough that Lila had to pound on the shop door. She was so desperate to get out of the dress she was wearing, it didn't matter what she found there if she just had the money to pay for it. And then the woman said to her, when she had taken a look at her, tried to get a look at her face, So what happened? You had a baby? Lila said, No, I didn't, and the woman studied her sidelong, the blood on her skirt where it showed below the hem of her coat, on her shoes, thinking she knew better, and said, Never mind. None of my business. Then she handed her a dress she said looked about right. That'll be three dollars. Not much wear. Lila gave her the money and one cent more for a parched bit of soap, and was leaving, since she couldn't try the dress without taking off her coat. The woman said, Wait, and wrote something on a scrap of paper and handed it to her. She said, There's a lady in St. Louis takes in girls who've got trouble. You look like you could use some help. Lila knew what that was about, but she put it in her pocket just the same. She thought, I suppose now I know what's going to happen next. Not that she could go anywhere so long as Doll was still living. But she thought a minute and then she stepped back inside that shop and said, "Then how'm I supposed to get to St. Louis?" She generally didn't look at anybody directly, because Doll never did, and the woman was a little while deciding about her, but then she opened a cash box and gave her a ten-dollar bill. "You show me a bus ticket, and I'll get you a suitcase, maybe a few things to put in it." So, Lila thought, maybe I can do old Doll a little bit of good. Maybe even figure some way to get Doll on a bus. It wouldn't be stealing if she paid the money back. That was her thinking at the time.

Soon she would hear the old man at the front door. He'd come in smelling all clean from the cold, his cheek would be cold, and his lips. If she put her face against the lapel of his coat, it would be cool, but if she slipped her hand under it, there would be the starch of his shirt and his warmth and his heart beating. She'd been thinking about herself hiding that filthy dress under her coat the best she could, all sweaty even in the cold, knowing anybody who saw her would think what that woman did. Guilty of the saddest crime there is. Nobody surprised to know she had that scrap of paper in her pocket. Old shame falling to her when it had been worn to rags by so many women before her. She could almost forget that the shame wasn't really hers at all, any more than any child was hers, not even a child cast out and weltering in its blood, God bless it. Well, that was a way of speaking she had picked up from the old man. It let you imagine you could comfort someone you couldn't comfort at all, a child that never even had an existence to begin with. God bless it. She hoped it would have broken her heart if she had done what that woman thought she had, but she was hard in those days. Maybe not so hard that she wouldn't have left it on a church step. How did that woman know it wasn't back at her room, bundled up in a towel and crying for her, waiting for her voice and her smell, her breast? The sound of her heart. God bless it. And she so desperate to give it comfort, aching to. Frightened for it, just the sight of so much yearning reddening a little body, darkening its face almost blue. Maybe that was weltering.

She told the old man she'd been thinking about existence, that time they were out walking, and he didn't laugh. Could she have these thoughts if she had never learned the word? "The mystery of existence." From hearing him preach. He must have mentioned it at least once a week. She wished she'd known about it sooner, or at least known there was a name for it. She used to be afraid she was the only one in the world who couldn't make sense of things. Why that shame had come down on her, out of nowhere. It might have been because for once she felt almost like somebody with something to say about herself, a girl with such an ordinary kind of trouble that there would be a bus ticket ready and a suitcase, a place to go because there was no place else to go. Knowing what to do next, even if it was the one thing Doll warned her against more than any other thing. "You think my face always looked like this?" Lila hid her own face half the time anyway. It wasn't much to look at. What matter if it had a scar, too. That's how she felt then, with the paper in her pocket and nobody in the world but poor old Doll, who was probably dying. If the Reverend had seen her then, she thought. Well, she'd have crossed the street to make sure that didn't happen. She'd have hidden her face in her hands. And he'd have followed her, and he'd have taken some of the shame away just by the way he touched her sleeve, "Lila. If I may." Strange to imagine him there, all those years ago, in that miserable damn place. She'd be young and he would not be old. He'd have on his preacher clothes, newer then, and his shoes would be polished for her sake, and he'd know the stain on her dress just meant she'd had to be kind. She wouldn't even have to tell him about it. And he'd walk along beside her, her hand in the crook of his arm. If only she'd known then what comfort was coming, she'd have spared herself a little. You can say to yourself, I'm just a body that thinks and talks and seems to want its life, one more day of it. You don't have to know why. Well, nothing could ever change if your body didn't just keep you there not even knowing what it is you're waiting for. Not even knowing that you're waiting at all. Just there on the stoop in the moonlight licking up tears.

She remembered how she felt that morning that she went walking by the jail, just to see if she could find out how Doll was doing, and there she was, bundled up in an Indian blanket, rocking in the chair the sheriff had set outside his office door for her, looking at the trees. The wind was taking the last few leaves. There was a little crowd of people watching her, since she was a curiosity, and a couple of men who were angry as could be to see her sitting there peaceful and at ease for all they could tell, though Doll never did give a stranger a sign that anything troubled her. The sheriff was standing on the step, talking with those men, already irritated with them.

One of them shouted, "You ought to be hanging her!"

"Doubt I can do that. She don't weigh nothing."

"Then shoot her."

The sheriff laughed. "I guess I wasn't brought up that way. To go shooting old women."

"Well, I'd be more than happy to do it for you."

The sheriff said, "Now, shooting a big fellow like you, I wouldn't have a problem with that at all. And you're about exactly the right size for hanging. Fine with me either way. You might want to keep that in mind."

"This town is a disgrace to the whole damn country, that's what it is! You're a disgrace to that damn badge! I never heard of such a thing in my whole life! Setting a killer outside where she can rock and watch the world go by, like somebody's dang grandma. If that don't beat all. And this ain't the only crime she ever done." He glanced at Lila. "She stole our baby girl, just took off with her. It was out of pure spite that she done it. We been looking for the two of them all these years."

The sheriff shrugged. "I wouldn't know about that. She's in enough trouble without adding to it. Just now she's gaining strength for her trial. Judge's orders. Gotta try her, you know. You're getting ahead of yourself with all this talk about hanging."

"The judge tell you not to lock her up?"

"The judge don't give a damn."

"Well," he said, "this ain't over. Not by a long shot."

"Never said it was."

From time to time one of the men would glance over at Lila, though Doll never looked at her, not even when Lila went up to her and put that molasses cookie on her lap. She just said, "I don't know you," and let the cookie lie there by her hand. So how those men would have known to watch her Lila had no idea. It might be she took after that family of hers she'd never heard of until a week ago. They looked at her as if they were asking which side she was on, and what was she supposed to do? They didn't even bother to tell her their names or say hello. When they decided she wasn't going to help them get their vengeance on Doll, maybe tell the sheriff that she'd been stolen by her as a child, they started looking at her with a kind of scorn, even laughing a little between themselves, like they couldn't believe this was what all the fighting had been about. It's just amazing how anybody at all can hurt your feelings if they want to. And she was wearing that dress she'd bought without even looking at it. It was tight across the shoulders. It had red pockets like hearts, with ruffles around them, and it was checked like a tablecloth. She kept her coat on, but still. Why you should have to stand there feeling ridiculous with a bloodstain still on your shoe, just at the time when other people are out to insult you, and not one part of it is your fault or your choice, that's the kind of thing she didn't understand. Because you do it to yourself. Why should she have cared for one minute what those people thought of her? Or cared that they never so much as spoke to her. She remembered a hot blush of something like anger, but more like damned old shame.

Then they came back, them and two others carrying a pine box, and set it down on the street right in front of where Doll was sitting. They took off the lid so the sheriff and all of them could see what was inside, that old man, bundled up in a sheet, just as pale as the moon. And one of them looked right at Lila when he said, "You see what she done to him. She bled him like a hog." Doll just kept on rocking, looking at the trees. Lila did glance into the box, since everybody else did and she didn't want to stand out. To keep her from drawing attention—that must have been why Doll acted like she'd never even seen her before, wouldn't meet her eyes. Somebody might notice. A grudge can pass from one person to the next just because it hasn't burned itself out yet. So you don't want to stand too close to it. None of it needs to make any sense. And Lila did have that knife, and now she meant to keep it. The dead man's lips were white as could be. So was the arch of his nose. It was a picture that stayed in her mind forever, no matter what, with the thought that he was her father, though that was more than she knew. With another thought, too, that maybe the grudge had meant more to Doll than the fact that he was Lila's father, and she didn't meet her eyes because she was ashamed to. Ah, well.

But there he was, in that box lying in the road, with those men sort of swaggering where they stood, shifting their weight, threatening by the way they kept their arms folded. The sheriff said, "He's dead, all right. You got a point there. Now I believe he has a train to catch." Doll's head didn't even reach the top of the chair, but there she was, proud in her captivity like some old Indian chief, and it was clear that the sheriff sort of took to her. He said, "When we set a date for the trial, you will be notified by mail." So the men knew they might as well close up the box. They carried it away to ship it home, wherever that was, to let the old man rest among his kin, whoever they were. Doll glanced after them once, and then she closed her eyes.

When that woman at the house in St. Louis asked Lila what she would call herself, since none of them used their own names, she said, "Doll, I guess," and the woman snorted, which is how she laughed. She said, "We already got a Doll. Had two of them till a couple months ago. The one ran off with some salesman. She'll be back pretty soon. Think she'd have better sense. So you ain't Doll. We don't have no Rose just now. Put a little henna in your hair—Rose'll do. Ruby. We'll think of something." Her knuckles were big, and her rings hung loose on the bones of her fingers. She was always turning them up the way they were supposed to be, and they wouldn't stay because of the weight of the stones. Bright red, bright green, big as gumdrops. Lila and Mellie used to keep bits of broken glass they found in the road sometimes, and they called them jewels. Why was she thinking about any of this? She was so scared that day, in that parlor with the drapes closed at noon and that damn credenza with the vase of dusty feathers sitting on it. Looking like a coffin. There was a stirring under her heart, so she said to the child, "I won't breathe a word to you about that place, but I guess you might know anyway. Because that fear has never left my body, has just hidden in it, waiting. You might feel it, down in your poor little bones. God bless 'em."

She heard the Reverend at the door, and she went down to meet him. He was smiling up at her as if he still hadn't gotten over the surprise of finding her, his wife, lowering herself down the stairs, with her hand on her belly so he would know she was being careful for the child's sake. And then his arms around her and his cheek against her hair. "So," he said, "how are you two?"

"Fine, I guess. We pretty much wasted the morning, day-dreaming. I keep trying to read the Bible, but my mind goes wandering off. You wouldn't want to know where. The things I find myself thinking about, with the Bible right there in my lap."

"Well," he said, "you know I'm always interested. If there's anything you want to talk about." He hung up his hat and his coat.

"One thing. Do you think the child knows what I'm think-ing? I mean, by the way it makes me feel? Do you think it might get scared or something? Sad? Because I do worry about that. Now and then."

He searched her face, abruptly serious.

"You don't know nothing about me," she said, because that was what he was trying not to think. "I got feelings I don't know the names for. There probly ain't any names. Probly nobody else ever had 'em. I tell you what, I wouldn't wish 'em on a snake."

"Well," he said. He cleared his throat. "Is there something I can do?"

"No. You haven't even ate your lunch yet."

He shrugged. "Lunch can wait." Then he made his voice just as gentle as he could. "Lila, I know I've said this any number of times. But people do talk to me. About all sorts of things. Sometimes it helps. At least that's what they tell me."

She said, "Then for the rest of their life you're gonna think about it. Every time you look at them. Hear their name even."

"True."

"Well, I spose it would have to be true, wouldn't it. The worse it was, the more you'd remember. Maybe I don't want you looking at me that way."

"Fine," he said. "Whatever you say."

"I don't know how those people go on living in the same town with you."

"A few of them do leave the church. Maybe because they've told me more than they meant to. I've suspected that was part of it. In some cases."

She said, "Now you're looking at me. Probly thinking it's worse than it is. Maybe it couldn't even be no worse."

He laughed. "I don't know how this happened. I hardly even step through the door and I seem to be in a whole world of trouble."

"Well," she said, "I ain't going to talk about it. I'm going to make you a sandwich."

"That's wonderful." He sat down at the table and picked up the newspaper he had read at breakfast. He glanced over it a little. Then he said, "I like to look at you, Lila. Lila my wife. There's a lot of pleasure in it for me. Of course I also like to talk with you."

"Well, that's probly because I never tell you nothing." She thought, Anything. I can talk better than this. I guess I just don't want to.

"You've told me a couple of things. I don't think either one of us is any the worse for it."

She almost said, There was a man. Why did she feel so mean sometimes? He would say, Well, yes, of course I assumed. Well, of course I knew—and he'd blush because he'd said that. There would be tears in his eyes, the poor old devil. What else could he say? He went and married her, and now he has to make the best of it. But she felt those words in her mouth and her heart was thumping. And she could have said something else. Probably worse. There was a child. She never did lie to him, and he knew it, so there were things she had to be sure not to tell him, things she could never say. She wanted to rest her head on his shoulder, but he was looking through the paper again. She could pull a chair up next to him and he'd probably put his arm around her. So she came and stood beside him, against him, and touched his hair. She said, "I never even thought of telling anybody what was on my mind, all those years. Not Doll, not any of 'em. I don't even think I knew people did that."

"Have I told you everything about myself? I suppose I have. Not much to tell, really."

She said, "Well, you never told me what you're scared of. There must be something, with all the praying you do."

He laughed. "You can probably guess." He glanced up at her. "I'm afraid to death some fine young man you knew once will show up at the door and you'll pack your bag. Just the things you brought with you. And you'll leave a note for me that says, Goodbye, Reverend. I won't be coming back."

"Will I take your mama's locket when I go?"

"No. But you'll have to ask the young man to help you undo the clasp. Then when I see it there, I'll know. That you'd left with somebody."

She shook her head. "Most likely I'd take it."

He said, "I'd be grateful if you did."

"Well, I believe you would. You're just the strangest man. I guess this better all happen after the baby comes?"

"I suppose so."

"It would have to. I never knew a man who would want to take on another man's child like that. I mean, before it was even born. Then I guess he'd make me leave it here anyway."

"I hope he would. I mean, I hope you would let me keep it. I'd work something out, hire a woman to take care of it. People would help. We'd be all right."

After a minute she said, "Well, I never made you that sandwich." But she sat down at the table across from him. He met her eyes. "You sure been thinking about this." She heard her voice break.

He said, "I have to believe I wouldn't die of it. For the child's sake. And for yours, if you ever wanted to come back. But I do feel that a child should have a living father, if the old codger can manage it. Someone to fall back on. As long as possible." He shrugged. "I think through things. It calms me. Otherwise I don't react as well as I could have. As I would have wanted to."

They'd been married a year, no, almost a year and a half, and he was still just as lonely as ever, and that scared her. So she said, "It's nice you think some man somewhere's going to bother to come looking for me. No chance of that happening, Reverend. You got me all to yourself. If that's what you want."

He said, "I guess I want it too much to believe I have it."

She said, "I feel the same way, pretty much."

He nodded. "That's good to know."

"I never thought I'd be living in a house like this, that's for sure. I mean a house where I was the wife and anybody cared if I stayed or left."

He nodded. "I hope sometime you'll feel—a little more at home, Lila. I hope sometime you'll move things around a little in here. These old pictures my mother put up—I probably haven't looked at some of them in fifty years. Most of them she just cut out of magazines. Well, you can see that, the way they've faded. My grandfather made the frames for them. I think it was mainly a way she had of keeping him out of her kitchen. He always wanted to be doing something. My point is that things don't have to stay the way they are. If you want to change them."

She said, "You ever heard of a credenza?"

He laughed. "A credenza. I've seen the word somewhere, I suppose. I'm not quite sure I know what one is."

"Well, I'm glad if you don't."

He nodded. "Happy to oblige."

"That's one thing I don't ever want around here."

"It might be hard to find one in Iowa. So that's good." He said, "Because this is your house, Lila, no credenza will ever come under its roof!"

"Now you're laughing at me."

"I've made a solemn promise! I gave you my word. I've never been more serious." He was at the cupboard, rummaging. "Sometimes I just laugh because I'm surprised. But I'd better have a little lunch. I get cranky on an empty stomach. Can't risk disheartening some poor sinner. You never know when one might wander in. Just a peanut butter and jelly sandwich will make me worthier of my calling. Till supper anyway."

"I was going to do that, then we got talking."

"I'm glad we got talking. I'm always glad when we talk. I

have so much to learn. Here I could have wandered in someday with a credenza, meaning no harm—" Then he looked at her. "I'm sorry!"

"It don't matter." She had put her hands to her face. "I was just thinking."

He stood looking at her. "Well, why don't you come down to the church with me. It's quiet today. Some people are coming from Des Moines to talk with me about a funeral. I didn't really know the fellow, he just happened to die here, and I have to have something to say about him. But you could wait for me in the sanctuary. Do your thinking there."

She shook her head. "It ain't that kind of thinking." She said, "It's on my mind now, so I might as well get it done with. It's so different here it makes me remember other places I been. I guess I have to do that. Sort things out a little. Seems like I don't even know myself, everything's so different."

"Yes. Well, as soon as I can get away I'll be home. Unless you want the afternoon to yourself."

"I'll come to find you like I always do."

"All right." He kissed her forehead. "Five o'clock, then."

It came over her, before he had even closed the door behind him, the thought of that house in St. Louis. It was just pure misery. Misery must have been what she was looking for, because she felt it the minute she walked in that door. The twilight of the parlor made her feel as if she had stepped into deep water with her eyes open. Breathing came hard and sound reached her a heartbeat after she should have heard it. She could hardly speak. Nothing was the way it was in daylight, but the place had its own ways and you got used to them. Like death, if something comes after it. That first day there were girls fighting over a hairbrush. Mrs. got up from her chair and went and took the brush away from them and put it in the credenza. When they saw her coming they shrank away from her, watching her.

"Now," she said when she came back to Lila, "you get a safe place to live, so long as you act right. Any trouble and you're gone. I don't like drinking or yelling. I don't want you out on the street. This is a respectable house. Quiet. Our gentlemen like it that way." She called them gentlemen. And the girls were supposed to be ladies.

But they were always fighting over something, a pair of shoes or a scrap of ribbon. And Mrs. would be slapping or pulling hair. The gentlemen brought in liquor, so they didn't have to steal it out of the cabinet unless they just wanted to. Mrs. went off sometimes to visit her sister and left the woman they called Peg in charge, and she'd let them drink if they let her boss them around a little. Then they'd fight over nothing at all, and cry for their mothers, and say they were going to leave that place and that life and never look back, and the gentlemen would say, "Sure you will, sugar. Just not tonight." But they never opened the shades or stepped out the door, and they never touched the credenza. Then they were glad when Mrs. came back. She'd yell at them for their cheap carousing and say she was going to toss them all out, and she'd add what she said was the cost of the liquor to the amount of money she said they all owed her already, and they'd just be glad she was back anyway, and they'd be so quiet and so careful to mind her that she had to calm down sometime. They'd be begging her to let them brush out her hair. A few of them had lived there since they were almost children, one or two of them probably feeble-minded. And two or three of them were just like Lila, no better and no worse. All crowded into two rooms, sleeping on cots so that the other rooms stayed nice for entertaining.

If one of them got sick they'd all get sick, or say they were, and Mrs. would close every blind and turn off every light, so the gentlemen would know they couldn't have company, she said, but really to make everything miserable enough to get back at them if they ever dared pretend. When a house is shut up like that in the middle of a summer day the light that comes in through any crack is as sharp as a blade. And there would be a pot of potato soup simmering from morning to night, and the steam from it would bring out the tobacco smells and the sour old liquor smells in the rugs and the couches and the drapes. And she'd put the poker deck and the checkerboard in that damned credenza, and anything else that could help the time pass. Not that they could have seen the spots on the cards, dark as it was. In a day or two they'd start saying they were better, and could they open a window a crack. Just the darkness made some of them cry. Then when she had turned on some lights and opened a window or two and they had put the place to rights, she would open the credenza and pass out the things she had put in it, the darning egg and the harmonica, and they'd be happy to have them back, as if she had done them a kindness. That credenza was the shape of a coffin, with little legs on it, and flowers of lighter-colored wood on the front of it, some of them peeling off, some of them gone, just the glue left. It was always locked. Any one of the girls could have figured a way to break into it, but they never did. One time Mrs. found some letters that belonged to the girl they called Sal and locked them up, for safekeeping, she said. That girl was begging for them until finally she just gave up, and that was when Mrs. got around to letting her have them back for a while. Lila had hidden her knife in a gap between boards in a closet floor. There were boxes stacked in that corner and the knife was underneath them, so she thought it was safe. Mrs. had nothing that mattered to take from her, nothing of hers to lock away.

Lila was called Rosie because no one else was Rosie, and the pink dress fit her well enough. Sal and Tilly showed her how to tie her hair up in rags so it would curl. They rinsed it with henna first. Mrs. charged her a quarter for the henna and five dollars for a pair of pink high-heeled shoes that were half worn out but she'd never find any cheaper. She could pay a couple dollars a week for the dress. Buying it would put her too far in debt, but she could rent it. So she was seven and a quarter dollars behind already, sitting there with her hair in rags and them about to punch holes in her ears with a darning needle. Then there was room and board, but that could wait till she'd made her start, Mrs. said. Once you're bringing in some regulars. Lila was just listening to all this, trying not to do the arithmetic. She should have walked out right then, but the other girls stayed there and put up with it, the damn credenza and the ugly gentlemen and all of it. After a while she was one of the older girls, and when a young one came to her all upset, she would say just what they all said, Don't you come crying to me and What did you expect when you come here? Then Lila would be patting the girl's hands or putting her hair in pin curls just to quiet her down. When they weren't working or fighting they were usually setting each other's hair.

That one day Mrs. asked her, "Do you have any little treasures you want to keep safe? Anything you want to give me?"

And Lila said, "I got a knife. That's the only thing. I been wanting to give you my knife." The words were just there, and she said them, and she meant them, too.

"Bring it to me. Let me keep it for you, dear. We don't want a knife lying around the house."

So Lila went to the closet and found it still hidden there and took it and handed it over, amazed as she did it, thinking, This is it. I'm here now. This is the life I'm going to have. Mrs. just looked at it lying there in her hand like it was an ugly thing, so Lila said, "Somebody killed my father with it." And then, because she didn't want to lie to the woman, she said, "He might've been my father." Mrs. smiled a little. She said, "I see." And Lila watched her lock it away. Well, she's got me now. And what sense did that make. But she felt that way, and it gave her a kind of ease.

Standing right there by the credenza, with the key still in her hand, Mrs. looked Lila over like she'd never seen her before and said, "You ain't a pretty girl, but you might try smiling, Rosie."

"Yes, ma'am. Yes, I will." Talking to her like that, calling her ma'am. It was a thing Lila blushed to remember, how much she was giving that woman. Doll's knife. But why shouldn't she stop being Lila Dahl and take another made-up name and let herself be glad there was someone telling her what to do every minute, no matter if she hated it. She could smile if she had to. People smile. When she was trying on that pink dress, Mrs. had the girl Lucy come in and pick up the dress she'd been wearing and her shoes and leave her an old flannel nightgown. Lucy said, "I guess you won't be going nowheres now." Lila blushed to remember how hurt she was that Mrs. thought she might run off. She'd thought, Now I gave her my knife, she's got it locked up, the one thing in the world I had that was mine. And she was glad that she'd given it up, that Mrs. didn't have to find it and take it from her the way she did that girl's letters. Lila had tried to think of anything *else* she could give her. As soon as she started earning a little money. My locket. What was she thinking? It was the old man's locket. She didn't even have it yet when she lived in that house. But if she had—she blushed at the thought that she'd have asked for her help with the clasp, and that she'd have been glad to feel her lift it from her neck, to see it lying in that claw of a hand. She loved it that much. Lila said out loud, "You poor child, your mother is a crazy woman."

The dress they gave her to wear had net under the skirt of it, like tiny little chicken wire, and the top just covered what it had to, and the rest was bare. Then those pink shoes she could hardly walk in. Peg would sing, You're all dressed up to go dreaming, and laugh, which was a mean thing to do because some of them just loved that song. It was bare feet and a raggedy old night-gown, except when there were gentlemen. Mrs. never even looked at her. She treated her like she was nothing at all. Lila tried smiling.

They'd be dressed up the best they could and dancing to the Victrola when the gentlemen started coming in, one uglier than the next, but all of them feeling rich because they could pay for an evening. There was one the girls were scared of because he was always drunk and mad and telling them he'd see to it that they all died in jail, telling them that he'd had his wallet stolen one time and when he figured out who'd done it he swore he would beat her within an inch of her life. Mrs. never made him go away. Ten dollars meant that much to her. It was the other gentlemen who put him out the door if anybody did, because some of them liked a little talk.

How could she tell the old man about things she didn't un-derstand herself? First there was Doll saying, I don't know you, and then there was that box with somebody in it that could have been her father, and all those cousins or whatever they were turning their backs on her, as if a bad joke had been played on them that she wasn't any more than she was. And then looking for Doll everywhere, creeping down through cellar doors, even, hoping she might be out of the weather, then walking out into the cornfields where a person could hide or be lost till the buz-zards found them.

There was one man they called Mack. He didn't have much of anything wrong with him, but he liked to come by, and the girls liked to have him there because he teased them and brought them chocolates and they thought he looked like a man you might want around even if he wasn't paying. He was always laughing or about to laugh, and it didn't matter if there was something a little mean about the way he did it. He was a working-man, you could tell, but he knew some ballroom dancing, the waltz and the fox trot, so they'd put the Victrola on and he'd dance with every one of them, even with Lila. The parlor wasn't big enough for more than three couples, but they'd push the chairs back and dance themselves winded. Sal said once, "This is what it *sposed* to be like!" They all loved Mack, but he favored one girl, the short, plump one they called Missy. And after a while he'd start up the stairs and she'd go tagging after him, because that's how it was.

Lila was horribly in love with that man. You can't go on forever thinking about nothing at all, and he had a nice face and that laugh, and what harm was there in it since she could hardly even bring herself to look at him. But he could tell somehow, and he started teasing her about it. Rosie, Rosie, give me a smile, he would say, and she couldn't do that at all because she just wanted to hide her face. Rosie, give me a peck on the cheek, just a little one, making a joke of her when he was the only thing she cared about in this world and he seemed to know it. When just a few gentlemen came, Lila was always left sitting, and if Mack saw her there he'd say, "Rosie here is the kind of girl a man could want to marry. There are good-time girls and there are girls you'd want to take home."

Missy would say, "Why, she's tough as a mule. I guess you might take her home if you needed some plowing done."

And he'd say, "A man wants a girl the other fellas ain't gonna come hankering after."

And she'd say, "Well, I guess that's old Rosie, all right. There's nobody comes hankering, that's for sure."

But it made Missy jealous that he said those things. Once, she flew at Lila for nothing and pulled her hair all this way and that so the pins fell out and the other girls laughed as if it was something they'd been wanting to do themselves and hadn't gotten around to it yet.

Lila never knew people could be so mean. She was mean, too, because the sadness in that house was like a dream that made everything strange and wrong. Mack could run his finger along her cheek and she would feel the warmth rising to follow it. He would touch her neck sometimes, and it would make the tears come every single time he did it, no matter who else was watching. It was terrible, and it was mostly what she lived for. The other girls laughed at her, and they were jealous because he paid even that kind of attention to her. So she made a kind of plan. There was an old man who was supposed to come before sunrise to stoke the coal furnace. Sometimes he did, and sometimes he just wandered in when he felt like it. There was nothing any of them hated more than getting up to a cold house. Lila liked that kind of work a lot better than what she'd been doing, or trying to do. She owed Mrs. more money by the day, and she couldn't think of any other reason she was kept on, except to make everybody else feel like they were better. She couldn't walk in those damn shoes and she couldn't keep "that look" off her face. A couple of times Mrs. slapped her for it, but that didn't help. Once, Mack touched her tears with the tip of his finger and then touched the wet to her lips. "She's a sweet girl, Missy. See that? Like a little child." She couldn't look at him. She couldn't even breathe. And there he was watching her, smiling.

So the next morning she went down cellar in her nightgown and bare feet, and stood there in the darkest dark with her back to the furnace for the warmth. If she stoked it too early, Mrs. would be after her for the coal she wasted, and if she waited too long, the old man might come to do it. If he did come she decided she'd shake the shovel at him a little and he'd probably run off the best he could, scrawny as he was. Mrs. had to pay him something, but Lila would be working off a debt, so Mrs. would see it was best to let her have her way. Then she'd scrub down the kitchen, which needed it something terrible. It was high time somebody beat those rugs.

Just standing there in the dark felt so good to her. She'd get all black and filthy with the coal dust, and when she came upstairs who knew what they would say, and that was all right, because she had this time to be quiet with herself. How long had it been. She was standing there, leaning against the warmth with her eyes closed, and she began to have bright dreams about waking up before dawn with Doll's arm for a pillow and the sound of a fire and Doane talking with whoever else was awake first. It was always Doane who got the fire going, and then Arthur would start the coffee when they had it. And Doll coaxed her awake. They would fry whatever there was, the light coming up and the birds singing. Dew on everything, beaded on cobwebs so it fell like a little rain when you broke one. Then Doll looked at her and said, "You're standing in a coal hole." No, Lila must have said that. She'd started talking to herself and they teased her about it. She knew nothing about anything but fieldwork and making change. And housekeeping, from the time in Tammany. When she lived in that town where they didn't hang Doll and she worked in the store, sometimes she would walk out at night, because then you can see into people's houses. The accounts always came out just right when she was working there, never a penny short. She was saving up a little money. There was nothing wrong with working indoors when a place was as clean as that and smelled so good. Ham and coffee and cheese and apples and flour. Spools of ribbon and bolts of pretty cloth. She'd watch how the women were dressed and what they did with their hair, listen to the way they talked. She'd really wanted to know those things. Well, she'd been learning some things lately, that's for sure.

"You're standing there in the dark in a filthy old cellar."

I like it down here. That was her talking to herself again. I ain't cut out for this life.

Doll said, "I tried to tell you about it. Didn't I tell you?"

No, you didn't. Just to stay away from whorehouses. Just that you got that scar. Anyway, I had a decent job, and then you come bleeding all over everything, fouling the place.

She nodded. "I shoulda give that more thought. But where's my knife? Why you let that woman have my knife?"

It's the only thing I had to give her.

That don't make sense. Lila was the one who said that. But Doll would have said it. If Lila had had the knife and a gold watch and chain, she'd have handed them all to that woman, seen them lying there in her hand and wished there was something else to give her. It was a bitter sorrow to her that Mrs. hardly even bothered with her anymore. Never smeared rouge on her face or told her she might try smiling. The gentlemen come here for a good time. You look at them like you hate them.

She hated them, for a fact. They were the worst part of the whole damn situation. It was them that made her think sometimes she'd like to have that knife back. No, because she couldn't go anywhere so long as it was locked away. Safekeeping. There was a picture in there of Peg's sister, and Mrs. only let her look at it once in a while. She'd say, Peg, I was going to let you look at that photo, but the way you been acting lately— Then there would be Please, and I'm sorry, and I won't do it again if you just tell me what it was I done, and Mrs. would say, Like you don't know! Next time I'll just toss it in the fire. Begging only worked sometimes, not quite never, but they did it anyway, till she slapped them for it.

Lila said, "I never knew there was such a place."

And Doll said, "Didn't I warn you." No, you didn't. But I guess you must have told me something. How else did I know to come here to just purely hate my life, hate everything about it, my damn body, my damn face, the damn misery in my heart because I got nothing to care about. How did that Mack get in there to devil me the way he does, when I never meant him one bit of harm? She thought, If I could hate him, too, that would make things easier. Nothing was supposed to be easier, she knew that. Once, when Mrs. was gone, somebody left a door unlocked and a preacher got in. He said a word or two about hell before they pushed him back out. She'd heard about it before anyway, at a camp meeting. Maybe that's how she knew to come here, thinking it might be where she belonged. But it was taking so long. Worse every day, because it was the same every day. It wasn't the end of anything. And she was beginning to think now and then about sunshine, and the smell of the air. Trees. She thought, I'm just doing that to devil myself.

Well, she better start shoveling the coal. She was only used to a wood fire. So she'd have to be careful not to put too much in too fast. Stir the coals and then build up the fire so she could see what she was doing. She knew a boiler could burst if something happened, it got too hot or heated up too fast. Then the coals would fly everywhere and the whole damn house would burn down, probably. She could fill it up, leaving just enough room for her to crawl in after and close the door. Boom! She'd go flying, a flaming piece of her right into that girl's face, that Peg, and another one into Rita's lap, where she was always picking at her fingernails until they were bloody, and another one into the room where they kept the dress-up clothes when the gentlemen weren't around. And Mack would see her, all fire like that, and he'd probably be laughing, thinking he'd done it. He'd touch her cheek and the fire would come away on his hand and he'd probably just lick it off. He'd say, Now, that's the kind of girl a man would marry! Telling that damn lie again just to see if she could burn any hotter than fire.

Doll said, "You're standing here in a cellar, barefoot in the dark, talking to yourself. This ain't how I brought you up."

Lila said, I got that plan about working around the place.

"You know how I got this scar? A girl just as crazy as you're getting to be heated up an iron skillet as hot as she could make it, and then when I come in the kitchen she hit me with it. Broke the bone in my cheek and who knows what all. I was as good as dead for a long time, and when I woke up, I had this face for the rest of my life."

Lila thought, How do I know that? Did she tell me sometime?

"You was a sickly child, and I told you old stories because my voice was a comfort to you. You remember."

I'm talking to myself. Seeing things in the dark. Slipping away. Maybe it don't matter.

Doll said, "Well, I tell you what. If I was still living I wouldn't waste it standing around in no cellar wishing I was dead. You sure never learned that from me. I'm surprised you can hold up your head."

Most times I can't.

Do it anyway. That was her way of speaking.

There she was, missing Doll again. For so many years she had belonged to somebody. The cow and her calf. That was all right, because Doll wanted her there beside her. The way they used to laugh together, half the joke being that nobody else would know what the joke was. Now here she had this preacher, maybe the kindest man in the world, and no idea what to do with him. And here she had his baby, and what did she know about bringing up his child? She was reading the Bible, thinking she might understand what he was talking about sometimes, what he and old Boughton were laughing about, arguing over, but her mind would go off on its own and she'd be back in the cellar, farther away than ever. Or she'd be slipping off with that child in her arms, and she'd be whispering right in her ear, her cheek against the child's hair, telling her what there was growing by the road that was good to eat and what was good to heal a sore, and they'd be whispering and laughing together when they found a way to get out of the rain, singing old songs together, the ones everybody knew that still felt like secrets when you taught them to a child. Sometime they'll begin singing, and these are the words, you know them, too. Shall we gather at the river.

She had thought about all that, stealing off with a child, in the house in St. Louis. She came up out of the cellar that first morning and went straight to the kitchen, filthy as she was, and began scrubbing. Everything was greasy, and there was food scorched onto the pots and pans so they gave off smoke every time they were put on the stove. Everything was dusky with old smoke. Mice in the pantry. Mrs. came in and watched what she was doing for a minute or two. Lila saw that shrewd look on her face she expected to see, as if the whole thing were her idea. A cleaning woman came in now and then and wiped up just a little, since Mrs. hardly paid her anything at all. But Lila was working off a debt, so there was still a savings for her, small as it was. "The floor needs mopping," Mrs. said, which meant what Lila was doing was all right with her. After a few days she decided to look around in the closets and drawers to find her own dress, and then she could go outside to beat the rugs. It made things nicer, so there was pleasure in it.

She hadn't been at that kind of work more than a month before she heard them saying Missy was going to have a baby. "She's so fat she didn't know it herself." Laughing, of course. "She was bawling all day yesterday, Mrs. is so mad at her. She don't want to tell where her sister is, so Mrs. got to get rid of it, and she don't like that one bit!"

"I guess we won't be seeing Mack around for a while."

"She'll just take it to the nuns is all."

"You ever see one of them nuns? I never did."

"Best not to wonder about it. There used to be an old man come around in the middle of the night."

"And then he took 'em to the nuns."

"Can't say he didn't. I wouldn't bet no money on it, though."

"What else he going to do with a baby, fool?"

"Well, you going to believe what you want to believe, fool."

And the other girl started crying. No end to the meanness.

That was when Lila started thinking she might just steal a child for herself. Nobody would mind. She could pick it up and walk out the door with it, for all they cared. Just so long as she waited till dark. And left through the back door. People don't like to think about babies coming out of a house like that, so she'd be careful and wait till the street was empty. The gentlemen didn't want to hear one word about babies. But that would just make everything easier. Mrs. would think it was her own idea. It would save her trouble, maybe a little money. So that would make up for most of whatever Lila still owed her. And the child would never be an orphan, because Lila would always be there looking after it, keeping it beside her. No tangled hair, no rickety legs. No cussing. She could hardly even sleep nights for the thought of it. She'd be out in the weather again, hugging a baby under her coat, watching for the minute that child would laugh, watching it play with a milkweed pod, a bit of string. Don't take much to please a child, if that's what you want to do. If Missy ever happened to find out what had come of her, she would be glad Lila took her, because Lila would show her every good thing she could think of, everything Doll had shown her. She would teach her how to get by. There was nothing so hard about it if you could read a little and you knew how to make change. All at once Lila was only there at that house waiting to leave it, waiting to take a child out into the good, cold night and show it the moon and the stars. Or out into the rain. It wouldn't matter. All at once it was only the child that mattered to her, and all that sadness and meanness wasn't her life at all. She could just walk away from it, taking with her one thing that would be worth the very worst of it. The surprise of it all made her laugh. She thought, Well, when was the last time I did that?

Lila had thought about what it might be like having a child of her own, but it never happened. Something must have gone wrong sometime and her body just wouldn't do it. Maybe that was what came of being a feeble child herself, that her body didn't wish that kind of life on anyone else. Or it could have been all the hard work. Once, in the old days, Mellie had gotten very curious about Arthur's boy Deke, so Lila was, too. Doane told him to stop bothering those girls, which really meant those girls should stop bothering him. When Doll found out what they'd been up to, she told them they were asking for a world of trouble messing around with boys. By then Mellie had found out whatever it was she wanted to know and had gone on to something else, trying to play an old fiddle somebody gave her. It had taken Lila a little longer. But no trouble had come of it for either one of them, maybe because Doane had put an end to it, maybe because Lila, at least, couldn't have that kind of trouble if she wanted to.

No matter. There was another way to get a child. If it happened to be one nobody else wanted around, then it was a good thing to take it up, tend to it. Who could know that better than she did. At the time she was thinking about this, making her plan, she'd had no idea there was anything about that written down anywhere. All she knew about the Bible was what she heard at the revival meetings she went to sometimes, in those days after Doll told her to go out on her own and live as she could, and she was so lonely that the crowds and the singing were a comfort to her. The preaching and praying were just something she put up with because she liked the rest of it. The best time to get a bag of popcorn. At one of those meetings she met a couple of girls who were on their own, too, and the three of them wandered around together for a while, looking for work, finding it sometimes, sharing what they had, going to the matinee, to the dance hall. There was a lonely kind of excitement about it because they knew it would only last for a while. Then one of them took up with a fellow and married him, the other one got a job working nights in a bakery, and Lila started clerking in a store. Things worked out more or less the way they had hoped, and that was the end of that.

Doll must have been following her from place to place somehow, even though Lila didn't know herself where she would be from one day to the next. Doll wouldn't have wanted Lila to see her panhandling, but it was hard to think how else she'd have been getting by. It might just have happened that Doll was in that town and saw her there, and watched to see where she lived. And it might just have happened that Doll and that old fellow had their knife fight there, close enough to Lila's room that Doll could come to her when she had to. It could have been that the man, maybe her father, meant to find Lila, and Doll threw her husk of a body and her dreadful knife into making sure that didn't happen. What might he have said to her, to Lila? She could only imagine him white as he was in that box, whiter at the bone of his nose. He'd stand there all slack in his joints like a zombie, stupefied by how dead he was, mumbling a little, and she would feel so sorry and so relieved that he couldn't tell her what it was he came to tell her. Things like that happen in movies. That was probably where she got the idea. He might have wanted to tell her that he and her poor dear mother hadn't meant to leave her long, but something happened. They were on the way to find her, and—what could he say?—the train went

203

off a cliff and all their arms and legs were broken, and when they came to, they didn't even know their own names. Years in the hospital. And while he was telling her some such thing Doll would come flying out of nowhere to cut him one more time. No wonder her thoughts were strange, considering what she had to think about.

But as long as the one thing on her mind was Missy's baby, she was just plain happy. The best of everything she remembered became the whole dream of what she could look forward to. So when the memory of some pleasant day she had put out of sight came back to her, even the taste of a clover blossom or the smell of the wind at evening, the pleasure of it was a sort of shock, and if she forgot that she shouldn't be talking out loud, she'd say, "Yes, yes," as if time could be coaxed into getting on with itself. She made a little garden out behind the house, a row of peas and a row of carrots, and planted some marigolds by the front steps. There wasn't really enough sunshine, the buildings were so close, but she wanted the feel of real dirt on her hands, not just the grime and mess she was always dealing with. The dirt would clean away the feeling and the smell of it. She walked a long way to find a store that sold seeds, the farthest she had been from Mrs. since she came there. It made her light-headed. Mrs. had begun talking about attracting a better class of customer now that the place had a little polish, and she mostly let Lila do whatever she wanted, pretending she was the one who had thought of it. The other girls wouldn't even go down the block to buy a loaf of bread because they thought people looked at them, but Lila didn't really care about that. She always felt strange in a town, but that was all right. It reminded her of the way she and Mellie used to steal a look at their reflections in a store window, waving their arms and making faces if they thought nobody was watching, laughing at the laughing ghosts of themselves for just the minute their pride let them risk, then walking on, thinking they had done something anyone else would notice or give a thought to, and laughing. Sometimes Lila walked away from that house as if she might just keep walking, block after block after block, imagining the night when she really would leave. Then she'd turn and go back to the house again, not because of Mrs., just waiting for the baby.

She hated to remember how swept up in it all she had been, how ridiculous she would have seemed to anyone who knew what she'd been thinking. That's one good thing about the way life is, that no one can know you if you don't let them. Oh, they noticed that she was acting different, and they tried to guess the reason for it, how she could have a boyfriend when she was so tough and wore out and never even curled her hair now that she was just a cleaning woman. Never you mind. He's some old bum on the street. No business of yours. Probly found him picking through a trash can. They were just mean no matter what, so she didn't even listen.

Lila spent her time waiting, working so far as anyone could see, but really just passing the time. Sometimes, when Missy didn't want to go downstairs, bringing a little supper from the kitchen. Missy didn't like her any better for it, but that was all right. She was so sad there was nothing she liked, nothing and nobody. Mack didn't come around, and she never mentioned him. She knew better than to trust him at all, but he had favored her for a long time, and she must have missed him. It got so that Lila had to open the seams of the biggest nightgown she could find, and pin up the hem of it, too, since Missy was no taller than a child. She'd bring a basin of water for her feet, thinking whatever comforted Missy might comfort the child. She tried to sleep lightly enough to hear, over the noise there always was in that house at night, any sound that might mean the birth was coming. Then one morning she came up from the cellar, and there was Missy with a coat she'd never seen before thrown over her and holding a carpetbag, standing at the door with a short, plump woman who had one hand on the doorknob and the other on Missy's elbow. "My sister," she said. "We're leaving. We don't want no part of this place."

The sister said, "Then let's go, Edith. The sun will be up."

But Missy just stood there, looking at the credenza. Lila said, "Something of yours in there?" The lower edge of the door hung an inch or so below the bottom shelf. She could just pull at it and pop the door open, it was so dry and shabby. She knew this from all the times she'd tried to polish it. So she did, and it opened, and she said, "Take what's yours." She saw Missy pause over the sad little odds and ends and then take at least half of them, even Doll's knife. "Well," she said, "that ain't yours, that knife. I don't know about the rest."

The sister said, "She don't want any of it. Put it back. You don't want nothing from this damn place, Edith, not one thing."

Lila said, "Where you going?"

"None of your business," the sister said. "A long way from here, that's for sure." So Missy left without whatever it was that had kept her lingering, and Lila had Doll's knife in her hand again, the shape and weight of it so familiar she felt as if it had always been there. Mrs. would yell when she saw what had happened to that cabinet. The little tongue of the lock had pulled right through the wood, splintering it. But Lila just stood there thinking, I never will see that baby. I've been almost feeling it in my arms, singing to it, and I'll never even see it. How could I have been so sure Missy would have it here, that she never would tell anybody where to find her damn sister? I never even believed she had a sister. Why did I think I knew how things would happen? It was because time was about to bring her back to the old life, where it seemed as though she could do what was asked of her. She had a dream sometimes that she was running along a road and there was Doll ahead of her, waiting for her, and she just ran into her arms, and she thought, It's over now, I'm not lost anymore, and the dream had all the sweetness of a mild day in summer. If you could smell in dreams, it would be the smell of hay on the softest breeze and sunlight warming the fields. She thought that was going to be waiting for her, that life, and she never even stopped to wonder about herself for thinking that way. I been crazy for a long time, she said.

The morning Missy left, Lila found a suitcase in a closet and put a few things in it, a hairbrush and a towel and a nightgown, slipped the knife into her stocking, and left the house. She walked until the sun came up, and until there were people in the street. There was just no end to the city. So she went into a hotel and asked if they could use a cleaning woman. And then the years passed. She didn't mind so much. It was just work. No need to smile at people you'll never see again. The other women would tell her to ease up a little. You start doing that, they going to start expecting it. Lila heard them talking about her, and they meant for her to hear. She don't have another job to go to when she done here. She don't have no children to look after. Nobody going to be hanging on her skirts, fussing for their supper.

But there's no pleasure in work if you don't break a sweat. Out in the fields you feel any little breeze. You know it's coming, you hear it in the trees, you almost can't wait for it, and then there it is, like a cold drink of water. Well, when she finished with her rooms Lila went to help another of the women finish hers. She didn't think of it as helping, it was just a way to pass the time. She'd hear them talking about their mothers and their children, so she kept to herself as much as she could. One woman gave her a jar of cream for her hands, and Lila couldn't even say thanks. She thought about doing it, but then pretty soon it was so long ago she gave it to her that it would probably seem strange to mention it. There was a time when I just quit talking, she said to the child. I'd go a day, a week, and never say a word, except to myself. To Doll sometimes. I'm probably talking to myself right now. No, you're there, I feel you there.

She had a room on the third story of a rooming house with a window that looked out on the street, and in the evening she would watch people pass by. She noticed when babies started walking, when an old man began to use a cane. At first there was a sway-back mule that pulled a wagon of odds and ends along the street, standing patiently while the junk man lowered the tailgate every block or so to let people see what he had to sell. At the end of the second winter they were gone. Somebody opened a sandwich shop. Now and then a new car came down the street. There were always papers blowing along the pavement, men talking and smoking by the streetlight. There were drunks, at night mostly. Sometimes she'd hear laughing or shouting or singing until morning, and she didn't mind it. Just people doing what they do.

She went to the movies. Every payday she put aside the money it would cost her to go two times a week, and then she got by on whatever was left after the rent. Those women were right, no children to feed. She could live on just about anything, but for a child you had to find something nourishing. So at least she always had a movie to think about. And when she was sitting there in the dark, sometimes, when it was crowded, with somebody's arm or knee brushing against hers, she was dreaming some stranger's dream, everybody in there dreaming one dream together. Or they were ghosts all gathered in the dark, watching the world, seeing all the scheming and the murder and having no word to say about it, weeping with the orphans and having nothing to do for them. And then the dancing and the kissing, and all of the ghosts floating there just inches from a huge, beautiful face, to see the joy rise up in it. Like sparrows watching the sun come up, all of them happy at once, no matter that the light had nothing much to do with them. Another day eating bugs, that was what it amounted to. Or maybe they ate the bugs so that they could watch another sunrise. Well, the movie was beautiful, even when it scared her. The music they played before the feature made it seem like something so important was about to happen that she could hardly stay in her chair. She could have watched that lion roar all day. Then the movie. If it wasn't very good, it was still all there was in her mind for an hour or two, a week or two. She might look like some woman going about her work, sitting by her window, but she'd be remaking a story in her mind. If they decided not to kill the old man but just took off in his car. They could pay him back afterward. She took most of the killing out of the movies, and most of the fighting. She kept the dancing and the weddings. But the best part was always to be sitting there in the dark, seeing what she had never seen anywhere before, and mostly believing it. If she had been a ghost watching Doane and Marcelle, so close she could have seen the change in their eyes when they looked at each other, it would have been there for sure. She imagined a wedding for them, both of them young, Marcelle with her arms full of roses. What to imagine for Doll. That she had never cut that old man. That she'd never held a knife or spat on a whetstone. That she was wearing a new shawl that was really the old one on the day whoever owned it first had bought it. She couldn't wish that scar away, or how Doll never forgot to hide her face from anyone but Lila. The ghost couldn't really be part of the dream. Lila would just be there, so close, seeing that tender, ugly face. Just her. Nobody else would even want a dream like that.

That was all the life she had for a long time. Three Christmases passed. She helped put up some garlands in the lobby one night, and a year later, and a year after that. Garlands. Tinsel. Everything has a name. Everybody else knows the name and they think you're stupid if you don't know it. Don't matter. The third Christmas passed, then the dirty part of a winter, then it was spring, and summer, and when she was walking home to her room one afternoon with her hair still tied up in a rag, thinking she might wash up a little and get a hot dog and walk down to the river looking for a breeze, she saw two men unloading some crates from the back of a truck and one of them was Mack. He saw her, too, and laughed, and said something to the other man, who glanced at her and then sort of shook his head the way people do when they don't want a part in something mean. She thought Mack took a step or two after her, but then she thought she heard him say, Lila, too, when he never knew her real name. How could it be that she had never told him her name? There was ringing in her ears. She almost thought she felt the brush of his fingertips at the side of her neck. The worst part of it all was that she knew better. He only teased her so Missy would be jealous. But she felt the rush of blood into her damn cheeks and even that damn sting in her eyes. And walking on away from him was like walking into a strong wind, or walking upstream in a river, and she hoped and hoped he couldn't see how hard it was for her, if he happened to be watching. The very worst part was that he would still know even if he wasn't watching. She thought she heard him laugh. Probably about something else. He'd probably already half forgotten he saw her.

So she left St. Louis. It wasn't just that one thing. It was her whole life. She had told herself that she went to the movies just to see people living, because she was curious. She'd more or less decided that she had missed out on it herself, so this was the best she could do. And it wasn't so bad. The women at work would talk about their children who used to be so sweet when they were little, and now they'd rather drink than eat, the boys *and* the girls, and they couldn't keep their mitts out of their mother's handbag. She'd be thinking how strange it was in that movie *Dorian Gray* that when the man's picture turned ugly from all his wickedness, the pants in the picture turned baggy, too. She couldn't make much sense of it. Half the people in the movie were dressed like Fred Astaire and the other half looked like they'd been sleeping in their clothes their whole lives. When that man goes off into the poor part of the city, he turns evil and ends up looking like he's been sleeping in *his* clothes. The more he goes there, the worse he is. Warts all over him. Maybe somebody stole his hat and the rest of it. Swapped with him. That could happen. Or somebody saw him there stripped naked and took pity on him, since every inch of that town he lived in was always soaking wet. What was she thinking about? It was the painting that changed. She couldn't remember if the man died in his good clothes and only the rest of him was ugly. Him lying there and the others clucking their tongues. Too bad he happened to have a knife to kill himself with. Then he was too dead to use it to make them stop staring, and that was a shame. She was wearing Doll's knife in her garter the day she saw Mack, but she probably wouldn't have used it even if it hadn't meant putting herself in reach of him, probably looking into his face. That damn face. Well, her life just rose up on her, and before she even knew quite what was happening she was walking away, struggling to keep from making a fool of herself, her heart beating in her ears. The life she'd decided she would never have was there the whole time, trapped and furious, and in that minute she knew that if a man she ought to hate said one kind word to her, there was no telling what she might do. Come along, Rosie. Give me a little smile, come along. He'd forgotten he ever saw her, and she was up in her room with the window shade pulled down, stuffing everything she had into her suitcase.

She walked over to the bus station to see where she could get to with the money she had. Wherever she went, she'd get there after the stores were closed, and the rooming houses. To get out of the city would take all her money, and then she'd have no place to spend the night and no supper. She went outside to sit on a bench and think about it. A car pulled up to the curb, and the driver, a young woman, called to her to ask her where she was going. Lila said, "Iowa," and the woman said, "Me, too!" as if she had been hoping to hear that very word. "Get in. I saw you sitting there with your suitcase and I thought, I'd sure appreciate some company. That's really why I came by here. It's not on my way." Lila wasn't sure what to think about sitting for hours beside someone who might expect her to talk or to give her more money than she had, but the woman said, "It'll save you the price of a ticket. I'll be driving all night, and I'd rather not do that alone." She was a tidy, freckly little woman with her hair in a knot. She was wearing a starchy white blouse she must have spent an hour ironing, it was so perfect. At the movies you could find yourself sitting next to anybody at all, some man with polished shoes and creased pants, some woman with rings on her hands, hugging her purse. They might tip their bags of popcorn toward her, she would hear them breathe and sigh as if they were sharing a pillow with her. Sometimes she could feel them looking at her, but she never looked at their faces or said anything to them. She'd just wait until the show began and they could forget each other. Now she would probably be sitting beside this stranger for hours with no way to stop thinking about her, which meant there was no way she could stop thinking about herself. Still, it would make some things easier.

The woman said, "Where you going?"

Lila thought she might try to get to Tammany, but the woman had never heard of it, so when she asked if it was near Des Moines Lila said yes, thinking that must be where the woman was going herself. It turned out she was going to a town called Macedonia, off somewhere in the cornfields, so she left Lila at a gas station in Indianola, which wasn't too far from Des Moines. Lila had no reason to be in Des Moines. In fact, she didn't want to be in any town that was big enough for anybody to know where it was. She had in mind one of those no-name places along a county road. A store and a church and a grain elevator. There must be a thousand of them, all just alike, and farms spreading out beyond them. But that woman had brought her clear from St. Louis, so she was glad for twelve hours of riding in a car. It stalled as often as it slowed down. Going up a hill was a trial every time. The woman said she was glad to have someone to talk to because driving made her sleepy, but then she was too nervous to talk. Every now and then she would say she was scared the car was going to break down, and she sure didn't want to be sitting there in the middle of nowhere all by herself. This was meant as a kindness to Lila, to make her feel welcome, but it was also true. She leaned into the steering wheel and peered out at the road as if that would help.

Lila was glad to be seeing the country again, the fields looking so green in the evening light. Knee-high by the Fourth of July. So it must be June. Every farmhouse in its cloud of trees. There is a way trees stir before a rain, as if they already felt the heaviness. It all just went on and on, the United States of America. It was so easy to forget that most of the world was cornfields.

The woman said, "My mama's sick, and there's nobody to help her out. I've got to get there fast." It was the first time she had driven any distance to speak of. "I got a letter from her. She never mentions a problem, she never wants to worry me. She doesn't have a telephone, so I thought I'd better bring a car in case I need to find a doctor. It might not even run after I get there. If I get there. I only bought it yesterday. Dang thief that sold it to me, I'd like to give him a piece of my mind." It began to rain. She was afraid to stop the car for fear it wouldn't start again, and they drove all night, except once when they needed gas. Then the man at the station had to push the car out onto the road. There was enough of a slope that the engine caught

213

and they went on again, with no light at all but the headlights, and they didn't show much but rain. The woman said, "I think I'd be scared if I were you, putting your life in my hands," and Lila said, "I don't much care what happens." Then she could feel in the dark that for a minute the woman was wondering about her, about to ask her a question, then thinking better of it. Lila thought, Maybe she suspects I'm the kind of woman who might keep a knife in her garter. Might sleep in her clothes. The woman said, "Do you hear that?" There was a soft thumping sound. "Is that coming from the motor?"

"Don't sound like nothing."

"You know about cars?"

"A little." She knew they had four wheels and a running board, and that she wasn't used to riding in one. But there was no point worrying when they couldn't even stop to see if there was a problem, and wouldn't know what to look for if they did stop. In the dead of night, without so much as a paper match to see by. And the rain would have put that out.

"I don't have a spare tire. There was one in the trunk, but I sold it for gas money."

"There's nothing the matter with your tires." Lila thought the woman could use a little comforting. It was kind of her to pick her up, even if she had her own reasons. It could take days of hitching rides to come as far as they had come in one day. If the car broke down she'd be hitching again, and that was just what she expected to be doing in the first place.

The woman said, "You're so quiet, sometimes I think you're sleeping. Or praying."

"Nope. I'm just sitting here wide awake."

"Good. It wouldn't matter, really, if you're tired. But I do feel better—"

"Sure." Then Lila said, just to say something, "You seen that movie *Double Indemnity*? Driving along in the dark like this reminds me of it."

"I can't go to the movies. It's against my religion."

"Oh." One more thing she didn't know about.

"I shouldn't have called that man a thief. I shouldn't have said dang."

"Something wrong with saying dang?"

"Well, it's practically swearing. Anybody knows what you really mean by it."

Lila said, "I didn't even know there was such a thing as practically swearing."

"In my church there is. Nazarene. We're pretty strict."

This is exactly why Lila kept to herself. She thought, It's a good thing I didn't get a chance to take that child. I'd have nothing to tell it about getting along. Don't lie more than you have to, don't take what ain't yours.

The woman said, "No drinking, no smoking, no dancing, no makeup, no jewelry. They're not too pleased with women driving cars. No stealing or killing, either, but that's not what they talk about most of the time. I don't mind it. I grew up in it."

"You give 'em your money?"

The woman laughed. "A dime on the dollar. That's usually about what it amounts to. Tithing. One-tenth of nothing. But we have a nice potluck every now and then. We try to look out for each other. It's cheaper than insurance. You have a church?"

"Nope."

"You might visit a couple of them. Just look in the door. If you're living away from your family, a church can be a help."

"I ain't living away from my family."

After a minute the woman said, "We're a mission church. So I'm supposed to try to bring you to Jesus. But I won't if you don't want me to. Try, I mean. Some people think it's irritating when I do that. I guess I'm not much good at it."

Lila said, "I wouldn't mind talking about something else."

"Sure. That's fine." They were quiet for a while. "So you've got family in St. Louis?"

"No, I don't." She would think that was what Lila meant. I ain't living away from my family. She was quiet again. Lila could feel her wondering, and she almost said, I was working in a whorehouse because the woman who stole me when I was a child got blood all over my clothes when she came to my room after she killed my father in a knife fight. I've got her knife here in my garter. I was meaning to steal a child for myself, but I missed the chance and I couldn't stand the disappointment, so I got a job cleaning in a hotel. You can't say dang or go to movies, and look who you got sitting next to you hour after hour. Look who you been offering half of your spam sandwich. She was laughing and the woman glanced at her. So she said, "You can try bringing me to Jesus if you want to. Might pass the time."

The woman was quiet for a while. The windshield wipers were groaning and the rain was pounding the glass. She said, "I'd better not. I'd better be trying to see the road." She said, "You've got to come to it in the right frame of mind. Otherwise it's just talking for the sake of talk. Passing the time. I might be making excuses here. Lord forgive me if I am. But you strike me as a woman with a lot of bitterness in her soul. I don't mean any offense. I might just make things worse."

Lila said, "I doubt you could do that." She was beginning to wonder how well the woman knew where the road was. She would steer away from the shoulder when they started hearing gravel.

"I'm a stenographer." Her voice was high with nerves. "I learned shorthand in night school. I'm pretty good at it—I'm not good at much else."

"Well, you're lucky you got the one thing." She had no idea what that thing was.

"My mama made me finish high school. I was so mad at her about that. Now I guess I'm glad she did. I wanted to quit and get married. He was five years older. She said, If he loves you he'll wait. He didn't. Wait. So I guess he didn't love me. He went into the army and came back with some girl he met in England. I was upset at the time. Cried my fool head off. Are you married?"

"Nope." I'm good at chopping weeds. I can change sheets well enough. I was bad at whoring. Lila didn't say anything, but she almost did. Why would she do that? The woman didn't mean any harm. She wasn't going to put her out beside the road for anything she said. If she hitched up her skirt to show her the knife, that might be different. She thought, I'm crazy, and laughed. She thought, I've got to stay away from people.

The woman was saying, "I always thought I'd have kids. A dozen of them. And now look at me. My mom said once the war was over and the boys came home I'd find somebody. She's still telling me I'll find somebody. I'm beginning to have my doubts."

Lila said, "I just wanted the one child. I didn't figure on—" and then she stopped herself. There she was anyway, rubbing her eyes. The woman glanced at her and said, "Well, God bless!"

It was just being out in that great, sweet nowhere that was making her remember. Sometimes they saw a light, mostly it was just darkness and rain. But she didn't have to see it to know. She could smell it. The window wouldn't roll up right to the top, so night air came whistling in, a little rain with it, but how could she mind. The woman was helping her regret the child she never had. Lila had thought, That would be the same child who wasn't the reason my dress was all bloody, who didn't get me sent off to St. Louis with a slip of paper in my pocket, who

217

wouldn't be carried out into the secret night under my coat, who wouldn't wake up to daylight and the birds singing.

Well, here she was in the Reverend's quiet house, as calm and safe as the good old man could make her. She hugged her belly. "I been waiting on you, child," she said. "You be good to your poor mama this time. No slipping away on me. Don't you go slipping away."

At the bus station in St. Louis that little woman had pulled over and rolled down her window and asked her where she was going, and that was one good thing. Then she wasn't at the service station at Indianola an hour or so when a fellow offered her a ride in his pickup truck, a shy fellow with rough skin and a bad cough, wanting company. Probably his girl had left him and he wanted just anybody beside him, because he didn't talk at all. Company does sort of settle people sometimes. They don't have to know anything about you except that you're sitting there.

He let her out where he turned off from the main road, and she walked along for a while till she was just about as tired of walking as she could stand to be, no cars passing at all, and she saw that old shack off in its meadow of weeds. Good things happen three at a time, and here was a place where she could take her shoes off and put her suitcase and her bedroll down. That road followed a river, so there wouldn't be much else to want. She could wash the dust off, get a drink.

Those first few days, clearing out the shack and washing at the river, finding dandelion greens and ferns still coming up and wild carrot, finding a rabbit burrow. Life is hard in the spring, and still it all felt like something she had almost died for the want of. She found a patch of violets blooming and lay down there, and ate every single flower, one by one, the way Mellie used to do. Mellie sitting there Indian-style with a blossom perched on the tip of her tongue like a toad with a butterfly, thinking about something else, some plan for the next ten minutes. Once, when she had that look on her face, Marcelle said, "Now what's she getting up to?" and Doane said, "She's just hatching a couple more freckles." Lila told the child, "I believe I really was a little crazy then, because things I remembered seemed so real to me. I don't wonder at it. I just hope nobody saw me acting that way." There was a time, when she was riding along in that car with the window down a crack, smelling the dark, wet fields, that she thought when she got the chance she might just lie right down on the ground in some lonely place and let the world take her life away. She felt that way when she saw those violets and remembered the old times, and she did lie down, but then the ants started bothering. There always was something bothering, and you had to be scratching and shifting around. The world don't want you as long as there is any life in you at all.

But a place like that, just waiting, unless somebody came along and said it was his. She'd left the bottles and tins where they were except in the one corner, so it wouldn't look like she meant to take the place if she didn't have the right. But she did spread out her bedroll and lie down, and next thing she knew, it was almost morning. She could hear the birds singing. What is it they know, when the sky is still dark? Mellie said if just one of them saw just one bit of light, it'd wake up the rest of them and then they'd all go at it, making sure none of them stayed asleep. That's what she did herself when she woke up first, no matter how early it was. Hum, hum, hum. I just wisht I knew where they put them matches. They got to be somewheres around here. Hum, hum, hum. I was thinking I'd get breakfast started. Tripping over Lila's foot once or twice. What would one bit of light look like? A star. The birds would never be sleeping at all. Mellie would say, That's all right, I know what I know.

She thought for a few days that she must have come to the end of her life, because it felt so much like the beginning of it.

She was waiting for something to happen and nothing did. Then she started thinking about the movies again, until she was afraid she would get tired of them, that she'd wear them out and wouldn't have them anymore to go back to. And then she decided she'd take a look at that town they'd passed through. Well, she had the money she didn't have to spend on a bus ticket, so she could walk into town and buy a few things.

She'd noticed there was a movie theater, which you wouldn't really expect in a town that size. She strolled by to see what was playing. *To Have and Have Not.* She'd seen it. That's the worst part about a small town. Well, pretty soon she wouldn't even know how long something had been showing in the city. Not that she should be spending money on a movie now anyway. Fishing line, fishing hooks, a pot, cornmeal, some matches. The man at the counter looked at her like Well, I never seen you around here before, meaning to be a little friendly, and she looked at him like Mind your own damn business. That same man gave her a big jar of cloves for a wedding present, wrapped in white paper. "Helps with the toothache," he said. He played third base and the Reverend pitched, back in the old, old days. At first she just hated having to deal with anybody. Then she got used to seeing how the gardens came along. Sometimes people would nod when she passed. She made up her mind about which house was the prettiest. That wasn't the one where she stopped to ask the lady if she might be looking for some help. Mrs. Graham. She was working in her garden and Lila saw her there and thought she might as well ask. There are women who take pride in how kind they are and jump at every chance, their eyes all shining with it so you can't help but notice. You keep clear of them if you can, but they do come in handy. Sometimes you want a bowl of soup. She said, "Why, yes, dear, I am! Yes, I am looking for help!" Just like that. She didn't give herself a minute to decide. Lila thought, I should mention the knife in my garter and see what she says then. But that was just a joke she made to herself. She said, "I've done housework and farm work. I'm good with growing things."

"Well, that's fine!" The woman rubbed her hands on her apron. "I'm behind on the weeding! I was hoping for a little rain yesterday or today, but nothing, so I thought I might as well get to it! If you could help with the onions," as hasty about it as if she might miss an opportunity. So Lila at least might have a door she could come to, someone who knew her name. The woman made such a point of not looking her over that Lila could see what she must have thought of her. "Lila! What a pretty name!"

It was a good-looking garden, though. A garden never really belongs to somebody else if you're the one that takes care of it. The soil was nice as could be, and the plants had all those good smells. Just brushing by the tomato plants, getting that musk on them, made her clothes seem clean. She was still waiting to hear somebody say the name of the place. It was painted on the water tower, so coming to town she walked along looking up at that word, wondering what it was supposed to sound like. Of course it was a Bible word. The old man would tell her that.

She said to the child, "Now I been in Gilead a pretty long time. A lot longer than I expected. And you're going to be born here. If I leave I'll take you with me, I will for sure. I'll tell you the name of the place, though. People should know that much about themselves anyway. The name of your father. Could be I won't ever leave. The old man might not give me cause." And then she almost laughed, because she knew he never would. She said, "That old man loves me. I got to figure out what to do about it."

She never stayed away from church anymore, for one thing. It still reminded her of that first time, when she was sitting there, rain dripping off her hair, down her neck, cold rain soaked into her shoes, hoping he wouldn't notice her. He was going on about baptism. A birth and a death and a marriage, he said. A touch of water and these children are given the whole of life. The sacraments remind us. She was thinking what sense did that make, but his eyes drifted across the congregation and rested on her face, as if he thought she might know what he meant and could say yes, it was true, what he meant if not the words he could find to put it in. Jesus drank from our cup and shared our baptism, he said, which meant He suffered and died like everybody else. And she was thinking how strange it was for them to be there singing songs to somebody who had lived and died like anybody. Doll would say, That's the way it is. They could as well be singing about Doll. And then she was thinking of that song they used to like in St. Louis, what a night to go dreaming, and his eyes drifted back to her again, and he looked at her until he remembered not to. When she thought about it afterward, she knew she couldn't have counted to five before he looked down at his papers and then at the people in front of him. Still.

Now that she was his wife he looked at her whenever he mentioned something they might have talked about, to let her know he thought about the questions she asked him, or questions she knew he asked himself. Sometimes he gave the sermon to her to read before he preached it. One morning he read to her at breakfast, something he had written during the night. "Very rough," he said. "Half of it I've crossed out. And this was supposed to be the clean copy." He cleared his throat. "So. 'Things happen for reasons that are hidden from us, utterly hidden for as long as we think they must proceed from what has come before, our guilt or our deserving, rather than coming to us from a future that God in his freedom offers to us.' My meaning here is that you really can't account for what happens by what has happened in the past, as you understand it anyway, which may be very different from the past itself. If there is such a thing. 'The only true knowledge of God is born of obedience,' that's Calvin, 'and obedience has to be constantly attentive to the demands that are made of it, to a circumstance that is always new and particular to its moment.' Yes. 'Then the reasons that things happen are still hidden, but they are hidden in the mystery of God.' I can't read my own writing. No matter. 'Of course misfortunes have opened the way to blessings you would never have thought to hope for, that you would not have been ready to understand as blessings if they had come to you in your youth, when you were uninjured, innocent. The future always finds us changed.' So then it is part of the providence of God, as I see it, that blessing or happiness can have very different meanings from one time to another. 'This is not to say that joy is a compensation for loss, but that each of them, joy and loss, exists in its own right and must be recognized for what it is. Sorrow is very real, and loss feels very final to us. Life on earth is difficult and grave, and marvelous. Our experience is fragmentary. Its parts don't add up. They don't even belong in the same calculation. Sometimes it is hard to believe they are all parts of one thing. Nothing makes sense until we understand that experience does not accumulate like money, or memory, or like years and frailties. Instead, it is presented to us by a God who is not under any obligation to the past except in His eternal, freely given constancy.' Because I don't mean to suggest that experience is random or accidental, you see. 'When I say that much the greater part of our existence is unknowable by us because it rests with God, who is unknowable, I acknowledge His grace in allowing us to feel that we know any slightest part of it. Therefore we have no way to reconcile its elements, because they are what we are given out of no necessity at all except God's grace in sustaining us as creatures we can recognize as ourselves.' That's always seemed remarkable to me, that we can do that. That we can't help but do it. 'So joy can be joy and sorrow can be sorrow, with neither of them casting either light or shadow on the other.'"

As he was reading, sitting across from her in his robe and slippers with his hair rumpled and his glasses unpolished and a silvery shadow on his jaw, he glanced up at her from time to time. He said, "It's very rough. I had a thought in the middle of the night, and I had to get up and write it out. Half the time when I write something that way it turns out the next morning to be nonsense. The sobering effects of daylight. But this still makes sense to me. It seems obvious, if anything. I believe. Of course it's early yet."

"Well," she said. "Near as I can tell, you were wanting to reconcile things by saying they can't be reconciled. I guess I know what you mean by reconcile."

He laughed. "Yes, clearly you do know. And I see your point. An excellent point." He was pleased with her. He'd mention it to Boughton.

She said, "You been worrying about Mrs. Ames." That poor girl.

"Yes. Yes, I have. I had an idea that I would be eternally loyal to her. I said as much to her. That was important to me for many years. The bride of my youth, and so on. After a while it may have been my loyalty I was loyal to. But I did the best I could."

"Then I come along."

"Yes, you came along. Thank the Lord."

She said, "If you thought dead was just dead, then you wouldn't have to worry about any of this."

"I guess that's true. It could be true. When I talk with people who aren't religious, I'm often surprised by what they tell me, though. I'm not sure anyone has ever said that to me, dead is just dead. They're loyal, too. Not like I was. But that was unusual. I believe I may have taken a certain pride in it."

"You're still loyal. You're up all night writing to her."

"Well, yes. In a way I suppose that's true. And writing to you. You asked me that question."

"It don't matter. She must have been a sweet girl."

He nodded. "She was. She was." He said, "So you covered her grave with roses. That was a wonderful thing."

She shrugged. "No folks of my own."

"I can't tell you what I felt when I saw that. I don't think there's a name for it."

"You didn't know it was just me doing it."

"Just you," he said. "If it had been a miracle, if an angel had done it, then there'd have been no one to walk with in the evening, no one to give that old locket to."

"No one to come creeping into your bed."

He laughed and colored. "True enough."

"No baby."

"Also true."

They were quiet for a while. Then he said, "God is good."

"Well," she said, "some of the time."

"All of the time."

She said, "I've been tramping around with the heathens. They're just as good as anybody, so far as I can see. They sure don't deserve no hellfire."

He laughed. "Well, that baby you talk about, cast out and weltering in her blood, the Lord takes her up. He looks after the strays. Especially the strays. That story is a parable, about how He bound himself to Jerusalem when He told her, 'Live.' It's like a marriage. More than a marriage."

"And then she takes to whoring."

"That means she starts worshipping false gods. Idols. And He's still faithful to her. To their marriage. That's the important point. Because in the Bible, marriage—" He said, "I used to think it was supposed to be eternal. Like the faithfulness of God."

"What do you think now?"

He was quiet for a minute. "I think I'm married to Lila now. Extremely married to her. And faithful as I know how to be. Not that that can mean much, I'm so old. And you'll want to make another life for yourself when I'm gone. I'll want you to do that. Especially if there's a child." He shook his head. "Since there will be a child."

"No," she said. "I'm going to have just the one husband." One was more than she'd ever expected.

"Well, you know, that's good of you to say, but it's not always wise to make promises. There can be a lot more involved in keeping them than it seems at the time."

She said, "That's not a promise. It's just a fact."

He laughed. "Even better."

And then he went upstairs to make himself into the presentable old preacher all those people had passed on the street every day of their lives, seeing him change and never thinking of it because his life never changed, all those years she was off somewhere or other getting by any way she could. And her life was just written all over her, she knew it without looking, because that's how it was with all the women she used to know. And somehow she found her way to the one man on earth who didn't see it. Or maybe he saw it the way he did because he had read that parable, or poem, or whatever it was. Ezekiel. The Bible was truer than life for him, so it was natural enough that his thinking would be taken from it. Maybe it never was normal thinking, since there were preachers in this house his whole life, quarreling about religion and talking to Jesus.

It could be that the wildest, strangest things in the Bible were the places where it touched earth. Doane said once that he saw a cyclone cross a river. It took the water in its path up into itself and crossed on dry ground, and it was just as white as a cloud, white as snow. Something like that would only last for a minute, but it showed you what kind of thing can happen. It would shed that water and take up leaves and branches, cats and dogs, cows if it wanted to, grown men, and it would change everything they thought they knew. Those women in St. Louis, they stepped into a place that looked like any old house and there was Mrs. and the damn credenza and the dress-up clothes that smelled like sweat and old perfume. And all you had to do was pierce your ears and rouge your cheeks and pretend not to hate the gentlemen more than they would stand for. It was as if that house had been picked up by a black cloud and turned around and dropped down again in the very same spot. Everything in it was still there, but it was changed, wrong, and from then on everybody in it knew too much about the worst that could possibly happen, even if they couldn't say what it was. Then it might be that she seemed to him as if she came straight out of the Bible, knowing about all those things that can happen and nobody has the words to tell you. *And I looked, and, behold, a stormy wind came out of the north, a great cloud, with a fire infolding itself, and a brightness round about it, and out of the midst thereof as it were glowing metal, out of the midst of the fire.* It says right there that even fire isn't hot enough to give you any idea.

It got to be Christmas time. They put a big wreath on the church door. Snow fell. People came to the house with plates of cookies and sat in the parlor for fifteen minutes talking about nothing. Lila's belly was rounder every day. The women told her that since she carried high it would probably be a boy. That wasn't how she'd imagined, but all right. One lady brought her two pleated smocks, one red and one green, both with rickrack around the pockets, which made her think of that dress she'd bought cheap, as she thought at the time. She wondered how

227

much Mrs. figured she'd left still owing her. That woman would know down to the dime.

The deacons brought in a pine tree and set it up, so she offered them some of the cookies their own wives had brought the day before, and they sat in the parlor for fifteen minutes. And then the Reverend went up in the attic and brought down a box with ornaments in it. He said, "It's been—I don't know how many years!" There was a tree in the church, and that used to be all he needed, those years when he was alone. He spent an hour untangling the strings of lights, and then he plugged them in, and when they didn't come on he started working through them to find the bad bulbs. He said, "This used to take a lot of the charm out of Christmas for me. When I was young and impatient." Finally they did light up, and he strung the tree with them and turned off the lamps. "I'd almost forgotten," he said. The room did look very pretty. "Next year we'll have somebody here to help us enjoy it." At the bottom of the box there were ornaments made of thread spools and colored paper and walnut shells. The children. "Nothing here we can use," he said. "I'll stop by the dime store tomorrow." And then he carried the box up to the attic again.

She just watched. He was thinking about next year, daring to say out loud that they'd have brought a new little Christian into the world who would take these things in with his baby eyes and believe them to be the way things are. For unto us is born this day in the City of David a Savior. A day so very long ago. Who is David? What is a Savior? He might never think to ask. It would seem to him that he'd known it all from the beginning. That's why we have to hang lights all over everything, and tinsel. That's why we sing all those songs. It was very nice, in some ways. People would come to the door, singing. The Methodists and the Catholics and the Lutherans, people they barely knew.

Sometimes in St. Louis a few of the gentlemen would stand

outside singing, things that didn't sound much like Christmas. Mrs. closed the house for the holiday, out of respect, she said, but also because she thought she might get shut down for good if she didn't. She kept the shades drawn and the lights off so no one would come to the door. She made the girls live on cold beans and cheese sandwiches so no cooking smells could drift into the street. She took the radio into her own room and turned it so low they could barely hear it. Those men knew they could devil her half to death and she couldn't even open the door to yell at them for it. So Christmas for the girls was just pinochle in the twilight of the drawn shades and then, when the sun went down, fighting and weeping and telling old stories everybody had heard and nobody believed except the ones who were just plain simple. Peg would be singing along with the dirty songs they could hear from the street sometimes, in that way she had of pretending she was in on the joke. Doane never said a word about Christmas, and Doll didn't either. They were always just somewhere trying to get through the winter. It was better for Lila while she worked at the hotel, but she never really liked it. Now here she was with an old man dreaming about his baby and humming "Silent Night." He was happier than he wanted to be. Someone knocked at the door with a plate of cookies, and when he brought it in, he said, "Gingerbread!" as if that was supposed to mean something to her. Somebody had put frosting buttons and collars and smiling mouths on them, as if they had the child there with them already.

She kept thinking, Wait. Don't hope, just wait. She couldn't help thinking how hard it would be for him to do these same things ever again if there happened to be no child. She had washed baptism off herself as well as she could. She had walked in the cold through those raggedy old cornfields that looked as though they had heard the first word of Judgment and couldn't believe what they heard and couldn't doubt it, either. She had

229

thought a thousand times about the ferociousness of things so that it might not surprise her entirely when it showed itself again. She wished she could warn him, even though he knew about it, too, and dreamed about it. This child must know about it, because it lived there under her scared, wild heart. It might not want the world at all. She could show it things that might seem wonderful to her because it meant you could live so the world wouldn't find you. Maybe heaven would be like that, with fields and fields of nettles and chicory, things anybody could take because nobody else would want them. Then if the thief on the cross went to heaven he could just thieve forever to his heart's content, nobody the worse for it. She pictured him as the boy at the shack, nails through those big, dirty hands. Her heart felt like a weight that would burden the child. She thought to him, It won't be that way for you. I promised your papa you'd know all the hymns.

The old man kept moving the lights around, trying to get them even. "My grandfather said this was paganism, bringing in greenery in the middle of winter, making fires. He said there were people in Maine when he was growing up who wouldn't have a thing to do with it. It's true, no one really knows anything about when Jesus was born, the time of year. But there's just a certain amount of exuberance that people have to burn off now and then, Christians and pagans. I like the idea—Druids rejoicing just because they felt like it. We took up where they left off. That's all the sense it has to make." Even his hair was rosy in that light. "Spring would seem like a better time to celebrate a birth. But it's even better for resurrection. Everything coming back to life. And Jesus did die sometime around the Passover," talking away because she wasn't talking at all. But if she just sat there watching, eating a cookie now and then, he was happy enough. He'd been alone for a long time.

He said, "A baby is born and the sky fills with angels. That seems about right. Calvin says every one of us has thousands of angels tending to us. There's an old hymn about the human body—'Strange that a harp of thousand strings should keep in tune so long.' Because the body is so complicated. Lots of work for those angels. For Calvin, angels are the effective attention of God, not separate creatures." And on he went.

Well, that's all fine, she thought. But I know there's more to it, and so do you. She just wished it was over and she had a child or no child and she could stop thinking how hard it would be for him to keep up all this talk if it came down to old Boughton again, struggling up those stairs to weep and pray and dampen a small brow, his bony self half a step from the grave and still without a sensible word to say about any of it. But then her husband smiled at her, and she could see in his face that he had had every one of these thoughts, that he knew everything about them. These thoughts were waiting and familiar, like a house where you knew you belonged though you just hated to go there and doubted once you were there you'd ever leave. He said, "You and I—" and shrugged.

She had to agree. There was night everywhere and snow, under a big moon. Beyond the few lights of Gilead the great white nowhere that the wind had all to itself, the frozen ponds and stricken cornfields and the ragtag sheds and shacks. The wind would be clapping shut and prying open everything that was meant to keep it out, bothering where it could, tired of its huge loneliness. Had she ever seen a windmill that hadn't lost half itself to the wind, like a blown milkweed? Maybe Doll was out there in some place so much the same that it was like dreaming to remember she was far away, far beyond any number of places with different names but all just the same. And that boy. And Mrs. Ames with her baby. And here were the two of them together in this warm light, the same dread feeding on the same hope, married.

———

There was snow on the ground when the baby came. It will snow in April sometimes, so there's nothing surprising about a blizzard or two in March. Still, it gave them a scare. One day they heard spring peepers, those same two notes, again and again, one higher, one lower. Then in the middle of the night it began to storm, and the next day they sat in the kitchen for the warmth and played gin rummy and listened to the wind howling. No one came to look in on them because the drifts were too deep to walk through and the wind was fierce. People can get lost in a storm like that and just die in the road outside their own gate the way they might if they were wandering through a country they'd never seen before, where nobody knew them at all, nobody was waiting for them. The old man would pretend he wasn't praying, and then his head would sink down on his chest and she would have to wait until he remembered to deal the cards. The deck would just spill out of his hands as if he'd gone to sleep or died. Then he'd say he ought to clear a path to the road and even get up from his chair, but the road was so deep in drifts there'd be no point in it. There'd be nowhere to go if he ever got to the road. The telephone wires were down and the electrical lines, too, but they had the woodstove and a kerosene lamp and Mrs. Somebody's meat loaf to warm in the oven. It would have been nice except that she was so pregnant and he was so old.

She said, "I guess you better discard."

"Yes, I guess I'd better. Sorry." But then he'd be studying her face, as if he'd never seen her before and there she was in his kitchen, and he had no idea what she might do next.

She said, "I feel fine. We're both just fine." And every time she took a breath she thought, when she was almost at the bottom of it, Will I tell him if it hurts, if there's some new kind of pain?

232

Could he stand to know it, when there was almost nothing he could do? And then she'd breathe again, deeply, carefully, hoping he would not notice. You always seem to need to touch the place it might hurt to touch. And not just once, either. Well, of course she felt different. Every day she felt different from the day before. There was somebody crouched under her ribs, shifting and fidgeting, growing. It was strange if you thought about it. She'd seen sows and ewes carrying young and birthing them. Hooves. That would be something. This was like a burden that had shifted and rubbed too long in one place. If there wasn't quite room for her to breathe without an elbow being in the way of it, then a little pain wouldn't mean a thing, especially since she would breathe again, then again, feeling for it. The old man was watching her.

She said, "I guess it's my turn." It was a little bit like a stitch in her side from running. It would go away if she stopped thinking about it, sooner if she could lie down. "Gin," she said. "I don't think your heart is in this card game, Reverend."

He said, "I wouldn't mind it if the wind died down a little. I never imagined it would be this bad. Just yesterday I saw crocuses coming up alongside the house."

She thought, He'll be worrying about old Boughton, too, wondering if he's trying to look after Mrs. Boughton all on his own, hobbling around in the cold with all his joints froze up till he can't strike a match. His children, except the one, were probably stuck in drifts along every road from wherever they lived to Gilead, trying to get to him, and he'd have that to worry about. The first break in the storm there'd be men and boys with shovels digging people out, but with the wind the way it was, they'd have to wait.

That wasn't pain, she thought. The child just arched his back.

The old man said, "I'm not too sure about Boughton's roof.

He loses track of the time, the years. There must be three feet of new snow. I'm not sure it's good for that much weight. I hate to think of him trying to light a lamp. Trying to deal with kerosene. Cold is such a torment for him."

She meant to ask him sometime how praying is different from worrying. His face was about as strained and weary as it could be. White as it could be.

He said, "I thought once we made it to March we were probably all right." Then he said, "As far as the weather is concerned." And then he said, "Of course we'll be all right. I didn't mean we won't be." His old head sank down again.

So she fell to wondering how his dread was different from Doane's, in those days when he began to realize that he had no way to look after them, stragglers who had no claim on him at all except that they had always trusted him. What would he have done with the hens that dog caught him stealing except to pluck them and gut them and roast them, handing the drumsticks around to the young ones as if it were just any ordinary supper in ordinary times, nothing so wonderful about it. He did have three silver dollars in his pocket, too, and he wouldn't say a word about where they came from. He never did anything with what he had except to keep things together as well as he could. But stealing is stealing, Doll said, especially if you get caught at it.

Now here she was again, worrying over people who were long past help. You can't even pray for someone to have his pride back when every possible thing has happened to take it away from him. She thought, Everything went bad everywhere and pride like his must have just drifted off the earth, more or less, as quiet as mist in the morning, and people were sad and hard who never were before. Looking into each other's faces, their hearts sinking. If she ever took to praying it would be for that time and all those people who must have wondered what had become of them, what they had done to find themselves without so much as a good night's rest to comfort them. She would call down calm on every one of them, on the worst and the bitterest ones first of all. Doane and Arthur walking away; Mellie, too, never looking back, leaving her an orphan on the steps of a church. Without the bitterness none of that would have happened. If Boughton dropped a lamp and set his house on fire, what would the Reverend say about that? He was looking at her then with as much fear in his eyes as she had ever seen anywhere, even counting those poor raggedy heathens who never thought the Almighty would have the least bit of interest in them.

That wasn't a pain, but he saw her pause over it, consider it, whatever it was. It was like listening for a sound you might only have thought you heard. She said, "He's frisky today. I guess he wants to be out in the snow."

He smiled at her. "I hope he can wait for another day or two."

That wasn't a pain, either. She said, "I might just go upstairs and lay down a while."

He stood up. "Yes." He said, "It's really cold up there. Those leaky old windows. I can put more blankets on the bed, but they'll be cold, too. I should have thought to bring them down by the stove. I don't know where my mind has been. I could have set up a cot here in the kitchen. This kind of weather—I didn't give it a thought. You'd think I'd know better." He might have said that if the child came then, he'd be earlier than they expected, or than he expected and she let on that she did. No, he'd never think that way.

"Well." She stood up from her chair, and that felt better. "I'm just thinking I might lay down."

"Yes." He put his arm around her and brought her slowly up the stairs to his room. He took off her slippers and found a pair of his socks to put on her feet and then helped her into his bed, pulling the blankets up to her chin. *His*, she thought, because it reminded her of that old gray sweater, when she loved how *his* it was. Loneliness and mice and the wind blowing and then that woolly old thing against her cheek, smelling like him. She'd put her head on his shoulder that one time when he hardly knew her name. She laughed to remember.

"What?"

"Nothing. It just does feel good. Cold and all."

"I'll put the skillet to warm on the stove. I can use it to take some of the chill off. There used to be a warming pan around somewhere. A perfectly useful thing. But I suppose it's ended up in the attic."

"Don't you go up in that attic."

"No, I won't. The skillet should work well enough."

"I'd rather you just crawl under the covers here until I get warm. That's the best thing you can do for me." The windows were rattling and the curtains drifting a little on the cold air, and the room was full of the light of a snowy afternoon.

So he did. "Here we are," he said. "It's as if we've floated out to sea on an iceberg. The two of us all on our own."

"The three of us."

"Oh, my dear."

She said, "Reverend, it seems to me you're about to cry."

He laughed. "I won't if you won't."

"Fair enough."

They were quiet for a while. He said, "I guess you're all right?"

"I think he must be sleeping."

Then he said, "It's all a prayer. You don't think to say, Let tomorrow be like today, because usually it is. For all purposes."

"Well, I wouldn't mind if tomorrow was a little different from today."

"That's a prayer, too."

"Now wait. It has to be different no matter what. One more day just like this one will be worse. More worrying, for one thing. That wears on a person. So it will be different even if nothing changes. Nice as it is right now."

"True. It is nice now."

"Old Boughton struggling through one more day."

"Ah!"

"Me trying to figure out what this child is up to. Not that I mind so much what he decides, so long as he waits till the road is plowed."

The old man sighed. "It's all a prayer."

"For you it is. I tried praying a couple times and nothing came of it."

"You're sure nothing came of it?"

"Well, how do you know anything ever does come of it? Boughton's roof won't fall because it's stronger than you think it is. He won't even try to light a kerosene lamp because he knows what might happen if he did. He's sitting in his morris chair, bundled up in that old buffalo robe, waiting for his children to come and take care of us all. And they will, whether he's praying or not. On snowshoes if they have to." Why did she talk to him like this? Here she was snuggled up against him, wearing his socks. She said, "The best things that happen I'd never have thought to pray for. In a million years. The worst things just come like the weather. You do what you can."

He said, "*Family* is a prayer. *Wife* is a prayer. *Marriage* is a prayer."

"Baptism is a prayer."

"No," he said. "Baptism is what I'd call a fact."

"Because you can't just wash it off."

He laughed. "Nope. Not with all the water in the West Nishnabotna."

Well. So he knew what she'd done, unbaptizing herself. She

probably had that river smell all over her that afternoon and he figured it out when she asked him later. And now the river was frozen and snowed under, and she wished she could see it, all pillowed like that, tucked in. By the time it thawed she would have her body to herself and she could walk in it barefoot if she wanted to, on those slippery rocks. She and Mellie used to pretend they were herding minnows, with their pant legs rolled up above their knees and wet anyway. Here she was, forgetting that there would be a child. It frightened her when she forgot. She must have started awake.

"What?" he said. The worrying had worn him out. He gave a sermon once about the disciples sleeping at Gethsemane because they were weary with grief. Sleep is such a mercy, he said. It was a mercy even then.

"I've just never had the care of a child."

"We'll be fine." He nestled against her. That sound of settling into the sheets and the covers has to be one of the best things in the world. Sleep is a mercy. You can feel it coming on, like being swept up in something. She could see the light in the room with her eyes closed, and she could smell the snow on the air drifting in. You had to trust sleep when it came or it would just leave you there, waiting.

She was thinking about the spring, how clear and stinging cold the water would be with snow still on the rocks and the sandbars. And summer. She might take the baby with her to the river. Little as it would be. Just to pick a few raspberries. And she might put it down in the grass by the road, just for a minute, just while she was picking berries. And then she forgot to come back soon enough, how long was she gone? and had to put it in a pail of river water because you never know. He would say, Why did you do this? Looking at her as if he didn't recognize her at all.

That woke her up. Her first thought was, I have to get that

knife off the table. She'd been having her worst dream, with the Reverend's arm carefully across her where her waist would be, with the Reverend breathing at her ear. She thought, There's a whole world of water in the West Nishnabotna. It's not the Mississippi, but it never begins and it never ends. *Wife* is a prayer. Because I'm his wife. I better think about that.

Sometimes when they were together in the kitchen, when he was drinking his coffee and reading the newspaper, he would fiddle with that knife, taking it up in his hand. He might have done the same with a piece of driftwood, with any harmless thing, just feeling how smooth it was, the shape wear had given it. She never got used to seeing it in his hand, but she never said a word about it except one time when he opened the blade. She said, "Maybe you shouldn't do that," and was surprised herself when she heard the words. She said, "It's awful sharp," thinking probably that the knife was like a snake, that it was in its nature to do harm if you trifled with it. She used to keep it by her when she slept, open, stuck into the floor so she could just grab it if she needed to. It was such a mean-looking thing, and if she had ever used it on anybody it would have been the knife that did it, because it was that kind of knife. Some dogs bite. So you keep them away from people. You can't just get rid of them for being the way they are. And now and then you can be glad to have them around, to snarl the way a good dog never does.

Say she took that knife away, put it out of sight. Would he notice and wonder what it meant? Would he ask her what she had done with it, look for it in her dresser drawer? Under her pillow? Could she put it anywhere at all that he might not just come across it and think, This is strange, why has she hidden it here? She had thought it through a hundred times. That knife was the difference between her and anybody else in the world. Ugly old Doll hunched over in the firelight, spitting on her bit of whetstone, sharpening and wearing the blade till the edge of it curved like a claw, readying herself for whatever fearful thing she turned over in her mind while she was working at it. And, knowing that the fearful thing might take even Doll, who stole her and carried her away from whatever she could have had of place and name and kin, Lila watched her, hoping the knife would take on the witchy deadliness she was conjuring for it.

Fear and comfort could be the same thing. It was strange, when she thought of it. The wind always somewhere, trifling with the leaves, troubling the firelight. And that smell of damp earth and bruised grass, a lonely, yearning sort of smell that meant, Why don't you come back, you will come back, you know you will. And then the stars, and Mellie probably awake, lying there thinking about them.

Lila could tell by the smell that the sheets had frozen on the clothesline. Then Mrs. Graham or whoever had the time had ironed them. But there was still that good, cold smell that made her think of the air after a lightning storm. New air, if there was such a thing, that the rain brought down, or the snow. She was still the preacher's bride, and those women still starched her pillowcase, blessing his happiness, praying for it. All those years of his loneliness were a weight on their hearts. Then he took a wife and he fathered a child, even if it wasn't born yet, and what else could they do? What more could they do? It made her think of the old days, when she lived her whole life just for the hours she spent at the movies, when everybody in the audience would sigh and weep and laugh for those beautiful ghosts in that unreachable place where people lived lives strangers could care about. She had a dream once that a woman's giant face turned and her giant eyes stared at her, and Lila was scared to death because, sitting there in the dark, nobody along with everybody else, she knew she was real to that woman. The look meant, Should I know you? as if to say, Who are you to be watching me like that? Now here she was under the covers with this man anybody in Fremont County knew better than she did, knew when he was first a married man and a father. All of them probably wondered now and then how the two of them passed the time together, what in the world they could find to talk about, different as they were. All of them thinking how sad any sadness that came to him would be, how sweet any happiness, the poor old fellow. And here they were, the two of them, waking and sleeping through the long afternoon, in the crisp sheets that smelled like snow, the baby stirring a little sometimes, the old man young in his sleep and his comfort and she as still as could be, wanting nothing. Those women, looking on at their life, would say oh, and ah, when the curtains stirred and let whiter light into the pale room. Doll there, too, watching. Damn that knife.

She said, "We got to do something with that damn knife."

He said, "I suppose." She could tell by his voice he'd been awake for a while, lying still, too. "It's handy to have around, though. Good for paring apples."

"You been using my knife to pare apples?" She'd have turned to look him in the eye, except for the heft of her belly.

"Once or twice."

"I never said you could use it."

"Sorry. I don't think I did it any harm. I believe you said you used to use it to clean fish."

"That's different." Why was it different? Because it was the only knife she had. And she never slit a fish without thinking she hated the need to use it that way. Hating the need almost made it seem all right. Besides, it was a kind of a little murder, gutting a fish, so when she did it she thought back over her life, and there was something to that. The knife was a potent thing. Other people had houses and towns and names and graveyards. They had church pews. All she had was that knife. And dread and loneliness and regret. That was her dowry. Other women brought quilts and china. Even a little money sometimes. She brought hard hands and a face she could barely bring herself to look at in a mirror because her life was just written all over it. And that knife.

But thinking about her life was another thing. Lying there in that room in that house in that quiet town she could choose what her life had been. The others were there. The world was there, evening and morning. No matter what anybody thought, no matter if she only tagged after them because they let her. That sweet nowhere. If the world had a soul, that was it. All of them wandering through it, never knowing anything different or wanting anything more.

Well, that wasn't true, either.

But one time she and Mellie cut across a field, and just beyond it there was a little valley, budding cottonwood trees letting morning light pass right through, new ferns and new grass all bright with it. In a few days it would be the valley of the shadow, but that day there were only traces of shade, the light just blooming, dandelion yellow in all that green. When you see something like that, it doesn't seem like anything you've ever seen before. She and Mellie were whispering. It would be their valley. They'd think of a secret name for it. Soon enough they heard Doane calling for them, and they had to leave it behind, and it felt like a broken promise when they did.

Remembering always felt almost guilty, a lingering where there was no cause to linger, as if whatever you loved had a claim on you and you couldn't help feeling it no matter what. There was nothing to do but leave, and still. That Mack. There was a time when she would have been so glad if he'd asked her for anything at all. If he had said one word to her, there in the street that day. The old man always pretended he was worried that some fellow would show up at the door. When she told him there was nobody coming for her, Mack was that nobody. She could just see the smile on his face, him standing at the Reverend's door, his eyes all sly with the evil he was doing. He'd have his hands on his hips, looking around at the neighborhood as if he couldn't quite believe people really lived that way. Cigarette hanging out of his mouth, laughing to himself. No decent man would look at every single thing in the world as if it had a price tag on it and he knew it wasn't worth half that much because he could see what the paint hid, where the rot was. He'd flip his cigarette into the bushes and say, So it's Mrs. Ames now, and laugh. He'd say, Good to see you, Rosie, hardly looking at her, and light up another cigarette and glance away from her like anything else would be more interesting, because nothing had changed at all. She'd probably shut the door on him, and then if he left she'd be thinking about him more than she usually did.

Or he might sit down on the step to finish his smoke, and if the old man happened to come walking up from the church, he'd tell him he was looking for a little work. If he happened to get a lift out of town, people always appreciate a dollar or two to help pay for the gas. The Reverend would nod, he could do something or other around the place, and he would say, Thanks, smiling, and then as soon as the old man had come inside to look for his wallet he would drift away because it was a lie that he wanted work or money. He would have said a few words to the old man just to make her worry about what he might say. He'd have been sitting there smoking, his back to her, making sure she remembered that the two of them were not strangers and never would be, either. That's just how it is. If she ever saw that child of Missy's, it would be the child she'd hoped to steal. No matter that it had never seen her face. If she heard it was in trouble, she would say, Come here to me, then. I used to dream I'd have you to comfort. That's how I kept myself alive for a while one time.

You. What a strange word that is. She thought, I have never laid eyes on you. I am waiting for you. The old man prays for you. He almost can't believe he has you to pray for. Both of us think about you the whole day long. If I die bearing you, or if you die when you are born, I will still be thinking, Who are you? and there will be only one answer out of all the people in the world, all the people there have ever been or will ever be. If we find each other in heaven, we'll say, So there you are! We'd be perfect in heaven, no regrets, no grudges, nothing to make you turn a cold eye on me the way you might do someday when you're old enough to really see me. When I tell you that that knife is the only thing I have to leave you. Then I'd be all hard and proud, like it didn't even matter what you thought. What else can a person do? And it would be the only thing that mattered, because no one else could say "you" and mean the same thing by it. But there would be years when the child would just want to sit on her lap. He'd favor her over anybody. He'd be crying and she'd pick him up, and then it would take him a minute to be done crying, but that would be all that was left of it, because she had her arms around him. Comfort. That's strange, too. When she used to lie there almost asleep, with her cheek on the old man's sweater, the night all around her chirping and whispering, the comfort of it was a thing she'd have promised herself the whole day long.

Thinking that way made her want to turn onto her back, to feel how good it was to be lying there, her body resting at a kind of simmer, the baby nudging a little, just so she'd know it was there. She could feel her body resting, the way you can tell that a cat asleep in the sun knows it's sleeping. The pleasure of it is just too good to go to waste. When she stirred, the old man sat up out of the covers. "Night!" he said. "Well. I guess the wind has died down. We slept through supper. How are you feeling? Can I get you a sandwich?" He fumbled for his glasses. It always took him a minute to collect himself. That's what he would say. Let me collect myself. Give me a minute here. Everything seemed strange when she thought about it. Where had he been? Nowhere at all, even lying there beside her. His hair was all pushed to one side, that longer hair that was meant to hide his baldness a little. He looked as though he had waked out of a dream, or into one, that made him feel he had to do something important and couldn't take the time to figure out what it was.

"You," she said.

He laughed. "Who else?"

She said, "Nobody else in this world."

There was more snow after that one, sugar snow, the old man called it, because his grandfather said that in Maine the last snow fell while the sap was running in the maple trees and they were catching it in buckets and boiling it into syrup. If he had ever visited Maine, it would have been in the spring. His grandfather talked about the wood fires and the sweet fog in the air and fresh syrup poured over fresh snow, the one earthly delight he would confess a craving for. "They ate it with a dill pickle. Afraid to enjoy it too much, I suppose." He was happier than he wanted her to see, relieved even though he knew it was too soon to trust that they were safe yet, and worried that he was too ready to be happy and relieved. After breakfast he set a little glass bowl on the porch railing to catch some snow as it fell, and when he saw it had stopped falling, he took the bowl out to the rosebushes to pluck snow that had caught in the brambles. He brought it inside and set it on the windowsill so the sun would melt it. It was pretty the way the light made kind of a little flame, floating in the middle of the water, burning away in there cold as could be. It was for christening the child, she knew without asking. If the child came struggling into the world, that water would be ready for him. If it had to be his only blessing, then it would be a pure and lovely blessing. That was the old man getting ready to make the best of the worst that could happen. Not my will but Thine. In his sermons he was always reminding himself of that prayer. She would wake up at night and find him sitting on the edge of the bed in the dark, his head in his hands. Maybe he never really slept.

Then there was a day of pangs and a night of misery, and after that the baby, scrawny and red as a skinned rabbit. When Boughton saw it he said, "Oh!" It was pity, startled out of him, and then he said, "My babies were always big, brawny fellows, except the one. And he grew up to be as tall and fine-looking as any of them. I always thought so. You can't tell by—you can't tell." Boughton had to be there because he was always there when he thought he might be able to help, bony old thing that he was, eyes full of tears. And the old man wanted him there, too, to help him when he decided he should bring that little bowl of water up the stairs. They didn't say so, but she knew. Teddy came the minute he could, probably afraid his father would die of grief. He was almost a doctor, there to keep an eye on the other fellow, his father said. She heard the phone ringing and the soft voices. People from the church. All the Boughtons would be coming from everywhere. Except the one. She wondered if she'd ever see the one. What did he do to make them all turn against him? "Well," the old man had said, "it was really more the other way around." She didn't tell him she sort of understood how that could happen.

The nurse washed the child and tied the cord, and Mrs. Graham and Mrs. Wertz bathed Lila and changed the bed with her in it. You could tell they'd done it a hundred times, they were so quick and gentle. It made her feel calm lying there in her clean nightgown, all the sweat wiped away with lavender water. How could she feel so calm? Had she died? All this quiet, as if no one could believe the saddest thing that could happen really did happen. Her old man was sitting there beside her, his hand on her hand, white as death. She thought, How many years has this cost him, how many will it cost? This was the moment before everything changed, and there was nothing else to do but watch and listen. The house was as quiet as a held breath. She said, "Well, you should give me that baby anyway."

He looked up at her and smiled. "Yes. Yes, the doctor has been checking him over a little. But he'll be wanting his mama. He's had a tough night." He said, "And so have you, precious Lila." So much regret.

She said, "You're praying for him."

He laughed and wiped his eyes. "Troubling heaven. You may be assured of it."

"Boughton, too."

"Boughton, too. Every last Boughton, in fact."

"Except the one."

He laughed. "I'm sure we would have his very best wishes." His face was so white and weary.

"Well now, don't you stop praying."

"I don't believe I could stop. For more than a minute or two."

"You might mention yourself," she said. "And Boughton. And the other one."

The nurse brought the baby and put him against her side. Such a little thing, he could get lost in the covers. But there he was, all bundled up like a cocoon. The nurse said, "Now he's happy." Nothing about giving him the breast. Teddy was leaning against the wall with his arms folded, just watching, not saying a thing, but when the old man lifted his head and glanced at him, he nodded, so slightly, and they all knew what that meant. The old man got up from his chair. "I'll get it. I don't know. It seems better than tap water, I suppose." He was a long time on the stairs, going down and coming back up again, with the little bowl of water trembling in his hands. She didn't see any light in it.

Boughton said, "John, let me hold that for you."

The old man took his Bible from the top of the dresser and opened it and read, "'But thou art he that took me out of the womb; thou didst make me trust when I was upon my mother's breasts. I was cast upon thee from the womb; thou art my God since my mother bare me. Be not far from me; for trouble is near; for there is none to help.'"

There was a silence. Boughton said, "Yes. I'm a little surprised you chose that text, John. It's a fine text. I just wouldn't have expected it. Don't mind me."

"No, you're right. I've had that psalm on my mind lately, I guess."

"Those verses in 139, 'For thou didst form my inward parts: thou didst cover me in my mother's womb'—very fine." He said, "The darkness is as light to You," and he shook his head. "Excuse me." He began groping for his handkerchief, holding the bowl in his weaker hand, and the water spilled, enough of it falling on the baby to make him mad, to judge by the look on his face and the sound he made.

Teddy laughed. "That was quite a howl." He came over to the side of the bed. "I think he's been playing possum."

Boughton said, "Yes, well, I don't think that was an actual baptism, though. I do apologize. There's still a little water left in the bowl here."

And Lila said, "We're going to get this wet blanket off of him, first of all." Teddy unbundled him and gave him to her, and there he was, a little naked man, not a Christian yet, needing comfort, then lying against her naked side where she unbuttoned herself so he could feel the softness of her breast. That wound when they cut him away from her, that dark knot, but never mind. He bumped his face against her side and pursed his mouth and found her breast with his wavering fist. She turned on her side to help him.

Teddy said, "Well, look at that! He's pretty spry."

Boughton was so upset with himself that all he could think of to say was "There is some water here. It hardly takes any at all." Then he said, "It's snowing again. That's good, I suppose, if you want snow. I never saw such a spring."

Teddy took the bowl out of his trembling hands and set it aside and put his arms around him. "Here," he said. "Just rest your head for a minute. You're all worn out." And he did rest his head against Teddy's chest, his sweater, crooked and small as he was, her old man watching the way he did when she knew he was thinking, that's how it would be to have a son. And then he turned back the sheet and looked at the son he had, so small he could fit in her two hands, but alive just the same, and he laughed. The tip of his finger on the little bird bone of your shoulder.

So that other life began, almost the one she used to imagine for herself when she thought she might just slip a baby under her coat and walk away with it. She knew better than to waste that time. There isn't always someone who wants you singing to him or nibbling his ear or brushing his cheek with a dandelion blossom. Somebody who knows when you're being silly, and laughs and laughs. So long as he was little enough to carry, she could hardly bring herself to put him down. She thought, I know what happens next. Old Boughton will tell you that story a hundred times. He will say he performed a miracle and that was why we had to name you after him, because he really was your godfather, yes! If anybody in the world has ever had a godson! And that is why you love the snow so much! You were christened with it! And you will wonder what such an old, old man could have to say to you, what it could mean. Putting his face down close to yours, making his eyes big, and you just staring at the way his flesh hangs off his skull, and how there are always whiskers in the creases of it. It's all strange. People never really believe they were taken from their mother's womb and laid on her breast. I could see your eyes behind your eyelids, and veins through the skin of your belly, and they were that blue that was never meant to be seen. It is so strange that it belongs in the Bible, with the seraphim and the dry bones. The day you were born there was just wind enough to stir the curtains a little, and there was just light enough to make it seem like evening all day long. And there was quiet enough to make it seem as though sound had passed out of the world altogether, leaving the wind behind to sweep up after it. And then you with your big belly and your skinny legs, like a wet cat, not half looking like the makings of a child. I'll never tell you that. It was a month before your father had the courage even to hold you in his lap. But when you were just two weeks old we took you to the church to be christened for sure, because Boughton kept on worrying until it was done. Your father said it was intention that mattered, and that didn't matter, either, because a newborn child is as pure as the snow. Boughton said if they did not act on the intention when circumstance allowed them to, then the seriousness of the intention was questionable.

"Robert, I hope I never have to be that serious again in this life."

"I can say that you were distracted from it. Your intention. I know what Calvin said as well as you do! Better! Don't even bother me with it!" Maybe you will remember how they sound when they argue about something,

Boughton thought it was all his fault, or he would have been the cause of any harm that came from it, which was just as bad. So when you were two weeks old we took you down to the church one cold Sunday, the first time you felt the air on your face. I carried you inside my coat, and I could see you peeking out at things. There you were, right against my heart, with a shawl around us both. Nobody but the two of us knew how plump and beautiful you were, because nobody knew what a pitiful thing you had been just a few days before, except Boughton, who was still scared to look at you and couldn't think of a thing except making a Christian out of you while we had the chance. Teddy told him to stop coming around so much, worrying everybody, and mostly he minded. Teddy had to be back at school, but he called every day and then every other day and then once a week, and then we all forgot to be frightened of you. You turned into a perfectly fine baby. Maybe your father has enough years left in him to see you turn into a perfectly fine boy. And maybe not. Old men are hard to keep.

Lila knew what would really happen next. One day she and the child would watch them lower John Ames into his grave, Mrs. Ames on one side and his father, John Ames, on the other, and his mother and that boy John Ames and his sisters, a little garden of Ameses, all planted there waiting for the Resurrection. She knew it was ridiculous, but she always imagined them coming up some June day, right through the roses, not breaking a stem or bruising a petal. Shaking hands, patting backs, too taken up with it all to notice her flowers. Except Mrs. Ames, who might stoop down and pick one to show that baby, This is a rose. See how cool it is, how nice it smells. Holding it away from the baby's hand because in the world as they left it there'd have been thorns. That day might come in a thousand years. But soon, before he was half grown, the boy would be standing beside her and he would ask where their places were, his and hers, because the plots were all taken up, and she would say, It don't matter. We'll just wander a while. We'll be nowhere, and it will be all right. I have friends there.

She would keep every promise she had made, the boy would learn "Holy, Holy, Holy" and the Hundredth Psalm. He'd pray before he ate, breakfast, lunch, and supper, for as long as she had anything to say about it. Every day of every year they lived in Gilead she would be remembering what happened that very day, reciting it to herself in her mind so sometime she could say, One time when you weren't even walking yet he took you fishing with him. He had his pole and creel in his hand and you in the crook of his arm and he went off down the road in the morning sunshine, striding along like a younger man, talking to you, laughing. He came back an hour later and set the empty creel on the table and said, "We propped the pole and watched dragonflies. Then we got a little tired." And what a look he gave her, in the sorrow of his happiness. He might as well have said, When he is old enough to understand, tell him about the day we went fishing. So she said, "You might as well be writing things down." Coming from him it would mean more. That was one of those days that is so mild and bright you know you'll never see a better one. The weather just flaunting itself. She might wait for another day like it to tell the boy how his father couldn't wait to have a son, because if you just say a day was fine, nobody makes much of it.

She could tell him how the old man looked standing in the pulpit, his hair pure white, his face all serious and gentle. He had looked into those faces in the pews for so many years, and couldn't look at any one of them without remembering the day he buried a mother, christened a child, soothed a parting as well as he could. And sometimes rebuked where he should have comforted—mainly when he was young, he told her. But he never forgot that he'd done it, and he said no one who heard one of those stories ever forgot either. So he spoke with a tenderness he wasn't even aware of anymore, that you could read if you knew how, like reading the bottom of a river from its pools and flows. He had paused over the word "widow" even before he knew her name, there were so many of them, but it was harder for him now. The word "orphan" troubled him after she told him a little about where she came from, and then after he had a child, he could hardly even say it. His preaching was a sort of pattern of his mind, like the lines in his face.

That old black coat he always wore to preach in was the one he put over her shoulders one evening when they were walking along the road together and he was throwing rocks at the fence posts the way a boy would do, still shy of her. But on a Sunday morning, with the sermon in front of him he'd spent the week on and knew so well he hardly needed to look at it, he was a beautiful old man, and it pleased her more than almost anything that she knew the feel of that coat, the weight of it. She'd be thinking about it when she should have been praying. But if she ever had prayed in all the years of her old life, it might have been for just that, that gentleness. And if she prayed now, it was really remembering the comfort he put around her, the warmth of his body still in that coat. It was a shock to her, a need she only discovered when it was satisfied, for those few minutes. In those days she had all the needs she could stand already, and here was another one. So she said something mean to him. That's how she used to be and how she might be again someday, if she was ever just barely getting by and somebody seemed to be about to make it harder just by making it different. They'd had their wedding by then, but she wasn't married to him yet, so she still thought sometimes, Why should he care? What is it to him? That was loneliness. When you're scalded, touch hurts, it makes no difference if it's kindly meant. Now he could comfort her with a look. And what would she do without him. What would she do.

Doll was hard that way. All of them were. Talking to strangers was putting yourself within the reach of sudden harm. What might they say? What might they seem to be thinking? Then you were left with it afterward, like remembering a bad dream, and nothing to do about it except to hate the next stranger a little more. Those times she used to think, I have a knife in my garter, and you don't know how you're pressing up against the minute I decide to use it. Doll told her, Don't cut nobody with it. You don't want all that to deal with. Just give them a look at it. Most of the time, that's plenty. But there were times when the merciless knife was a comfort to her. Even when she only thought somebody might have looked at her the wrong way, she'd tell herself she had that furious old knife and it had done the worst already. That was before she had a child to look after. You have to stay out of trouble for the sake of your child.

She still actually thought like that, when she let her thoughts sink down to where they rested. She had never taken a dime that wasn't hers or hurt a living soul, to speak of. But that's what her heart was like sometimes, secret and bitter and scared. She had stolen the preacher's child, and she laughed to think of it. Making him learn his verses and say his prayers would be like a joke, when they were off by themselves, getting by as they could. She did steal that Bible, and she'd keep it with her, and she'd show him that part about the baby toiling in its blood, and she'd say, That was me, and somebody said, "Live!" I never will know who. And then you came, red as blood, naked as Adam, and I took you to my breast and you lived when they never thought you would. So you're mine. Gilead has no claim on you, or John Ames either, or the graveyard that has no place for you anyway.

Oh, if the old man knew what thoughts she had! She could make a pretty good meat loaf now and a decent potato salad. He told her he'd never liked pie very much anyway. She could keep the house nice enough. People passing in the road stopped to admire her gardens. The boy was as clean and pretty as any baby in Gilead. A little small, but that could change. And the old man did look as though every blessing he had forgotten to hope for had descended on him all at once, for the time being.

She couldn't lean her whole weight on any of this when she

254

knew she would have to live on after it. She wouldn't even want to see this house again after they left it, or Gilead, at least till the boy had outgrown the thought that they belonged there. So she thought about the old life. She never really hated it until Doll came to her all bloody and she went to St. Louis. But it was a hard way to bring up a child. And she would tell him he was a minister's son, so he might blame her because she couldn't give him what his father would have given him, the quiet gentleness in his manners, the way of expecting that people would look up to him. She surely couldn't teach him that.

Still, there was this time, this waking up when the baby started fussing, this scrambling eggs and buttering toast in the new light of any day at all, geraniums in the windows, the old man with his doddering infant in his lap, propped against his arm, reading him the funny papers. So one morning, standing at the sink washing the dishes, she said, "I guess there's something the matter with me, old man. I can't love you as much as I love you. I can't feel as happy as I am."

"I know," he said. "I don't think it's anything to worry about. I don't worry about it, really."

"I got so much life behind me."

"I know."

"It was nothing like this life."

"I know."

"I miss it sometimes."

He nodded. "We aren't so different. There are things I miss."

She said, "I might have to go back to it sometime. The part I could go back to, what with the child."

"Yes," he said. "I've given that some thought. I know you'll do the best you can. The best that can be done. I'll be leaving you on your own. We've both always known that. I can't tell you how deeply I regret it."

"You have told me, plenty of times. But for now," she said, "things are good. If hard times are coming, I'd just as soon wait to start worrying. That's not really the problem." The problem is, she thought, that if someday she opened the front door and there, where the flower gardens and the fence and the gate ought to be, was that old life, the raggedy meadows and pastures and the cornfields and the orchards, she might just set the child on her hip and walk out into it, the buzz and the smell and the damp of it, the breath of it like her own breath, her own sweat. Stepping back into the loneliness, a dreadful thing, like walking into cold water, waiting for the numbness to set in that was the body taking the care it could, so that what you knew you didn't have to feel. In the dream it was always morning, and the sun already a little too hot. She was glad she had seen the boy brand new, red as fire, without a tear to give to the world, no ties to the world at all, just that knot on his belly. Then he was at her side, at her breast, a human child. The numbness setting in. But it never sinks right to the bone. That orphan he was first he always would be, no matter how they loved him. He'd be no child of hers, otherwise. She said, "What is it you're missing?"

He shrugged. "Pretty well everything. You. This old fellow." He patted the baby's leg. "Evening. Morning."

"You aren't as old as you think you are, Reverend."

He said, "It's just arithmetic. That's what it comes down to. Boughton has married four or five of his children. Baptized a dozen grandchildren by now. And maybe I'll teach this fellow to tie his shoelaces. The years of a man's life are threescore years and ten, give or take. That's how it is." He said, "I feel like Moses on the mountain, looking out on the life he will never have. Then I think of the life I do have. And that starts me thinking about the life I won't have. All that beautiful life." He shrugged. "I guess I'm pretty hard to please."

"I'm going to make us some more coffee. Did I ever say that?

That I love you? I always thought it sounded a little foolish. But the way you talk, sometime I might regret putting it off."

"I believe you said it a minute ago. You can't love me as much as you do love me. Something to that effect. Which I thought was interesting." He said, "All those years, were you as sad as you were sad? As lonely as you were lonely? I wasn't."

"Me neither. I'd have died of it."

"I had the church, of course, and Boughton. I had my prayers and my books. 'And my ending is despair, Unless I be relieved by prayer, Which pierces so that it assaults Mercy itself and frees all faults.' Quite a life, really. A very good life. But there was such a silence behind it all. Over it. Beneath it. Sometimes I used to read to myself out loud, just to hear a voice."

"You do that now."

"Do I? Well, by now it's just habit."

"And I think about Doll." Then she said, "I'm keeping that knife. I'll put it out of sight somewhere, but I'm keeping it."

"Fine."

"It ain't very Christian of me. Such a mean old knife. I hate to think he could want it sometime, but he could."

The old man nodded.

Here she was practically calling herself a Christian, because when the Reverend had baptized their infant at the church that day and put him into her arms, he touched the water to her head, too, three times. He turned his back to the people and murmured to her, "I don't really know what I'm doing here. I should have asked you first. But I wanted you to know that we couldn't bear—we have to keep you with us. Please God." That late new snow made the window light very cool and pure, and she was a little faint from standing, so soon after the birth. Mrs. Graham took her into the study to wait with her for the service to end.

She sat down in the preacher's chair and held the baby against her, and she thought, Did I say, It's all right with me, I guess? thinking that if she'd said it she wasn't sure she'd meant it, and if she hadn't said it she was sorry she had not. The old coat he had put over her shoulders when they were walking in the evening was as good to remember as the time Doll took her up in her arms. She thought it was nothing she had known to hope for and something she had wanted too much all the same. So too much happiness came with it, and happiness was strange to her. He said, We have to keep you with us. In that eternity of his, where everybody will be happy, how could he feel the lack of her, the loss of her? She had to think about that. Sometime she would ask him about it. It must always be true that there are the stragglers, people somebody couldn't bear to be without, no matter what they'd been up to in this life. That son of Boughton's.

And then there were the people no one would miss, who had done no special harm, who just lived and died as well as they could manage. That would have been Lila, if she had not wandered into Gilead. And then she thought, I couldn't bear to be without Doll, or Mellie, or Doane and Marcelle. Even Arthur and his boys—not that they had mattered so much to her when she was a child, but because fair was fair and none of them ever had any good thing that the others didn't have some right to, even Deke. If there was goodness at the center of things, that one rule would have to be respected, because it was as important to them as anything in this world.

She thought maybe, just by worrying about it, Boughton would sweep up China into an eternity that would surprise him out of all his wondering. God is good, the old men say. That would be the proof.

Can a soul in bliss feel a weight lift off his heart? She couldn't help imagining— Oh, here you are! Your dear weariness and ugliness as beautiful as light! That boy, weeping over what he was, his big, dirty hands that had done something he couldn't quite believe, and then there he would be, fresh from the gallows, shocked at the kindness all around him, which was the last thing he expected. He'd had the idea "father." That was what made him so desperate that his father in this life never said a gentle word to him. And there that mangy old father would be, too, because the boy couldn't bear heaven without him. He'd say, See, you was lucky to have me for a son, after all! Look what I done for you! And, Ain't this better than anything! Better than money! He'd be as proud of heaven as if he'd come up with it all on his own.

So it couldn't matter much how life seemed. The old man always said we should attend to the things we have some hope of understanding, and eternity isn't one of them. Well, this world isn't one either. Most of the time she thought she understood things better when she didn't try. Things happen the way they do. Why was a foolish question. In a song a note follows the one before because it is that song and not another one. Once, she and Mellie tried to count up all the songs they knew. How could there be so many? Because every one was just itself. It was eternity that let her think this way. In eternity people's lives could be altogether what they were and had been, not just the worst things they ever did, or the best things either. So she decided that she should believe in it, or that she believed in it already. How else could she imagine seeing Doll again? Never once had she taken her to be dead, plain and simple. If any scoundrel could be pulled into heaven just to make his mother happy, it couldn't be fair to punish scoundrels who happened to be orphans, or whose mothers didn't even like them, and who would probably have better excuses for the harm they did than the ones who had somebody caring about them. It couldn't be fair to punish people for trying to get by, people who were good by their own lights, when it took all the courage they had to be good. Doane tying that ribbon around Marcelle's ankle. If that wasn't good or bad, it was something she was glad to have seen. Mellie singing to soothe some borrowed baby.

That's what she was thinking. The Reverend couldn't bear to be without her. Nothing against Mrs. Ames and her baby. Eternity had more of every kind of room in it than this world did. She could even think of wicked old Mack in the light of that other life, looking it over, wondering what the catch was, what the joke was, somehow knowing that she had brought him there. And his child. She couldn't bear to be without them. It was eternity that let her think like that without a bit of shame.

There was no end to it. Thank God, as the old men would say.

But the baby started fussing and Mrs. Graham took him and jostled him a little in her arms and let him suck her finger—such a good boy, such a good boy—and Lila heard the final hymn and the benediction. Then the Reverend came in, looking a little worried as he always did when he thought he might not have been attentive enough, and then she realized how tired she was. But she knew she would come back to what she'd been thinking about. And also to "the peace that passeth all human understanding," which was the blessing he said over his flock as they drifted out into Gilead, the small, frail, ragtag work of their hands.

So when she told him she meant to keep that knife and he nodded, she could explain to herself why she meant to keep it. There was no way to abandon guilt, no decent way to disown it. All the tangles and knots of bitterness and desperation and fear had to be pitied. No, better, grace had to fall over them. Doll hunched in the firelight whetting her courage, dreaming vengeance because she knew someone somewhere was dreaming vengeance against her. Thinking terrible thoughts to blunt her own fear.

That's how it is. Lila had borne a child into a world where a wind could rise that would take him from her arms as if there were no strength in them at all. Pity us, yes, but we are brave, she thought, and wild, more life in us than we can bear, the fire infolding itself in us. That peace could only be amazement, too.

Well, for now there were geraniums in the windows, and an old man at the kitchen table telling his baby some rhyme he'd known forever, probably still wondering if he had managed to bring her along into that next life, if he could ever be certain of it. Almost letting himself imagine grieving for her in heaven, because not to grieve for her would mean he was dead, after all.

Someday she would tell him what she knew.